ADAM and EVE
on a
RAFT

RON GOULART
(Photograph by Elana Lore)

ADAM and EVE
on a
RAFT

MYSTERY STORIES

RON GOULART

Crippen & Landru Publishers
Norfolk, Virginia
2001

Cover illustration and design by Gail Cross

Crippen & Landru logo by Eric D. Greene

ISBN (limited edition): 1-885941-57-9
ISBN (trade edition): 1-885941-58-7

FIRST EDITION

10 9 8 7 6 5 4 3 2 1

Printed in the United States of America on recycled acid-free paper

Crippen & Landru Publishers, Inc.
P. O. Box 9315
Norfolk, VA 23505
USA

Email: CrippenL@Pilot.Infi.Net
Web: www.crippenlandru.com

To the memory of Anthony Boucher,
who bought my first short story
and was the closest thing to a mentor I ever had.

CONTENTS

INTRODUCTION

This collection gathers together stories from two series that appeared originally in *Ellery Queen's Mystery Magazine* and *Alfred Hitchcock's Mystery Magazine.*

One deals with Scrib Merlin, a somewhat opportunistic would-be comedian and disgruntled advertising copywriter. Scrib has an affinity for being on hand when expiring murder victims deliver their last words, coupled with a knack for solving cryptic dying messages. He's based in Manhattan.

The other series centers around a nameless advertising man who seems to number a great many ill-fated and often homicidal people among his acquaintances. He's based in Southern California.

I myself was in advertising, with occasional escapes into freelancing, for thirteen years. During that time I was based in San Francisco and Hollywood.

The anonymous adman is a sort of parallel world version of myself, what I might've become had I remained in the advertising game. I became a copywriter immediately after graduating from college. While I chose not to make the profession a lifetime one, I am grateful that it saved me from my earlier intention of becoming an English teacher. Had the head of a San Francisco ad agency not noticed my contributions to the humor magazine at the University of California and concluded that I ought to be able to write what was then called offbeat copy, I might today be a retired academic planning to start my first novel any day now.

The adman never actively participates in any of the murderous activities, but simply listens and observes as a succession of prideful and compulsive focal characters confide their assorted schemes on how to achieve success, revenge, love and money. The format I worked out for the stories was inspired, oddly enough, by the novels of W. Somerset Maugham. Quite late in my reading career I came across *Cakes and Ale* and *The Moon and Sixpence.* I was fascinated by the way Maugham telescoped time. He told somebody else's story, casting himself as a moderately involved witness to some of the events. He could say things like, "I didn't see him again for six years, but ..." and then fill in what had happened to the central character, based on hearsay or speculation. It occurred to me that I could use a similar technique in short stories and thereby cover a longer span of time and include more events than usual.

I sold the adman mystery stories to both *EQMM* and *AHMM* from the early 1970s to the middle 1980s. The late Eleanor Sullivan was the editor who bought most of them. When she seemed to lose interest in him, I, after a couple of rejections, stopped writing about him. The adman occasionally encountered people who got themselves into supernatural situations. Accounts of that sort appeared in *Twilight Zone* magazine, *Amazing Stories* and the sedately named and short-lived *Haunt of Horror*.

Those of you who've read my mystery novel *Even The Butler Was Poor* will notice that I swiped the basic plot notion from the adman story called "Barbecue Bob." And speaking of swiping, the dying message in that same novel first surfaced in the Scrib Merlin story "Ninety-Nine Clop Clop."

Initially I was only planning to do a single story about Scrib. He gets his comeuppance at the end of "Ninety-Nine Clop Clop" and that should've been the end of him. But then I got to feeling that I'd treated him badly, never giving him a chance to redeem himself. And, frankly, I realized that there was more fun to be had with the venerable dying message tradition. Back in junior high school—as we called it then—and high school I'd considered becoming a standup comedian. I actually put together an act and performed in public a few times. So I could identify with a character who was a frustrated comic. At any rate, Scrib returned and, over the course of several stories, worked at becoming a better person. He had quite a way to go.

His career, too, began in the early 1970s and ended in the middle 1980s—after Eleanor Sullivan also grew tired of him. Scrib, I'm fairly certain, finally got his own ad agency. He's still involved in advertising and only now and then regrets never becoming a professional comedian. He married Salty Warbeck, whom you'll meet in several of the stories. She now uses her real name of Sally Ann. She gave up the idea of becoming a model and has been drawing a very successful newspaper comic strip for nearly ten years now. She and

Scrib live near the beach in Southport, Connecticut, and have an eleven year old daughter who wants to be a ballerina.

The adman, I imagine, has been retired for a few years. He lives very comfortably in a Southern California beach town. He and his wife play tennis together at least two afternoons a week.

Ron Goulart

SCRIB MERLIN

NINETY-NINE CLOP CLOP

He came staggering into the dressing room, stumbled against a chair, skidded, stepped into the waste basket with one foot, clomped, fell down, and started to die. His expensive suit was splotched with dirt.

"Jockey, are you kidding?" Scrib Merlin was alone in the communal dressing room of the Joke Box Club when Jockey Metz staggered in and tumbled down. Stuffing his stack of file cards into his jacket pocket, Scrib scooted to the older comedian and knelt beside him.

Jockey was a small man, in his middle sixties, and nearly bald. It was evident up close he'd been worked over and thoroughly beaten. There were welts and bruises on his face and scrawls of dry blood. His hands were in even worse shape, with one finger obviously broken and two of the nails gone.

Scrib thought he knew what had happened. "Jockey," he asked, lips close to the dying comedian's swollen ear, "were they after—"

"Scrib," Jockey managed to gasp, his eyelids flickering. "Scrib, maybe you ... take over ... "

"Okay, sure, be glad to, but—"

"Ninety-nine clop clop," said Jockey in that familiar high voice of his. Then he died.

"What?" Scrib grabbed him by his narrow shoulders and shook him. "You've got to give me more than that, Jockey. You're one of my idols, an inspiration since I was—damn!" He shook the dead man a few more times before letting him drop to the straw floor mat.

Scrib rose, sucking in air, and shook his head. He absently slipped a hand into his pocket and fondled the packet of routine cards. "Better call the police," he decided.

✗

"I can see where that would be very depressing to you," said lovely blonde Texas Blender from across the table. "I'm more used to that

15

sort of thing because of my work and I doubt if I'd—"

"Used to dead men walking in and falling over at your feet?" Scrib scowled.

"I've been on *Mercy Hospital* for three seasons. I guess that gives me a pretty thoroughgoing knowledge of life and death and—"

"Soap," he said. "I'm talking about real life."

"To a great many people *Mercy Hospital* is real life." Texas glanced a the few patrons scattered around the late afternoon pub. "You ought to see the mail I receive, Scrib, addressed to me as though I really was an anesthetist. People with all sorts of problems which—"

"Which call for an anesthetic, sure." He drummed his fingers on the table top.

"You're very grouchy today."

Scrib watched a pair of advertising men playing darts at the other end of the dim pub. "Sorry," he said finally. "It's just that I'm very down. Things were going badly even before Jockey Metz dropped dead right in front of me."

"It's like the proverbial straw which breaks the camel's—"

"You've been babbling soap dialogue too long, Texas. It's made your brain—"

"Good thing I'm fond of you." She put a hand over his nervous fingers. "You're being very irritable today."

"I know, I'm sorry." He shook his head. "I've been really busting my brain on my new comedy routine, to try out at the Joke Box. I was figuring to go on last night. I was signed up and Lanza said he'd give me another chance if I had new material. Then Jockey comes in and dies and the police arrive and I had to answer questions for half a dozen stocky guys who need shaves and ... " He sighed forlornly. "I lost my turn."

"New comics are trying out at the Joke Box every night, except Sunday," said the girl. "I'm sure Lanza will fit you in again next week sometime. The important thing is to forget about poor Jockey so you—"

"No, that's exactly what I don't want to do." He leaned toward her. "Jockey's been my best friend for years, my mentor sort of. If it hadn't been for him I wouldn't even have got the chance to try out at the Joke Box the first time. Because Lanza didn't really care for my type of material."

"You've got talent. I know that. Sooner or later—"

16 Adam and Eve on a Raft: Mystery Stories

"Later looks like the time," said Scrib. "Look, I'm twenty-eight. I've been trying to break into comedy for eleven years. This is as far as I've come."

"You'll get your chance. It's the people who hang in there and—"

"Doing dumb clerk jobs, living on unemployment half the time, scrounging," he recited. "Having to polish my damn act into shape in my spare time, begging people for a chance to show what I can do. Damn it, Texas, I *know* I'm a comedian. If I'm not ... then I'm nothing."

"You *are* a comic, of course you are. I think you're very funny," she told him. "And Jockey thought so too."

Frowning, Scrib said, "I don't know if he did. Sometimes I got the idea ... well, I had the feeling he was sort of stringing me along. Almost making fun of me. I don't know, I guess he really liked me. He liked to talk to me a lot, about his career, his life, his wives. I'm going to miss the guy."

"This may not be the time to mention it," said the girl," but I never thought Jockey was that terrific. Yet he did dozens of specials for NBC, had his own show for three seasons, and you saw him on *Tonight* and Merv and he practically lived on Larry Finger's *Now* show. I think if Jockey could make it, you sure can."

Scrib glanced around, hunched, and lowered his voice. "This is confidential," he said. "But I think, in recent years anyway, part of Jockey's continued success was due to the fact that ... well, he had something on somebody."

Texas' eyes went wide. "What do you mean? He was blackmailing somebody?"

"Don't holler it," Scrib cautioned. "But, yes, blackmail. He hinted at it more than once. 'Face it, kid, I'm a second-rate comic,' he'd tell me. 'But I've got one hell of an ace in the hole.' " His voice went quieter. "Texas, I think that's why they killed him."

"The person he was blackmailing?"

Scrib nodded. "I figure it this way. The police are certain Jockey was worked over and tortured. Somehow he managed to get away from whoever had him, managed to come tottering to the club and me. He must have known I'd be there and could help him."

"He should have gone to a hospital instead."

"Maybe the Joke Box was closer, maybe he was so far gone he wasn't thinking straight."

Texas said, "Why'd they torture him? Just to be mean?"

"To make him talk," he answered. "Obviously he had some piece of physical evidence on whoever it was he was blackmailing. Could be his target got tired of paying after all these years and hired some people to make Jockey tell where the incriminating stuff was hidden."

"A photograph," suggested Texas. "I bet it was a picture."

"Yeah, Jockey was a camera buff. He had half a dozen of them in his room at the Troupers Club."

"We have no way of knowing if he did talk."

Scrib shook his head. "Don't think so. He gave me the impression his secret was still a secret."

"He talked to you before he died? You didn't tell me that."

Edging his chair nearer to the girl, he said, "I didn't tell anyone."

"But you ought to tell the police."

"Jockey was my closest friend. I'm not about to tell them I think he was a blackmailer and that he got knocked off by one of his victims. Wouldn't look very good in his obit."

"It might help them find out who killed him."

"I can do that," Scrib assured her. "I've got a pretty good mind for analyzing things. You have to if you're a comedian."

Her pretty face took on a look of concern. "No, that's dangerous, Scrib. You can't do any—"

"Suppose I figure out who Jockey was blackmailing. Then I, very subtly, drop a hint to the police," he said. "First, though, I get rid of anything which might hurt Jockey's rep. Then I nudge the cops in the right direction."

"Motive," said the girl. "Without the blackmail motive, why are the police going to think this particular person did Jockey in?"

"I can hint that this guy threatened Jockey and I just now remembered it, that it might be a good idea if they checked his alibi, inquired if he'd hired any goons. Million ways to handle it."

"All of them dangerous."

"Give me credit for being able to be sly."

"Okay, but how are you going to find out who Jockey was blackmailing?" asked the girl. "Or is that what he told you before he died?"

"He didn't name names, no. He was able to give me a clue, though," said Scrib. "It was a dying message. All I have to do is figure out what it meant and I'll have the whole business solved."

"What," she carefully inquired, "was the dying message?"

He jiggled his chair farther around the table. Closer to her he said, "Ninety-nine clop clop."

Her face stayed blank for a few seconds, then a smile touched it. "That's silly. That can't be what he said. I mean, what kind of last words are those?"

"This isn't a funny situation, Texas." He jiggled his chair away from her.

When she stopped laughing, Texas said, "Okay, forgive me. Do you have any idea what he was talking about?"

Scrib studied his lap. "Not at the moment," he admitted.

✗

It came to him a night later, near midnight.

Scrib was alone in his small apartment in the West Eighties, watching Larry Finger's *Now* show. This was a favorite talk show of his, one which showcased a lot of comedians and had helped launch some of the most successful. A successful tryout at the Joke Box might, eventually, lead to a spot on *Now*. From there it would be onward and upward.

Sitting in his lopsided wicker armchair and making infrequent notes for his routine on a pad of yellow lined paper, Scrib absently watched the television screen. He had a sudden unplanned insight. "A joke," he exclaimed aloud. He stood up so rapidly that his pad fell to the worn rug. "A joke," he said, clapping his hands together. "That's what Jockey was telling me—part of an old joke."

Scrib circled his small bedroom-living room. He actually smacked the heel of his hand against his temple, the way people did in old movies to get themselves to thinking, cudgeling his brains. "Sure, he was like Berle and Henny Youngman, he knew thousands of jokes. Used to brag about how many—a joke for every occasion, a joke on every subject. So he's dying and his mind isn't in the best of shape, but he wants me to understand something important. What's more natural for an old comic than to use an old joke."

Fine this far. Except Scrib couldn't force himself to remember what the rest of the joke was.

"Somebody with a cane? No, and it isn't the little-old-lady-sick-upstairs switch." Muttering, he made a wider circle of the room. He wandered over to his alcove of a kitchen. Sometimes a cup of coffee helped him think better.

When he reached for his nearly empty jar of instant coffee a large cockroach came scurrying out from a patch of shadow next to the jar on the shelf. Scrib automatically reached out to flick the bug into oblivion. He didn't. He put the jar down with a clack on the stove top.

"Bug," he said, excited. "Joke about a bug. Yeah, that's it. You're getting warm. Cockroach? Nope. Fly in the soup?" He shut his eyes, his lips pressed tight. "Caterpillars? Something like … centipedes! 'Who goes ninety-nine clop clop? A centipede with a wooden leg.' That's the joke!"

He spun and did a jig in the confined space of his tiny kitchen. He'd remembered, he'd got the joke Jockey Metz had been trying to tell him when he died.

All at once Scrib ceased celebrating. He realized that, although he knew where Jockey's dying words came from, he still had no idea of what they had to do with the blackmail operation.

He went back to his wicker chair, returned the notepad to his lap, and started making notes.

✗

"It helps you think."

"It helps me wheeze. Hey, is there a gag there? 'My girl says jogging makes you fit, but me it makes wheeze.' Not quite right. Maybe a play on fit. 'She says it keeps you fit. I tried it and, sure enough, I had a fit.' Naw, still not good enough."

"We're supposed to be thinking of other things," Texas reminded him. Clad in a scarlet warmup suit, the lovely blonde girl was jogging effortlessly along a Central Park path.

It was a warm clear Saturday morning. Scrib, in his regular weekend outfit of sneakers, khakis, and an ancient pullover, was trotting beside the girl, breathing through his open mouth. "Okay, I agree Jockey wasn't trying to give me the name of who he was blackmailing," he said, gasping in air between every few words.

"A caterpillar with a wooden leg wouldn't have much money."

"You're always accusing me of being sarcastic, whereas it's you, Texas, who—"

"Suppose he wasn't trying to tell you a darn thing? It's possible all dying comedians mutter old jokes as they depart this life." Her blonde hair flicked rhythmically as she ran.

Avoiding a sprawled drunk, Scrib said, "You're missing the whole and entire significance of dying messages. They're intended to convey something. That's the sole purpose of a dying message, no matter how cryptic."

"Where he stashed the pictures or whatever," she suggested. "Could Jockey have been trying to tell you that?"

Scrib brightened. "Hey, you've got it," he said. "Sure, that's what he meant. He wanted me to find the stuff, to avenge his death. So he tried to tell me where it was hidden."

"Did he have any friends with wooden legs?"

"You were at his funeral with me yesterday. Did you see anybody like that?"

"Without pulling up trousers one can't always be sure."

A scruffy terrier joined them in their run, nipping at Scrib's heels. "Go away, scram!" he said. "Somebody with a wooden leg. It would have to be somebody famous for having a wooden leg."

"Long John Silver."

"Quit kidding around."

"I meant someone noted for playing Long John Silver, an actor," said Texas. "Most of Jockey's friends were in show business."

"You're right," said Scrib. "In fact, he even used to go out to Long Island once a month to put on shows at the Coldport Actors Home. I went with him once and did my act, but those older people don't seem to care much for contemporary humor. They really loved Jockey, though, and—" He halted on the path.

The terrier caught up and made another try for Scrib's leg.

After helping scare him off, Texas asked, "Why did you stop running all at once?"

"One of the old guys at the home. He was even in the show with us. Well, several of them were, but this one guy ... he was in vaudeville and then on TV back in the early days. He was still on once in a while when I was a kid." His head was nodding vigorously up and down. "This guy—"

"Has a wooden leg?"

"No, no. He's a ventriloquist. Maybe you remember him. Kenyon and Bugsy. Get it? Bugsy is the nitwit dummy's name. What is a centipede? A bug. And what is this dummy but a bug with a wooden leg."

Texas arched one eyebrow, considering. "You think possibly Jockey hid whatever it is inside the dummy?"

"I think it's worth a drive to Coldport, Long Island, to find out,"

Scrib said.

✗

"Dead? He can't be dead."

"It is often difficult to accept the death of a loved one, but nevertheless—"

"When?"

"Only two days ago," answered the plump grey-haired woman in the grey pants suit.

Scrib gave an unseeing glance at the chill white lobby of the Coldport Actors home. "He died of natural causes?"

The director of the home frowned. "Mr. Kenyon was in his eighties," she said slowly and carefully. "He passed away quietly in his sleep. I do think it might have been partially due to the shock over the death of his old friend, Jockey Metz." She studied Scrib's face. "You came here with Mr. Metz at least once, didn't you?"

"Couple of years ago."

"You ought to visit again. They love entertainers here."

"I had the impression my type of comedy material didn't—"

"What," put in Texas, dressed in a tweed skirt and cable-stitch pullover, "what became of Mr. Kenyon's personal effects?"

"Oh, he had nothing in the way of possessions."

"We were wondering about that marvelous dummy of his," persisted the girl. "Bugsy."

The plump woman touched at the corner of her eye with a knuckle. "It's a very sentimental thing," she said. "Somewhat unusual as well, but I got all the interested parties to agree. Mr. Kenyon has no immediate relatives, so I had only to persuade the mortuary and they—"

"Wait," said Scrib, stiffening. "You're not trying to say the dummy was buried with old Kenyon?"

"Yes, that was his last request. It was little enough to do for him, poor man."

"When was he buried?"

"Oh, the funeral isn't until Monday," said the director. "So if you'd care to pay your last respects you'll find him at the Plaut Brothers Funeral Home on Wharf Lane. It might be nice to drop in before you go back to Manhattan."

"Yes," agreed Scrib. "Yes, we'll pay our last respects."

"It's not graverobbing," explained Scrib. "Graverobbing is when you dig somebody up with a shovel."

"Okay, but it's the next closest thing," said Texas. "They call it, technically, being a ghoul."

"Nobody's been arrested for being a ghoul on Long Island lately," he told her. "Besides which, we're not disturbing the body. We're only going to disturb the dummy."

"You're going to, I'm staying out here."

They were parked on a tree-lined side street, watching the rear of the funeral parlor from Scrib's rented car. It was a few minutes to midnight.

"We haven't seen any cops go by all the time we've been here," Scrib said. "The last employee left half an hour ago. I'm going to make my move, Texas."

"What we should have done," the girl said, folding her arms, "is gotten hold of the dummy while we were in there pretending to view the remains."

"Too obvious."

"I could have distracted both Plauts while you frisked Bugsy."

"Not with the organist watching."

"She wasn't going to rehearse forever."

"This is the best way," he assured her. "I stuck that matchbook in the side door of the room Kenyon's in. All I have to do now is sneak inside."

"It still sounds unwholesome." She shivered.

"A wooden dummy, what's unwholesome about that?"

"The dummy happens to be lying there with that dead old man's arm around it."

"Listen," he said, "Jockey was murdered a week ago, beaten to death. He's dead and buried and the police haven't a notion of who did it." He pointed in the direction of the dark funeral home. "I think the answer is inside that place. I'm going after it."

"All right." She patted his arm. "Be careful, honey."

"Sure." He eased silently out of the car, and keeping in shadows as much as possible he made his way to the side of the white wooden building. There were no cars passing through this part of Coldport at this time of night.

The door still had the matchbook preventing it from closing

completely. He pushed the metal door, listened at the narrow opening. He pushed harder and entered. There was thick flower-scented darkness all around him.

Tugging out the flashlight he'd bought at a hardware store that afternoon, Scrib clicked it on.

The coffin sat on a cart at the front of the small chapel-like room—an inexpensive coffin surrounded by only three small floral pieces. He hesitated a few seconds before striding up to the casket.

He tried not to look directly into Kenyon's wrinkled old face. Balancing the light on the shut portion of the coffin lid, Scrib got hold of the dummy, pulled hard, and got Bugsy up off the satin pillow.

Retrieving his flashlight, Scrib squatted beside the casket and inspected the dummy. He held it by the shoulders and shook. Something rattled faintly. He brought Bugsy closer to his ear and shook again.

"Left leg." He crouched on the padded steps, rested the dummy on his lap, and pulled up its checkered trousers leg. "Yeah, there."

Along the pink-painted leg a faint crack was visible. Scrib inserted his thumbnail and made the crack widen. He fiddled a bit more and the two joined halves of Bugsy's leg came apart.

A small paper cylinder fell out. Tossing the dummy on its back, Scrib scooped the cylinder off the rug. It was composed of three photographs and three negatives, wound round with a rubber band. Holding the flashlight between his knees, he unfurled the pictures. There were three separate shots, taken at short intervals, aboard a yacht, showing a lean blond man in the act of shoving a struggling dark-haired girl over the side and into the night sea.

"Damn, it's Larry Finger," he said out loud. "The host of the *Now* show."

✗

Scrib figured it this way. The girl in the pictures was a model named Donna Klay, who had supposedly committed suicide in 1967 while on a yacht party. The boat belonged to Larry Finger and among the other guests had been Jockey Metz. That much Scrib got from the accounts in the library's microfilm files of the *Daily News*.

But Donna, rumored to be a girl friend of Larry Finger's, hadn't taken her own life. Finger, who had been earning over $200,000 a year as far back as 1963, had killed her. Killed her without ever realizing Jockey was nearby with one of his cameras. Funny about

Jockey. He'd chosen to snap pictures instead of trying to save the girl. He must have realized, in an instant on that dark deck, it would be more lucrative to have the pictures. The pictures would assure him an income for the rest of his life.

Scrib had nothing like that in mind. He knew exactly what he wanted. After he'd told Texas there had been nothing hidden in the dummy and that he might as well give up the search for Jockey's killer, he set out to get an interview with Larry Finger.

That took him nearly three weeks, but he finally managed to see the *Now* host alone. He gave Finger one of the pictures and one of the negatives. He promised he'd hand over the other photos and negatives as soon as Finger gave him what he wanted.

Finger agreed.

Scrib had it all worked out. He knew, always had, that once he was exposed to a large audience he'd start really succeeding as a comic. So that was all he asked of Larry Finger. Not money, not a lifelong income, but only a chance to do ten minutes of his own comedy material on the *Now* show.

Finger gave him that chance.

There was only once thing Scrib had overlooked.

He wasn't funny.

CHRISTMASTIME IN PRISON

They all skirted the dying man, avoiding his sprawled body, stepping off the late-afternoon park pathway. He was lying face-down across the sidewalk, a thickset man of sixty in a rumpled tweed suit, his legs touching the burgeoning grass of the slanting Central Park field.

Scrib Merlin, muttering, "Another halfwit drunk," almost went by too. But then he recognized that suit and the close-cropped grey hair.

Dropping to his knees, he touched the man gingerly. "Yoyo, what's wrong?" Carefully, he tried to ease him up and over into a sitting position.

That's when everybody saw the blood, the people who were shortcutting through the park as another workday wound down. Most of them stopped, forming a lazy half circle around Scrib and the man whose chest was splotched with growing red.

"Scrib, old buddy," said Yoyo Hobbs, recognizing him through glazing eyes.

Putting his arm around the dying comedian's shoulders, Scrib turned to the growing crowd. "Get an ambulance, somebody!" Three lean men in runners' warmup suits on the path across the way, walking and preoccupied, caught his eye.

"Stabbed," murmured a frail woman. "Stabbed and it isn't even dark."

"Payoff," muttered Hobbs. "Scrib, I—he fooled me. No payoff—"

"Who? Who knifed you, Yoyo?"

"Big money—big—"

His face close to the older man's, Scrib repeated, "Who knifed you?"

The crowd kept growing. There were maybe forty people now, edging nearer, watching, whispering.

Hobbs became aware of them. "Audience, huh? Too many ears," he said. "But I—I'll tell you."

26

Scrib moved his ear up to the parted lips. "OK, tell me."

"It was—it was Christmastime in prison and—he was—the one who couldn't tell a joke."

Yoyo made a funny sound then. A sound you don't often hear. The sound people make when they die.

"Here comes a cop!" said somebody.

"Too late," said the frail woman. "They always get here after you're dead."

✗

Darkness was filling the space between his dusty office window and the brick wall across the alley. Scrib, hunched slightly at his typewriter, two-finger-typed the last line of the radio commercial for the Dunkirk Hotel. " 'The convenient and moderately priced Manhattan hotel out-of-towners habitually flock to,' " he read aloud from his yellow copy paper. "You'd really have to be a yokel to think West Seventeenth and Eighth Avenue is convenient to anything."

"I bet if you put your mind, which is basically, it seems to me, a good one, to work, you could find positive things about your job, Scrib," said the young woman who was sitting, upright and knees together, in his only other chair. She was pretty, thin, and blonde. "Take my case, for example. I'm doing just fine, or at least fine by the modest standard I apply, as a contributing cartoonist on *The National Buffoon*, yet I'd much rather be gainfully employed at my first love, which—"

"You're never, Salty, going to make it as a nude model." Scrib yanked the copy out of his ancient machine and tossed it into the outbox.

"That's a negative attitude."

"The average halfwit reader of skin magazines wants to slobber over girls who are much heftier than you are."

"Trends come and go, that's what mass culture is all about," persisted Salty Warbeck. "One year it's hefty, the next—"

"It's never going to be skinny," he pointed out, frowning. "You're never going to see a skinny *Playpen* Cutie of the Month or a skinny *Houseboy* Honey of the Month."

Salty smiled. "I'm lean, not skinny."

"I like you exactly as you are," he said. "But I don't have mass taste."

"Don't underestimate yourself, Scrib, because, honestly, if you weren't able to identify with the mass, you couldn't work here at Amthrax & Associates as a copywriter and be doing so darn well at it."

"I'm not doing well at it," he informed her. "Which is why you find me here at seven in the evening, batting out copy for the Dunkirk and Waterloo Hotels, two of Manhattan's—"

"Mr. Amthrax told me once, when I ran into him in the elevator, that you're doing very—"

"You're an attractive girl, naturally he'd lie to you," Scrib said. "Me he hollers at and calls Dimbulb and Peabrain. You don't know what it's like to be thirty-two and have to sit here and have a dwarf heap—"

"He's not a dwarf, he's a midget."

Scrib shrugged. "He's smaller than me, whatever he is, and running his own agency even though he's not more than a couple years my senior. If only I could've made it as a comedian, instead—"

"I know why you're so especially grumpy today." Salty stood, gracefully, up and crossed to his worn wooden desk. "It's because you found that body in the park."

"He wasn't a body when I found him," Scrib said. "Yoyo was alive, trying to tell me something. Something important."

"Let the police worry about that," she advised, touching his shoulder.

"They don't know about this."

"But isn't that against the rules? I mean, when you hear a dying message from someone aren't you obliged to inform the author—"

"It isn't exactly a law, Salty."

"Wasn't it something like this that got you into trouble before?"

"Not exactly."

"Yes, it *was* another dying comedian you told me about once, Scrib," she said. "You seem to specialize in finding dying comics who are determined to—"

"The other business was three years ago and that comedian found me," said Scrib. "Today I was just simply crossing the damn park on my way back from the halfwit Lincoln Center library and—well, there was Yoyo Hobbs in the act of dying."

"You must feel truly awful, finding a friend bleeding out his—"

"Yoyo wasn't exactly a close friend," Scrib corrected. "He did some radio spots for us a few weeks ago for the Nuts 2 U Candy Shops. Yoyo played one of the singing cashews. Originally he was cast as a peanut, but—"

"Still, he was someone you knew and, being a comedy buff yourself, I just bet you used to talk to him about his better days, when he was a bigtime comic on TV."

"Yoyo was never exactly bigtime—he went through his life being a second banana," said Scrib. "Which still put him several bananas ahead of me."

"Maybe, you know, you could still try to be a comic." Salty stroked his nearest shoulder. "After all, thirty-two isn't exactly over the—"

"I can't do that," he said quickly. "What I would love to do, though, is have an agency of my own. A small shop with just a few clients, specializing in humorous copy. I know I could take the Nuts 2 U account if—"

"That would, wouldn't it, require a lot of—"

"Money, yeah, I know." He stood. "I've been thinking though. If I can solve Yoyo's murder I may be able to get hold of the dough I need."

"Is there a reward?" Her lovely grey-green eyes widened.

"Who'd pay a reward to find out who killed a second-rate comedian? What I'm talking about is this," he said, moving clear of her and toward the doorway. "From what Yoyo told me I've figured out he must've been involved with something that was going to bring in big bucks."

"Could be, Scrib, he was merely babbling. People often do that when they're dying." Salty followed him out into the small shadowy reception room of the Amthrax & Associates agency. "They talk about things they've done, things they had, things they miss. Like Orson Welles in *Citizen Kane* remembering his wagon that—"

"Sled," he said. "And Yoyo wasn't goofy at the end, he was struggling to convey something important to me." Scrib shook his head. "The trouble is, he noticed all those halfwit gawkers and he got cagey. Tried to tell me who to go after without giving it away to anyone else."

"What was it he whispered? Something about Christmas?"

"He said, 'It was Christmastime in prison and he was the one who couldn't tell a joke.' "

"Wrong time of the year for Christmas." Salty coughed into her slender hand. "Sounds to me as though he was just babbling the way—"

"No, he gave me an important clue."

"So what does it mean?"

"Right at the moment I don't know," admitted Scrib. "But maybe after we search his apartment I will."

✗

They were not the first.

"Used this fire escape in here," said Scrib from the small bedroom of the late comedian's small walkup apartment. "Jimmied the window, left a handsome muddy footprint on the rug."

Hesitating between the bedroom and the disordered living room, Salty said, "I hope you'll accept this suggestion, Scrib, in the spirit in which it's given. Let's get out of here. Let's, really now, phone the police and—"

"Tell them we just happened to break into Yoyo Hobbs' apartment, by jobbing his front door, and we noticed that another housebreaker had been here before us?"

"Listen, it just occurred to me—maybe the police themselves, you know, did this," she suggested hopefully, taking a tentative step across the threshold.

"Nope, they don't break in by way of windows and they most usually wipe their feet first." Scrib was scowling down at the footprint on the worn pseudo-oriental carpet. "This guy was pretty obvious—turned drawers upside down, tossed the mattress—wanted anyone who came in after him to write this off as a break-in and burglary. Except—"

"Except what?"

"He didn't," said Scrib, walking around her and back into the small buff-walled living room, "bother to take the television set or that clock radio by Yoyo's bed."

"It's a pretty old TV," she said. "Probably only the Museum of Broadcasting would want such—"

"And look at this." Scrib was looking through a desk calendar on the lame little desk against the wall. "Six days missing from last month, torn clean out."

"Your friend Yoyo might've done that."

Calendar in hand, Scrib sat down on the swayback green sofa. "March 17 through 22. What could he have been doing—"

"Marching in the St. Patrick's Day parade maybe."

"Let's refrain from the Nora Charles wisecracks." Scrib paused to snap his fingers. "That was the week Yoyo phoned and asked me if I had a videocassette player. I pointed out that on the salary Amthrax pays me, a salary that wouldn't even keep a dwarf alive in—"

"Midget."

"That I could barely afford a small-screen TV let alone a Betamax," said Scrib, resting the calendar on his knee. "Yoyo was very anxious to get access to a video machine, but when I suggested he use the one at Audio-Video Studios, where we tape commercials, he told me he had something he wanted to view in private."

"A porno movie," suggested Salty, perching on the fat arm of the sofa and causing it to issue a wheezy groan. "There are hundreds of those available, you know, offering every sort of vile—"

Scrib shook his head. "Yoyo was an old man, but not a dirty old man. Not that he was moral or especially trustworthy, but he didn't go in for porn stuff."

"How's his anxiety over viewing a videocassette tie in with the missing leaves off that calendar?"

"I don't exactly know," said Scrib, rising and returning it to the dead comic's desk.

"Do you know where he finally did see his cassette?"

"Nope." Scrib stood in the center of the room, looking slowly around. "Damn. He assured me there was big money in this somewhere."

"He also got killed," Salty reminded him.

✗

The loft studio was long and narrow, one immense room rather haphazardly divided into sectors. The most space was given to Salty's work area, which was cluttered with, in addition to her yellow-painted drawing board, a half dozen unmatching chairs, imitation Greek vases, plaster casts of classic sculpture, an articulated skeleton on a wheeled stand, scarves, pairs of boots, peacock feathers in a green glass bowl, a canning jar jammed to the brim with glistening glass marbles, a windup monkey musician who'd lost one of his drumsticks, a frilly black-lace bra, an empty banjo case, stacks of back issues of *The National Buffoon*, a framed cartoon drawing of *Krazy Kat* that leaned against an eagle-head brass hatrack, one red roller skate, and an imitation jade Buddha some two feet high with a coin slot dead center in his ample stomach.

Scrib was seated in an ice-cream-shop chair, fidgeting, absently watching the television set in the next living area over.

The place had an abundance of windows, in the high walls and in the ceiling. Most of the wall windows were recessed and accompanied by window seats. Salty was on one, tugging off a boot. "My suggestion would be, if you don't mind my giving you some helpful advice, to abandon—"

"I'm not about to abandon big money." Scrib turned to watch her. "Hey, remember what I said about sitting there? Those old windows, most of them, are so weak that if you lean back hard you're likely to go crashing out and—"

"It's only five floors up." She tugged off the second boot. "You really are, and keep in mind that I'm uncritically fond of you, Scrib, a fussbudget. I've lived here—what is it now? Sixteen months and I've never fallen out of a window yet."

"One fatal plunge is all it takes."

Making a demure snorting noise, she stood up, barefooted. "If I'd kept track of the number of times you've—"

"Numbers!" Scrib leaped up.

"What's wrong?"

He beat both fists on his chest, the way silent movie actors did when confessing great sins. "Another damn joke! Why do all these dying comedians tell me jokes? Why don't they simply—"

"Are you getting an insight into what Yoyo Hobbs was raving about in his final minutes on earth?'

"It's a joke, a venerable one, that Yoyo was still telling all the time," he said as he slowly settled back into the wrought-iron chair. "A favorite of his, one I've heard a dozen times and should've rememb—"

"So what's the darn joke?" She glided closer to him on pretty bare feet.

"It's Christmastime in prison," he explained, "and this social worker visits the prisoners at dinnertime with the warden as his guide. All of a sudden a prisoner gets to his feet and says, 'One ninety-six,' and all the rest of them start laughing like crazy. Another con pops up and says, 'Twenty-seven,' and that brings down the house. Even the guards are chuckling. 'Fifty-eight,' says another convict and gets a tremendous laugh. The visitor asks the warden what the heck is going on and he explains that the prisoners are telling jokes. They've heard them so often that they know them all by heart and to save time they just mention the number of the joke. Just then a wrinkled-up old prisoner totters to his feet and says, 'Two thirty.' There isn't so much as a snicker. The social worker asks why and the warden tells him, 'Oh, he never could tell a joke.' Yeah, that's what Yoyo was alluding to."

Salty's face was expressionless. "That's not much of a joke, even for a dying man to tell."

"He wanted to pass that number on to me," said Scrib. "Sure, two hundred and thirty."

She wrinkled her faintly freckled nose. "You sure that's the number he always used for the one who couldn't—"

"Yeah, yeah, I heard it enough to memorize it," said Scrib, standing again. "He was stabbed about four o'clock. Two thirty can't be the time he was attacked."

"An address?"

"Could be, except he was knifed in the park and didn't, according to what the cops let me overhear while I was hanging around, stagger more than a few hundred yards after he was stabbed up in that patch of trees. A nice secluded spot it was, without a single witness."

"Maybe it's the number of a locker."

"If it was a locker, Yoyo'd have tried to slip me a key or a claim check."

"Maybe he was too far gone to reach for a key."

"Two thirty. What sort of numbers do taxis have? —Hey! Look!" He pointed a the TV screen he'd been watching out of the corner of his eye.

"Runners," she said, puzzled. "There was a ten-kilometer fun run in the park this afternoon. Some kind of Executives For Fitness-sponsored race. I got the promo piece at the *Buffoon* offices."

"See what those people have pinned to them?" Sprinting to the set, Scrib turned up the sound.

"Over four hundred executive types, male and female, participated in this afternoon's run, Bud," one announcer was saying to another, "and if you'll look closely you'll spot me bringing up the rear. Panting along in my orange running togs, number 316—and that's about where I finished in—"

Scrib killed the sound. "That race was going on when Yoyo was killed," he said, tapping a finger against the glowing screen. The jogging parade of runners faded and was replaced by a closeup of a steaming bowl of noodle soup. "Suppose a rendezvous had been set up, Salty? A runner drops out for a couple minutes to meet Yoyo. Yoyo had something to sell and this was going to be the payoff. Instead he gets a knife in the ribs."

"A videocassette?" she suggested. "Is that what Yoyo was selling?"

"Sure, it must be." He sat on the edge of his chair, tapping his feet on the hardwood flooring. "The killer takes the cassette and instead of handing over cash he pulls a knife. Yeah, you can hide a cassette and a knife under a sweatshirt."

"Now," Salty said, "would be a good time to phone the law."

"No, now is a good time to find out who wore number two thirty this afternoon."

"That number, Scrib, might pertain to a post-office box or—"

"It could even be the waist measurement of an elephant," he said. "But let's try to connect it to one of those runners."

She sighed. "I guess I can phone Roscoe in the morning."

"Roscoe?"

"Roscoe Chu—he edits the *Gotham Running Tab*," explained Salty. "They cover all the local running events, list all the participants."

"Must make for stimulating reading."

"If you were a runner, it would. Roscoe'll have the list of people who entered the race."

"OK, good. Find out who was number two hundred and thirty and where he finished," he told her. "I figure two thirty came in toward the end, since he had to take a few minutes out of the race to do away with Yoyo."

"Are you sure you—"

"I'm sure," he said.

✗

The next night it rained, a hard-falling rain that hit at all the many windows of Salty's apartment-studio.

Salty, clad in nonfashion jeans and an old college sweatshirt, was at her tilted drawing board, scanning a nearly blank page and biting on the end of a pencil. "It's basically," she said, "dishonest."

"Sure," agreed Scrib, who was slouched in a nearly authentic Morris chair. "Same as murder."

"Just because this—what's his name again?"

"Talbot Sondeck," he said. "A very wealthy man, family money. Also a chap who's had a bit of trouble now and then with the law."

"That doesn't mean he killed Yoyo Hobbs."

"Right, could be the guy's merely a philanthropist," said Scrib. "He's going to pay us $200,000 to keep quiet about—"

"Not us," said Salty, twisting on her high stool, "you."

"You mean when I collect the cash tomorrow you don't want so much as—"

"Not a penny, no."

He shrugged one shoulder. "It ought to be nearly enough to set me up in business."

"Blood money," she said quietly. "And you really aren't certain if Talbot Sondeck is—"

"Of course he is." Scrib straightened, held up his left hand, and began ticking off his fingers as he went over the explanation again. "Talbot Sondeck, age thirty-eight, was number two thirty in the race yesterday. Sondeck, I found out from microfilm files of *The Times*, was picked up three times in the past five years for suspected unsavory activities with underage girls. He is also, I discovered by asking some discreet questions in the video shops in his posh East Side neighborhood, a video nut. Has not one but two recorders and his very own video camera. He's noted in that same neighborhood for still having very young and sexy ladies up to his penthouse. What's the logical conclusion?"

"Very well, this dippy semi-millionaire maybe likes to take video movies of himself and his young lady friends."

"Exactly." Scrib chuckled. "Yoyo got hold of a couple of the roughest cassettes probably. How? Simple. On March the eighteenth he was hired to entertain at a party Sondeck threw. He did his surly-waiter routine, swiped from Vince Barnett, which was something Yoyo did now and then to earn extra dough."

He'd run out of fingers and started on his other hand.

"We now have Yoyo in Sondeck's penthouse on the eighteenth, something I confirmed from Yoyo's sleazy agent. What did Yoyo do? Obviously he prowled around the place while the party was going on. Could be he was hoping, his financial state being what it was, on borrowing a little jewelry or some cash out of the coats and purses in the bedroom. Somehow he stumbled on Sondeck's little cache of incriminating cassettes and, curious as to what might be on them, he swiped one or two."

Salty tried to concentrate on the drawing in front of her. "All you have is conjecture, not—"

"I've got Talbot Sondeck." He grinned broadly. "Because when I phoned him this afternoon and hinted at what I might know the guy absolutely panicked. Pleaded with me not to go to the cops, begged for a chance to buy my silence."

"Could be he put on the same act with Yoyo Hobbs."

"I'm not as dumb as Yoyo," Scrib pointed out. "He gets the cash ready and tomorrow, midday, I phone him again. I set up a meeting in a nice public place where there are no trees or shrubs."

"And Talbot Sondeck turns up with the police and they grab you for attempted blackmail."

"This guy has a record, Salty," reminded Scrib. "He can't keep bribing his way out of trouble forever. If I talk, the police'll maybe dig into his latest activities. Even if they can't tie him in with Yoyo's murder they'll find out lots of other—"

"Yes, exactly."

Salty dropped her pencil and it rolled down across her board and hit the floor. "Scrib, is—"

"Yeah," Scrib verified unhappily, "he's Talbot Sondeck."

The man who'd stepped out of the shadows beyond the lighted work area was tall and lean. Tanned, slightly handsome, his sandy hair close-cropped. He wore dark jeans, a navy-blue pullover, and black sneakers. In his black-gloved right hand he somewhat casually held a .38 revolver. "Amateurs are always so easy to outfox," he said in a smug, very nasal voice.

Salty said, "Roscoe."

Nodding, Sondeck eased closer to them. "Yes," he said, smiling. "For all his devotion to nonconformist life styles and natural foods, Roscoe Chu has considerable respect for a man of my means. After some soul-searching, Roscoe decided to phone me to mention someone had been asking after me. By the time he did, I'd already had Mr. Merlin's quite unsettling extortion offer. Asking if the curious Miss Warbeck had, by chance, a gentleman friend, I was told she did indeed and his name was Scrib Merlin. I really am going to have to take care of the pair of you."

"Going to make it look like a burglary?" Scrib asked.

"Exactly, yes."

"Too many people to kill," Scrib said. "First Yoyo, then the two of us."

"Not at all," cut in Sondeck. "You forget you're living in one of the murder centers of the nation. You are also, forgive my snobbishness, not very important people. Neither was Yoyo Hobbs. The law won't spend much time in—"

"No, no," sobbed Salty, doubling up on her stool and hugging her middle. "I don't want to die. Oh, no, no. Please!"

"Not so much noise," warned Sondeck.

She stumbled off the stool, bent and shivering. "I'm an artist, I want to live a long time. Oh, no, please—don't kill me!" Salty dropped to her knees next to the skeleton on the wheeled stand and sobbed loudly and forlornly.

Sondeck exchanged glances with Scrib. "I've never liked women who crack under pressure."

Scrib said, "Look, suppose you let her go and—"

"Not possible. You both have to die."

"*Die?*" cried Salty. "Oh, this is so awful, so dreadful. Oh, please, please!" Then she shouldered the skeleton hard.

It rolled, as she'd anticipated, right into Sondeck.

"Get him!" she shouted at Scrib.

Scrib dived for the backpedaling murderer.

But he never managed to tackle him.

Sondeck did an unexpected backwards somersault over the banjo case, stumbled, and fell into a window alcove.

His full weight hit against the wide window frame and his body hesitated there for a long second framed against the wood and glass. Then there was an awful rending sound as the window gave way. Sondeck, gun in hand, tangled in squares of glass and fragments of wooden frame, went slamming out into the rainswept blackness and fell in silence down to the wet street five stories below.

Scrib got up, shaking his head. "Why the hell did you do that?" he asked Salty.

She was still on her knees on the floor. "To save your life," she answered, "and mine."

He stalked to the window and jabbed a finger toward the black opening. "There went $200,000," he said.

"I'm sorry. It won't happen again," she promised.

SIX TABLESPOONS MOLASSES

He heard the pots and pans falling first, then the screams. A thumping thud came next and more screams.

Anxious to get out of the big department store, Scrib Merlin had almost passed the commotion by. But when he'd glanced in its direction, he'd seen a crisp white chef's hat go rising up above the heads of the gawking customers here on the Gourmet Floor of Mitgang's Mammoth Store. The hat had apparently popped free of the head of whoever'd taken that rattling fall. That aroused Scrib's curiosity.

He pushed his way through the startled, whispering, murmuring patrons who surrounded the Model Kitchen Korner.

"Awful, awful," a plump woman was remarking. "And so typically New York."

"I was thinking of buying a set of those very knives."

"Don't look, Kevin."

A plump man was sprawled face down on the almost spotless white floor. About fifty-five, he was wearing a white chef's jacket and there was a wooden-handled carving knife planted deep in his lower back. The price-tag still dangled from the polished handle, like a tiny flag of surrender. The cloth around the blade's entry point was a soggy red. Blurry dots of blood led from the fallen body to the half-open doorway at the rear of the three-walled room.

"Kevin, it's not something to laugh at. Behave now."

Scrib recognized the dying man. "Chef Pastore," he said aloud, nudging free of the growing crowd. Although he'd worked with him several times over the past three years, Scrib wasn't sure what his first name was. Everybody always called him Chef.

"Chef?" Kneeling next to him, avoiding a smear of fresh blood, Scrib took hold of his plump hand.

"Who ... ?"

"It's me, Chef, Scrib Merlin. You know, I'm a copywriter with

Amthrax & Associates here in Manhattan. I wrote most of the Pizza Ona Stik TV commercials you've been in."

After groaning, the chef, with great effort, lifted his head and gazed up at Scrib. "Sure ... my friend, Scrib. How you doing, Scrib?"

"I'm okay, but you—"

"I'm dying ... and this isn't what I planned. I used to be big time. My cooking show on TV. Not just a chef at a cut-rate hotel then but a big person—somebody. Didn't have to moonlight and do cheap commercials. Meaning no offense ..."

"Listen, Chef, tell me who knifed you," urged Scrib. He glanced up at the surrounding crowd. "Did somebody send for a doctor?"

"Aren't you a doctor?"

"Scrib ... I was almost on top again ... was going to have money ..."

"But who stabbed— What kind of money?" Scrib moved his head close to that of the dying chef.

"This isn't what we anticipated. No, not at all." A lean man in a sedate grey suit had come fluttering up to the edge of the model kitchen. "The chef is supposed to be over in the model dining room demonstrating how to make canapés out of leftovers. Young man, what exactly are you—"

"Hush," advised Scrib. "Go ahead, Chef."

"You a nice boy, Scrib. Maybe you ... get the money and don't mess up like me ..." His plump face was turning to a strange white color and his words were thinning. "All you got to remember is ... six tablespoons molasses ..."

"Hum?"

"Six tablespoons molasses ... and ..." The words stopped coming. Chef Pastore's head twisted away from Scrib and dropped with a thump to the white floor.

"This is terrible, absolutely," said the floor manager. "A man actually dying right smack in our model kitchen. With one of our knives sticking out of him. Dreadful."

"Stand aside, please. I'm Doctor Reisberson."

"Too late, Doc. The old man bought the farm."

"Kevin, be still."

Shaking his head, Scrib stood up and away from the dead man. He backed off, skirting the copper pans and skillets Chef Pastore must have knocked off the butcher-block table when he came staggering into the room.

Scrib looked at the doorway that probably led to an employees-only passway behind the model kitchen and the other displays. No use trying to poke around back there now, the killer was long gone—either out of Mitgang's already or lost in the hundreds of late-afternoon shoppers.

The chef had talked about money, presumably a lot of money. All Scrib had to do to get in on it was remember the words.

"Yow!" he said, suddenly and out loud. Someone had poked a finger in his back—at about the same spot the knife had gone into Chef Pastore.

"You really and truly do make a habit of this, don't you?" inquired the slim, pretty red-haired young woman who'd nudged him.

"Afternoon, Miss Cashin," he said without enthusiasm. "Habit of what?"

"Stumbling over dead men," said Molly J. Cashin. "From what I hear, corpses fall at your feet like rain in the Brazilian jungle."

"*Two* dead men," he said, holding up the appropriate number of fingers. "Two in five years. That sure as hell doesn't make me a dousing rod for defunct citizens. So don't go sounding like some bubbleheaded reporter from the *National Intruder* or—"

"Three," she corrected amiably. "This corpse today, poor Chef Pastore, that makes three. Doesn't it? You always seem to arrive on the scene just as some poor fellow of your acquaintance is breathing his—"

"Speaking of arriving on scenes, what are you doing here? The word at the agency today was you were felled with a bug."

"Do I look as thought I have a bug running around inside me?" Molly asked, reaching into the canvas bag slung over her shoulder and fishing out a tiny square mirror. "I look, and if you weren't such an oaf you'd mention it, Merlin, pretty near terrific. I took the day off today to check on the Nolan Hosiery displays in various department stores and boutiques around Manhattan. That's my big account at Amthrax, after all." Flashing herself a smile in the mirror, she put it away. "I happen to be the Senior Account Ex on the Nolan account, even though I'm only twenty-seven."

Scrib, who was fast approaching thirty-four, said, "Right. And you make more money that I do. Due no doubt to your talent and not your terrific looks. Goodbye, Miss Cashin."

"Call me Molly."

"I'd just as well not."

"I know I've only been at the agency four months whereas you labored there several long weary years and—"

"Three and a half years isn't exactly—"

"I know you resent my meteoric rise," she continued. "Be that as it may, Merlin, I want you to call me Molly from hence on. We're going to be partners."

Scrib took an uneasy step back from her. "Partners in what?"

"Partners in finding all that money Chef Pastore just gave you the clue to," she answered, smiling up at him.

✗

"Tell me about the first corpse you stumbled on," called Molly from the kitchen of her penthouse apartment.

Scrib, his hands in his pockets, was gazing down at the twilit Central Park far below. Tiny people were hurrying in and out of it and a few of them were traveling in tiny carriages drawn by tiny horses. "Nope, I don't talk about that."

"Well, then, the second one." She appeared in the doorway, a fresh white apron on over her dark skirt and yellow blouse. "You can come into the kitchen and talk to me while I'm fixing our dinner."

"I'm not particularly hungry or—"

"Surely seeing Chef Pastore expire didn't upset you? You should be used to—"

"Seeing three people die over a period of five years doesn't exactly qualify me to run for coroner."

"True, yet you have to admit you seem to have an affinity for being at the right place at the right time. Take the Yoyo Hobbs Case last year, Merlin. You found his body, solved his murder, caused the demise of the killer, and—"

"And didn't make a penny. So there's no need for you to—"

"You didn't have me working with you then." Giving him a follow-me nod over her shoulder, she returned to the kitchen.

Shrugging, Scrib followed. "You have an impressive apartment here."

"Family money. That's what pays for it, which is what you've probably been wondering." Molly stopped in front of the stove, resting her hands on her knees, and watched the three pots on the burners. "What do you know about Hungarian goulash?"

"I've eaten it."

Using a wooden spoon, she pointed a the Pyrex pot nearest him. "Should it be doing that?"

The plastic cooking pouch had obviously sprung a leak and the ingredients were spinning and dancing all through the hot, bubbling water and staining it a deep orangish brown. "The sack's got a hole in it."

"Well, I know that. I poked it with the ice pick is why."

"On purpose?"

Straightening up, Molly said, "No, when I was chopping it free of the ice in the freezer compartment. I had the package stored for quite a while."

"We can send out for—"

"No, absolutely not. I like fixing meals. I don't get to do it half as often as I'd like. The noodles look okay, don't they?'

He scrutinized another bubbling pot. "They seem sort of limp."

"Noodles are supposed to be limp. Hence the expression, limp as a noodle."

"Not that limp."

Molly gave a short sigh. "While I'm doing the cooking, let's get to work solving the mystery."

"What's in the third pot, the one with the lid?"

"A surprise," she answered. "What form do you think the big money Chef Pastore alluded to is in?"

Scrib watched things bubble for a few seconds. "My past experience leads me to believe he was probably blackmailing somebody," he answered finally.

"Good, that makes sense." Molly nodded. "Now usually the Chef, who'd fallen from his former glory in recent years, worked in the kitchen at the Hotel Waterloo down at Twenty-second and Fifth Avenue. That's one of our Amthrax & Associates accounts, isn't it?"

"Yes, one I write copy for," he replied. "The Waterloo and the Dunkirk, the two hotels to think of when you want high-class accommodations and low low prices. A couple of fleabags, but a lot of bubbleheaded tourists seem to flock to them."

"The chef, because of his background as a former well-known television cooking-show host, also did commercials."

"That's how I got to know him, when he played a part in one of my Pizza Ona Stik spots. He had a pretty good singing voice, too, and we also used him on radio as a singing anchovy for—"

"The point I'm leading up to is, he knew you and trusted you."

"I'm basically a trustable person."

"I found out while you were chatting with the police that—"

"Chatting isn't the exact word. Grilling is more like what went on. They have the notion that because I happened to find a body in Central Park once, and then, months later, happen to be in Mitgang's when—"

"Let's concentrate on the murder at hand and not get into your personal—"

"Being labeled as another Jack the Ripper or Son of Sam doesn't exactly make me feel—"

"The police don't suspect you of being anything more than some kind of Jonah," she told him. "That cute Sergeant Hunsburger told me that while you were talking to the Eyewitness News girl with the wig."

"That's gratifying."

"Okay, Chef Pastore was working on a special one-day job at Mitgang's." Molly scratched her chin with the handle of the wooden spoon. "Obviously he made an appointment to meet someone behind the scenes and collect some money."

Scrib nodded. "There are a lot of little corridors and hallways behind those display rooms," he said. "The cops say they found blood in the passage just behind the kitchen where Chef Pastore collapsed. That must be where he met his killer."

"Only he didn't know it was a killer. He thought the gentleman was going to hand him some money."

Scrib leaned back against the sink and folded his arms. "We don't know for sure if it's a man or a woman."

"Yes, that's true. And a kitchen knife is a woman's weapon more or less."

"The killer had to bring those knives from a display several hundred feet away from where the killing took place." Scrib added. "Meaning he or she intended to use one and this wasn't a spur-of-the-moment thing."

After giving the disconnected goulash a tentative poke with her wooden spoon, Molly said, "Which brings us to the dying message. You have, so says rumor, a knack for working out this sort of thing."

"The other times," said Scrib, looking away from her, "the final words happened to be from old jokes. For a while there, it looked like every dying comedian in Manhattan was going to gasp out his last words to me. In this instance, though, Molly, the chef just muttered some gibberish about—"

"What specifically did he say? You can tell me." She held out her hand. "I know you're capable of solving this enigma and making us a lot of money. To show you my good faith, we'll split forty-sixty in your favor. A deal?"

He shook her hand. "It's a deal," he said. "But I really am unsure of what he was trying to convey. The important part, the message that's supposed to be the key, consists of three words. 'Six tablespoons molasses.' "

"Six tablespoons *molasses*?"

"Yep."

"So that's what he said. I wasn't quite close enough to catch it." She poked at the goulash once again. "Sometimes I wish I was a better cook, but when it comes to reading a recipe I—"

"Recipe!" exclaimed Scrib, straightening up. "Sure, of course. He was a chef, not a comic. He didn't tell jokes, he told recipes."

Molly was watching his face, a puzzled frown spreading. "Beg pardon?"

"Six tablespoons molasses," Scrib explained slowly and carefully. "That's the way you list ingredients in recipes. You know, three pounds bananas, two cups sugar, six tablespoons *molasses*."

Molly laughed. "Great, you've solved it," she said. "What does it mean?"

"I don't know," he admitted. "But maybe if we look through some cookbooks we—"

"I only have one, actually."

"That's a start. I'll run through the index and find all the recipes that call for molasses and then—"

"This one won't help much. It's the *Girl Guides Campfire Cookbook* and I don't recall we used much molasses when we were tramping in the—"

"That's all you have?"

"Mostly when I have lavish dinner parties like tonight, Scrib, I thaw things."

"We'll have to go to the nearest D. Trumbo Bookstore and—" He took a few steps toward the doorway, then halted. "Wait now. Chef Pastore wouldn't give me a tip out of just any cookbook. It had to be something special that— Got it!" He gave a happy snap of his fingers.

"What? What?"

"About six months ago he presented me with an autographed copy of his old cookbook—the one he wrote when he had his national television show in the Fifties," explained Scrib. "Yeah, the *Chef Pastore TV Cooking Guide*. It was on *The New York Times* list for weeks back in—"

"Where is the darn thing?"

Scrib considered. "I never got around to taking it home," he remembered. "Nope. So the book must still be in my office at the agency."

Molly whipped off her apron, flicked off all three burners, and said, "Let's go get it."

✗

Coming into his office out of the shadowy hallway, she observed, "Dinky."

Scrib nodded toward the small window that looked out on a drab stretch of brick wall. "Not much of a view, either," he said, clicking on his desk lamp.

"No wonder you've been resentful of me," she said. "Only four short months with A & A and I have a spacious office that makes this one look—"

"Account people always fare better than copywriters." He crouched down in front of the forlorn little grey bookcase next to his ancient desk.

The shelves were packed with reference books, broken-spined paperbacks, piles of old commercial scripts, bundles of advertising newsletters, a Betty Boop penny bank, a folded-up coat sweater, and a jar of peanut butter.

"Yep, here it is." When Scrib tugged the fat book free, the jar of peanut butter hopped to the floor.

Placing the book on his stained green blotter, he dropped into his swivel chair. It gave a keening moan. "Let's see now. Molasses— molasses—"

Molly rubbed at the edge of his desk with her fingertips and then perched on it to watch him as he ran a finger along the index column. "You really ought to be doing better than this," she said. "You're not a bad copywriter and—"

"I've had a few setbacks. Page 117, page 226, page 394—"

"Were you sick or—"

"Nope, I got sidetracked. Into trying to be a comedian."

"I didn't know that."

"Few people do."

"What went wrong?"

"Numerous things." He turned to page 117. "This calls for two cups molasses."

"Ugh," Molly remarked.

He leaped ahead to page 226. "What I'd like to do now, as soon as I accumulate enough money, is start my own advertising agency. Merlin, Limited, specializing in humorous copy."

"That'll take considerable money."

"Exactly ... Nope, this one's for molasses cookies and calls for half a cup."

"If and when you start your own ship," Molly said, "I might come along."

He paused to look up at her. "Can I afford you?"

"Depends on how much money Chef Pastore helps us make."

"Hey! Here it is," he announced, returning his attention to the late chef's cookbook. "The first ingredient is six tablespoons molasses."

Molly put her hand on his arm. "Is there a clue in there anywhere?"

"Well, it's a recipe for Boston Brown Bread," said Scrib, a shade disappointed.

"Meaning maybe he was killed by a man named Brown?"

"Or a lady from Boston."

"Or someone who owns a bakery."

"Damn, it doesn't look like much of a lead to anything." He turned again to the index and then began flipping pages at random. "That seems to be the only damn recipe in this entire bubbleheaded book that uses six tablespoons of molasses."

"I never much liked molasses," she said. "It has such a dark brown taste."

Shutting the book, Scrib leaned back. The chair groaned. "Okay, the chef wanted me to read this recipe—and then what?"

"Bake some bread?"

Scrib tapped his thumb and forefinger on his desk. "Where did he figure I'd go next?"

"He was breathing his last, remember? Maybe none of what he said means a darn thing and we're simply wasting—"

"No. Boston Brown Bread has to mean something," insisted Scrib. "He's dying, he's got a secret worth money and on top of that he doesn't want whoever it was who killed him to get away free and clear."

"I hate to sound pessimistic, but—"

"The Hotel Waterloo." Scrib sat up.

"That's not in Boston, it's right down on—"

"He had a room there, they threw it in as part of the deal. He was head chef and got a free room." He stood up. "The next part of the answer's got to be in his room."

✗

It wasn't, though.

At least not any more—if it ever had been.

"Someone anticipated us," said Scrib, who was standing by the tumbled bed.

"I don't think it was Sergeant Hunsburger," said Molly, surveying the disordered room. "He struck me as being much more fastidious than—"

"No, this was the killer," Scrib told her.

All the drawers in the woebegone bureau against the blotchy green wall had been yanked out, shaken, and dropped. The threadbare rug had been rolled up, the two suitcases taken out of the narrow closet and searched. There were clothes, papers, two fresh chef's hats, and a silver cake-server scattered on the floor.

Molly reached into her heavy canvas shoulder bag. "Mind if I smoke? I've cut down to about one cigarette a day and this feels like a good time to indulge."

"You ought to quit." Scrib dropped to his hands and knees. "Damn, there's no way of knowing if the killer found what he was looking for or not."

Molly held a package of cigarettes in her left hand. "One a day isn't a very big habit."

"None is better."

"Oh, the hell with you. I need a cigarette." She shook one out, lit it, and took a deep drag. "I'm not as used to finding bodies as you are."

Scrib began pacing off a slow circuit of the dead man's room. "I guess I better go through all this scattered stuff and see if there's anything pertaining to brown or Boston."

"Whatever the killer was looking for is pretty small and flat, right?" She exhaled smoke and ribbons of it began snaking up toward the peach-colored light fixture dangling high above the bed.

"Yep, something you could slip under a rug. Pictures, letters, money."

"Interesting how many valuable things are small and flat." She exhaled more smoke.

Within fifteen minutes Scrib and the red-haired young woman had sifted through all of Chef Pastore's belongings. There was nothing that told them anything.

✗

Scrib gave the room key back to the desk clerk in the lobby. "Thanks, Hermie."

"Anything to oblige, Mr. Merlin," said the dark young man. "Have you been considering my suggestion?"

"Which one?"

"To use me as an actor in the next Waterloo TV commercial you guys do," the clerk reminded him. "Seems odd to me to bring in actors to play the clerks and bellhops when you got—"

"I mentioned you to Mr. Amthrax, but—"

"Did you tell him how much I look like Treat Williams? That's a plus."

"Forgot to. Next chance I get." He rested an elbow on the sign-in desk, looking over at Molly, who was sitting demurely in a fat armchair near the switchboard girl's cubicle. She really was an attractive girl. "Hermie, did Chef Pastore ever talk much with you?"

"Lou? Naw, he thought he was still cooking at the Waldorf or someplace."

"Was that his first name—Lou?"

"Sure, didn't you know? No, he probably insisted you all call him Chef."

"I'm curious about who he might have known around the hotel here. For instance, is there anyone named Brown who—"

"Lou wasn't friends with anybody. Except Marina."

"Who? One of the maids or—"

"She works the switchboard on the eight-to-midnight shift," answered Hermie, nodding at the alcove. "She was pretty thick with

Lou and I didn't expect she'd even come in tonight, him just dead and all. She's here, though, but tearful."

Scrib crossed over to the switchboard. "My name's Scrib Merlin," he said to the plump blonde woman sitting there. "I was a friend and associate of Lou Pastore and—"

"The poor man, the poor dear man," said Marina, rubbing at her nose. "He was a genius, a marvelous person, and—now—"

Along the wall on the sobbing woman's left was a low bookcase. There were two dozen phone directories lined up on the top shelf. As Scrib casually glanced at them the word *Boston* suddenly leaped out at him. "Hey! That must be it," he said. "I have to phone someone in Boston, a friend of Lou's up there. May I borrow that phone directory for a moment?"

"Certainly." She reached out, unlooking, took it off the shelf, and passed it to him.

✗

Molly made an angry noise and turned away from the six photos spread out across her living-room coffee table. "So it's true," she murmured.

"Hum? What's true?"

She coughed into her hand. "I mean, it's true the chef was blackmailing somebody."

"I warned you about looking at this kind of picture," Scrib said, frowning at the girl. "Pictures of people in this sort of situation can upset you."

"I'm not at all upset," she assured him. "Seeing people in bed making love doesn't sicken me or anything."

"You know who the guy in all the photos is, don't you?"

She said, "He looks sort of familiar."

"Sometimes people look different without their clothes," said Scrib, shifting each of the photos a half inch to the right.

Each of the pictures showed the same blond forty-year-old man in what used to be called compromising positions with two different young women. The pictures had been shot through a transom and the bedroom in question was obviously one at the Waterloo Hotel. Chef Pastore had enclosed copies of his six shots, plus the negatives, in a white hotel envelope and then taped them to the inside back cover of the Boston phone directory. He had been intending to retrieve them himself.

"This is great," said Scrib. "Before us we see none other than Rodlow Neeb."

"Is that who he is? I know I've seen him around the agency a few times."

"So had the chef, probably, which is how he came to recognize Neeb when he went sneaking into the Waterloo for his assignations," said Scrib, leaning back. "Yep, Rodlow Neeb. He's the ad manager over at one of our biggest clients, Jarvis Drugs, makers of Snooz, No Sneez, and Snoz." He slid each photo a half inch to the left. "Neeb earns around $150,000 a year *and* he's married to Dinah Corkin."

"Who's she?"

"The Corkin Paper heiress." Scrib grinned. "He'll want to buy these pictures—he'll have to. If his wife saw them, he'd be in considerable trouble. Corkin also owns a share of Jarvis. Yep, Neeb is going to pay money. Big money."

"Scrib—"

He glanced over at her. "What?"

Impulsively she kissed him on the cheek. "Just be careful, will you? You don't want to end up like Chef Pastore."

✗

It was a little after 11 a.m. on a near-perfect Saturday morning. Scrib was whistling sedately as he pushed through the heavy glass doors of the Museum of Advanced Art. He'd phoned Rodlow Neeb last night from Molly's penthouse and made his pitch. Everything had gone well. Neeb had been scared silly and agreed right off to paying $100,000 in cash for the photos and negatives that the chef had more or less willed to Scrib.

And Scrib had picked a near-perfect place to make the exchange, the Food Is Art/Art Is Food exhibit in the main gallery at the AA. A huge well-lighted room on the ground floor was where the exhibit was being staged. No chance of Neeb's ambushing him or dragging him into a dark corner to do him bodily harm. Nope, Scrib would hand him the pictures, take the briefcase full of cash in return, and that would be it. He'd have $100,000, which would give him a hell of a good start toward setting up his own business. Well, even though he had to turn over forty percent to Molly, he'd still have $60,000. That wasn't bad, even these days.

A smile touched his face as, walking across the bright airy foyer of the museum, he thought of Molly. She was an attractive young woman—bright, too. Up until now, none of the women he'd been involved with had been able to understand his somewhat mercenary outlook. But Molly did. She even shared it. She'd be waiting for him back at her apartment. So, when he'd divided up the money he might just mention to her that—"

"Holy Hannah!"

Molly wasn't home at her penthouse apartment. She was right here in the bright and airy main exhibition room of the Museum of Advanced Art. He'd just seen her ducking behind a twenty-foot-high plaster BLT sandwich.

"What kind of bubbleheaded behavior is this?"

Keeping his face unclouded, he wended his way through the scatter of other patrons.

"Don't touch the iron pickle, Kevin."

"Marvelous, marvelous. A giant rubber blintz sums it all up, doesn't it?"

By stationing himself behind an immense slice of Swiss cheese, executed in some kind of rubbery plastic and hanging like a curtain in the middle of the room, Scrib found he could, peeking through one of the holes, watch Molly unseen. He was also near enough to the gigantic sandwich to hear what she was saying to the big blond man in the conservative grey suit. It was Rodlow Neeb, with a fat briefcase tucked up under one arm.

"Relax, Molly," Neeb responded to the redhead. "I can explain the—"

"Explain my fanny!" Molly's face was pale and blurred with anger. "You swore to me I was the only woman you were seeing."

"You and my wife, yes. I can't drop her without a great deal of financially embarrassing things happen—"

"Here I compromise my principles, carry on a torrid affair with a married man, I let you pay the outlandish rent on that seamy love nest on Central Park—"

"It's not exactly a love nest, Moll." Neeb made hushing motions with his free hand. "Even if it were, dear, shouting the details in public isn't—"

"Don't talk to me about going public, you oaf!" Her voice kept getting angrier and louder. "You, who've been carrying on with not one but two other bimbos at that tacky Waterloo Hotel. How could you?"

Neeb glanced anxiously around. A thin old man who had been admiring a huge inflated tomato was now eyeing him. "Quit now, Moll. Let's go someplace quiet for brunch as soon as—"

"We're not going anywhere, Rodlow," she told him. "Oh, I'm so glad I followed you yesterday instead of going into the agency. Yes, I followed you down to Mitgang's. I thought you might be off on another of your furtive assignations, as I'd long suspected, but instead you were slaying poor Chef Pastore."

"Quiet, quiet. You don't want to make that sort of allegation too loudly, Moll."

"I'm also glad I attached myself to the poor simp who took over from the chef. That way I found out the whole truth."

Poor simp? said Scrib to himself.

"Yes, that way I got to see the photos, Rodlow. You never do take a good picture, do you? It's that flabby double chin of yours and—"

"Control your temper, Molly. We can—"

"No, my controlling days are over," she said. "I came here this morning for just one thing. Well, two actually. I wanted to see your simpy face while you still thought you were going to get those photos and be home free."

"Just a little family squabble, folks," Neeb said to the half dozen food-art patrons who were staring at them.

"Remember what I told you I'd do to you if you were unfaithful to me, Rodlow?"

"Oh, sure, you said you were going to kill me. But I assumed— Moll!"

She yanked a .32 revolver out of her canvas shoulder bag. "I'm a person of my word," she told him and shot him three times in the stomach.

Neeb's placating smile remained on his face for several seconds. Then all expression dropped away, his mouth fell open, and he collapsed to the bright floor. The briefcase, splashed with blood, was pinned beneath him.

Scrib took a deep breath. He thrust his hands deep into his pockets. As more people came running to the scene of the shooting, he walked out of the museum and into the street.

The sun came shining down on him. It was a near-perfect morning.

ADAM AND EVE ON A RAFT

He wasn't dead when he landed at her feet.

But nearly so.

He'd come hurtling out of a third-story window of his vast stone mansion and landed with an unsettling cracking, splattering sound on the rose-colored flagstones of the courtyard.

Salty Warbeck, tossing her portfolio clear of the spatters of fresh blood, moved up and knelt beside the dying man.

A flutter of something up at the open window made the slim blonde glance upward. A white lace curtain was waving faintly. Up from the gabled roof a single sooty seagull went rising into the midday air, circling away toward nearby Long Island Sound.

"Mr. Hoogly," said Salty, bending her head low and brushing at his ruined old face with her hair, "how are you, or is that a dumb question? You'll have to excuse me since I'm really not used to finding dying people. Oops, I shouldn't say that, since it may dampen your spirits, but— What happened?"

The plump millionaire gazed up at her through dimming eyes. "Hello there, my little—cutie—" he wheezed. "And—such a gifted artist."

"Listen, don't think I don't enjoy flattery as much as the next person," she informed him. "The thing is, though, Mr. Hoogly, that you actually ought to be talking, at a crucial time like this, about yourself, you know, and explaining what happened and all."

"Want you to have—a little bonus," gasped Munson Hoogly, making a dreadful sound that was part chuckle and part death rattle. "Little cutie—done lots of nice ads for me. Hidden money—tell you where."

"No, really, Mr. Hoogly, you've paid me more than adequately, especially since those dippy account executives in the ad agency that handles your account don't think I'm really a commercial artist at all.

53

See, they just can't get used to the fact that I'm a woman *and* a regular contributor to *The National Buffoon*. Even though, as we've chatted about many a time in pleasanter circumstances when I've dropped by here to deliver finished art, my main ambition in life is— But you were saying?"

"Hidden money, Salty," muttered the expiring old man. His eyes flickered from side to side. "Don't want rest of them—to know—but give you a hint. You'll find—smart kid—"

"Please don't go trying a dying message on me, Mr. Hoogly. I mean, if that's really your last wish, well, okay, but I'm not at all good at this sort of thing. I did have, which I may have mentioned during one of our nice chats over ice cream, a gentleman friend who had a knack for solving cryptic stuff like that. People were continually dying when he happened to be in the vicinity and gasping out all sorts of puzzling—I guess, though, I ought not to keep interrupting you."

"Pay attention, Salty," gasped Hoogly, his bloodied head raising up slightly off the stained flagstones. "Here's how to find some cash—lots of it—"

"Well, I'd prefer a clear-cut statement, but go ahead."

"Adam and Eve," Hoogly choked out. "Adam and Eve—on a raft."

"Beg pardon?"

"Adam and Eve," he repeated in his rapidly fading voice, "on a raft." His head sank back, his body quivered, his hands fluttered like the wings of a fledgling bird.

His eyes drifted shut. "By the way," he added. "I was pushed."

He shuddered twice and died.

"Oh, darn," said Salty to the dead millionaire, "you should've told me that part right off at first."

Shaking her head sadly, she stood back and away from the corpse. A new wind came blowing from the Sound and the young woman hunched her narrow shoulders, shivering.

"Adam and Eve on a raft," she said to herself. "I don't really much want to, but I guess I'm going to have to get in touch with Scrib Merlin."

The carved oak door of the Hoogly mansion now burst open. The chubby butler came puffing out, followed by Hoogly's only son and his latest wife.

"I'm afraid you're a little late," Salty told them as they came running toward the body.

Scrib Merlin poked at his ancient typewriter. "I wonder what kind of muse presides over copywriters," he muttered. "Specifically copywriters who bat out one-minute radio commercials for Bowling Green Toilet Cleaner. New Improved Bowling Green Toilet Cleaner with SaniScrub 36 added."

Dusk was descending on Manhattan and the brick wall a few feet outside the dingy window of his minute office was slowly turning an ominous black.

The phone rang.

"Amthrax & Associates," he answered. The switchboard girl went home at six.

"Don't scream or yell or call me foul names," requested a familiar voice. "Okay, Scrib?"

He frowned. "Salty?"

"I intended to call you much earlier but I got tied up with the police and some reporters and all."

"For two years?"

"Oh, you mean, which is a perfectly natural question really, why haven't I called you for over two years and then am suddenly doing it now," said Salty. "Well, we broke up, you knew that."

He nodded. "I was aware of the fact, yes. I also recall your statement that you never wanted to see me again."

"I still don't much like you, Scrib, if you want the honest-to-gosh truth," she admitted. "I mean, I was very fond of you at one time and, I do think, fairly supportive. I tried to listen to your many and varied complaints about Mr. Amthrax, even though he always seemed to me a very nice man although a bit on the short side and—"

"He's a midget. He is no more than four feet high even when standing on tiptoe."

"Size isn't everything. Look at me. I'm slim, yet I'm very attractive and eventually I'm going to move out of cartooning, even though I have a great affinity for it, and become a model in—"

"Why did you phone me, Salty? Why were you with the police?"

"These were Long Island police," she said. "In fact, I just now got back from Cold Harbor, Long Island. That's in Suffolk County."

"I know. It's where that halfwit you've been doing newspaper ads for resides. Munson Hoogly, owner of ninety-six Cone-Y Island Ice Cream Shops in the tri-state area. Perpetrator of the worst radio spots ever to defile the human ear, a man who has set back the cause of communication several score—"

"You ought to speak well of the dead."

"Hoogly's dead?"

"He fell out a window," she explained. "Well, he didn't fall. At least, he said he was pushed. Except a fairly unimaginative man named Detective Bonfigli, which is pronounced, as you just heard, Bon-feely but is spelled, for some dippy reason, B-o-n-f-i-g-l—"

"Did you want to get together with me, Salty, or what?"

"Well, yes," she said in a somewhat, for her, timid voice. "The thing is, the time that playboy got killed in my apartment, or actually by falling out of it, and you had solved that dying message business with the old comedian, well, as I tried to make perfectly clear at the time, Scrib, I respect your ability at solving puzzles like that, but I don't want us to get involved in any other way. But if you could help me out now I'd be most—"

"Wait, now. You're telling me Hoogly passed on some kind of dying message to you?"

"Yes," Salty said. "I didn't mention that to the police, though I did inform them Mr. Hoogly hinted he'd been pushed, except this detective Bonfigli doesn't much accept that at all."

"Hoogly was murdered?"

"Yes, but that's not really what I want you to work on. You don't actually hate me, do you?"

"Not exactly, but—"

"Good, and I, even though as I once explained, think you're much too crass in your outlook on life, still admire your ability to—"

"Ha." He sat up in his chair. "That old coot gave you a lead on something you think'll make you money, right? Sure, and you didn't tell the cops. So that makes you as crass as—"

"A lot of money may be involved. Everybody knows how eccentric Munson Hoogly was."

"Yeah, I've heard he squirreled wads of cash all over that ten-acre estate and marina of his out there."

"Now, from a strictly legal point of view the money ought to go to his heirs," said Salty. "Perhaps to his only son, Beauford Hoogly, and his most recent wife, Sabrina Destino Hoogly, who claims to be just thirty though she's got all kinds of squiggly little lines around her eyes and her—"

"She's still attractive. I've seen her picture in *The Times*."

"Anyway, Scrib, I don't imagine Mr. Hoogly got around to mentioning me in his will, even though he was quite taken with the drawings I've been making and all. So since he really made it clear, with his dying breath just about, that he wanted me to have this little bonus, though his idea of little may not match mine—"

"What exactly did he say?"

"Will you help me then?" She sounded pleased. "For a split of—um—how does thirty percent sound?"

"Better than twenty-five percent, not as good as fifty percent."

"Well, I might go to fifty percent, depending on how much there turns out to be. See, I know you'd like a big lump sum to start your own advertising agency and—that's still your goal, isn't it?"

"Yep."

"And you haven't come up with the money on your own since I saw you last?"

"Nope. How much did Hoogly say there was hidden away?"

"He didn't. I imagine it has to be in the thousands, wouldn't you?"

"Could be, yes."

"You'll really help me?"

After a few silent seconds, during which he stared out at the darkening brick wall, Scrib answered, "Okay. So what was the dying message he—"

"One thing further, which I hope won't discourage you," Salty said carefully. "Even though in the past we were intimate and had a somewhat pleasant relationship, I don't want to start up anything like that again. What I'm suggesting is a strictly business relationship. Anyway, for all I know you're passionately in love with some new creature who—"

"No, there's nobody special," he answered. "But we'll keep this a business thing, Salty. What was the dying message?"

"I'll tell you day after tomorrow, while we're driving out to Cold Harbor to look around."

"Day after tomorrow? Aren't you anx—"

"The funeral's the day after tomorrow. It seems rather sudden to me, but that's what the widow wants," she replied. "Since Barnum—did I mention that the butler's name is Barnum and he's fairly fat and I'm not at all sure what sort of strange sex life he may lead but he's very fond of me and he's going to let me in the place to poke around while everyone else is away at the funeral and all. Can you get off work, commencing around noon?"

"I've been putting in a lot of extra time, so I can take the whole day off."

"Are you still living in that depressing apartment house in the East Eighties?"

"Yep."

"I'll pick you up exactly at noon," Salty said. "Oh, and Scrib?"

"What?"

"It's been nice talking to you again." She hung up.

✗

"C'mon, c'mon, nice baby," urged Salty. "You can do it."

Seated uneasily in the passenger seat next to her, Scrib inquired, "Why do you keep talking to the car?"

"It seems to help," she answered as she guided the ancient green Volkswagen into another lane of the expressway. "Some machinery is very sensitive and you have to sweet-talk it quite a bit. I have a toaster that's the same darn way and if you don't flatter it the toast pops out like charcoal. Plants are that—"

"Suppose you fill me in on Hoogly's alleged dying message."

The afternoon was a grey, rainy one. The VW's windshield wipers did their work in a jerky, complaining way.

"Okay," she said, her eyes on the rainswept road and her shoulders hunched. "Well, the actual message itself was pretty dippy. Mr. Hoogly led up to it by saying he wanted me to sort of have a bonus because of all the splendid drawings I've been providing for his Cone-Y Island Ice Cream Shop newspaper ads. Then he seemed to get the notion we were being eavesdropped on and he turned sly."

"Saying what?"

"Adam and Eve on a raft."

"Hum?"

" 'Adam and Eve, Adam and Eve,' he gasped out. 'On a raft.' Not certain I'd heard him correctly, I asked him, even though he was breathing his last, to repeat it. He said, 'Adam and Eve on a raft,' all over again. People do say some odd things while they're—"

"Didn't Hoogly start life as the owner of a greasy-spoon café?"

"He did, yes. That's where he invented his Special Creamy Hoogly Ice Cream and began his climb to success. It's a real American success story how he parlayed that stuff into a chain of—"

58 Adam and Eve on a Raft: Mystery Stories

"The point is, Salty, that 'Adam and Eve on a raft' is old short-order slang," Scrib cut in. "You know, waitresses used to holler back to the frycook things like, 'Hounds on an island,' or 'Shimmy in the hay.' Meaning hot dogs on baked beans and strawberry jello."

"So what does 'Adam and Eve on a raft' mean?"

"Two poached eggs on toast."

She sighed and the car swerved slightly to the left. "I don't see where that gets us," she said, disappointed. "What kind of dying message is that?"

"It suggests several things to me. All of which we can check out when we get to the estate."

Salty brightened some. "I knew I'd picked the right man for the job." She reached over and patted his hand approvingly.

✗

The funeral procession was quite impressive. Three glittering Mercedes, a sparkling Rolls, and then a string of expensive domestic automobiles came rolling somberly through the open ironwork gates of the sprawling Hoogly estate. The black hearse itself was impressively long and highly polished.

"Poor Mr. Hoogly," observed Salty.

Her Volkswagen, quivering and rattling, was idling across the rainy street, waiting for the cortege to depart.

From his side of the car Scrib could see the turreted mansion and the private docking area beyond it. "Is that Hoogly's boat down there?"

"Yes, it's a fifty-eight-foot yawl, or at least I think that's what he told me once." She was watching the funeral parade disappear around a bend in the road. "Mr. Hoogly, rest his soul, showed me around it one afternoon and it's really quite handsome even though he named it the *S.S. Tutti-Frutti*. After, you know, his favorite ice-cream flavor."

"It figures," said Scrib.

Salty drove the car onto the estate grounds and parked it on a patch of white gravel near the row of garages. As she was getting out of the safety belts, she cautioned, "Be nice to Barnum."

The massive front door of the mansion creaked cautiously open while they were still on the bottom step of the stone porch.

A plump pinkish face was floating in the shadows of the foyer, looking out. "Bless my soul, if it isn't Miss Warbeck, right on time."

She hurried up the steps and hugged him. "This must be a trying time for you, Barnum."

"That it is, Miss," he admitted, snuffling. "Dear Mr. Hoogly and I were— Ah, but you'd best scoot inside before you're noticed."

"Noticed? I thought everyone was away at—"

"Not her, oh, no." He pointed a fat thumb at the beamed ceiling. "Prostrated by grief, she claims. Prostrated by booze is closer to the mark."

"The widow?" inquired Scrib.

Frowning over at him, Barnum replied, "You can call her that. Too unsteady on her pins to attend the funeral. Shameful."

Salty asked, "Is she likely to notice us if we poke around?"

"You'll likely have to steer clear of the third floor, Miss. Otherwise I don't imagine you'll have anything to worry about."

"Barnum," she said, tapping at Scrib's arm, "this is Mr. Merlin. He's a—um—very dear friend of mine."

Barnum looked him up and down. "And a fine strapping lad he is, too. Pleased to meet you, sir." He bowed slightly. "Where would you two dears like to begin?"

Salty glanced at Scrib. "Well?"

"The kitchen," answered Scrib.

✗

"Experimental farm?" he asked as he finished putting the last toaster together again.

"You're very handy with appliances, Scrib. I didn't realize—"

"This halfwit farm—where is it, Salty?"

"Right on the estate here. It's small, only an acre or so."

Scrib set the toaster back on its breadboard resting place. "And there are chickens there? And eggs?"

Her head bobbed up and down. "Dozens of both. There's a model chicken coop there where he was experimenting with chickens. He was trying to get better eggs so his ice cream would taste even—"

"Okay, his last words to you were about eggs and toast," said Scrib, starting to pace the big white kitchen where they'd spent the past forty-five minutes. "We've checked out the eggs in the refrigerator, the bin they're kept in, and the powdered eggs in that pantry yonder. Also all the toasters, of which there are five, as well as the breadbox, packages of melba toast, and even the flour bin. We haven't found a damn thing."

"There was that twenty dollars in the sugar bowl."

"You can't call that much of a legacy. Probably belongs to the cook, anyway."

"That's why I didn't take it."

He drummed his fingers on the edge of the sink. "We'll have to search the chicken coop, dig into all the nests."

"His dying message to me was in café jargon," she said thoughtfully. "Could my legacy, maybe, be in the old restaurant?"

He stared at the pretty young woman in a questioning way. "What old restaurant?"

"Mr. Hoogly, didn't I mention this before, Scrib, was a very sentimental old gentleman and he built, oh, it must be about six years ago, a replica of that first restaurant of his."

"And where is that?"

She pointed at the rain-speckled window over the sink. "Out on the other side of the farm."

He let out his breath slowly. "Okay, we'll search the farm. If we don't find anything there, it'll be this sentimental café."

"Don't be downhearted."

"What gave you the notion I was?"

✗

Scrib sneezed again, brushed white feathers off his elbows and then his knees.

"That's very interesting," remarked Salty as she opened the door of the little reconstructed restaurant. "I wasn't aware people could be allergic to chickens in that form. I mean, I have an aunt who breaks out in hives if she eats chicken soup, but you're sneezing over living chickens."

Stepping in out of the grey rain, Scrib looked around the place. It had a counter, stools, and three small booths. The menu was scrawled on a blackboard up over the grill and the prices were from another era. "Anybody'd sneeze with feathers in their nose," he said. "That's not an allergy."

Salty perched on a stool and rotated around one full turn, then did it twice again. "Sixteen chicken nests and not so much as a plug nickel, whatever that might be." She looked thoughtful. "It's funny how one uses everyday expressions and yet isn't at all—"

"Hush," he suddenly advised.

"Don't go taking your frustration out on—"

"No, I'm telling you to fall silent for practical reasons." He made a be-still motion and went easing over to the still-open door.

"What's wrong?" Salty whispered.

He stood listening, hearing nothing but the rain falling down through the branches of the surrounding oaks and maples. "Nothing, I guess," he said finally, closing the door quietly. "I thought I heard someone out there."

"Everybody's still at the funeral except Mrs. Hoogly and she's up in the mansion dead drunk," reminded Salty. "No one'll be back for a good while since the cemetery's way over on the other side of the island almost."

Scrib went around behind the counter. The old-fashioned refrigerator was still in working order, although there was nothing inside it but a box of saltine crackers. There was a small white shelf with six shallow depressions in it and the word EGGS lettered on it.

Scrib crouched a bit, trying to determine if you could somehow hide a wad of money under it.

"Scrib?"

"Hum?"

"You did hear something."

He turned away from the open refrigerator and saw a lean man of about fifty standing near Salty. He wore a dark suit and a somber tie.

"Go right ahead," he urged, smiling some. "I'm as interested in this as you are."

"This is Beauford Hoogly," said Salty in a voice not filled with enthusiasm.

"That same Beauford Hoogly who's supposed to be away at the burying ground?" Scrib shut the refrigerator door.

"I thought I spotted Miss Warbeck coming in when we were driving off," said Hoogly.

"He was in the second Mercedes." Salty folded her hands in her narrow lap and gave a forlorn half turn on the stool.

"It occurred to me that, by golly, the old boy'd been playing tricks again," explained the ice-cream heir. "She was with him at the end and that would've been just like him. Did he tell you where he'd hidden one of his packets of cash?"

Salty kept her lips pressed shut for nearly a half minute. "Well, yes, but not exactly. I mean, your father told me he wanted me to have a little bonus and he gave me a sort of clue that might lead to money, but we've been at it for a couple of hours without any luck to speak of."

"I know," said Hoogly, brushing chicken feathers from his sleeve. "I've been tagging along in your wake for the past hour. At first I was dead certain you knew exactly where to look. Now I'm losing my certainty."

"We'll find it," said Scrib.

"When do you think?"

"Eventually."

"What's the use of finding it now?" said Salty. "It's Hoogly money and if we unearth it, we'll just have to turn it over to him."

"No, no, Miss Warbeck," said Hoogly. "You don't understand quite what I have in mind. I'm no good at these scavenger-hunt things at all, even though my late father doted on paper chases, treasure hunts, and the like."

Scrib leaned over the counter, like a frycook who's anxious for an order. "You have a deal in mind?"

"Fifty-fifty?" suggested Hoogly. "You see, I have a dreadful suspicion Dad's left a big chunk of everything to Sabrina. I think I can fight that in court, but I'll need some ready cash meantime."

"You're willing to split half and half?"

The heir smiled from one to the other. "I'll even put you two up at the mansion. Take your time, and if you don't find any loot today try again tomorrow. What say?"

Salty tossed Scrib a quick affirmative nod.

"It's a deal," he told Beauford.

✗

At eleven that night the rain was falling hard and heavy. Scrib was sitting up in bed, alone, reading a book he'd borrowed from the Hoogly mansion library.

After trying the opening paragraph for the third time, he set it aside. "Guess I'm not in the mood for Albert Payson Terhune," he decided and swung out of bed.

Up here on the third floor of the house you could hear the night rain loud and clear.

"What a nitwit day this has been," he said to himself as he paced on the thick Persian carpet. "Looking under chickens, taking a 1930's greasy spoon apart, and finding not one thin dime."

On top of which Salty was sleeping by herself in the next room.

With the door between—he'd tried it carefully an hour ago—locked tight.

"No romance, no money. The story of my life."

Barefooted, he continued pacing.

"That old tutti-frutti tycoon must've meant something."

But what?

"Adam and Eve on a raft," muttered Scrib. "Eggs—on a raft. Eggs on a boat? On a boat! Holy moley!"

He started hurrying into his clothes.

✗

No use waking Salty. Let her sleep—safely behind her locked door.

The collar of his sportcoat turned up, a borrowed flashlight clutched close to his chest, Scrib slipped free of the house by way of a back door.

The rain attacked him, splashing and pelting.

He ran, splattering water and mud, down toward the private dock.

He sprinted up the gangway, head ducked low.

Clicking on his flash, he found his way to the galley. He located the light switch and flicked it on. Thin yellow light blossomed and showed him a huge refrigerator hulking in one corner of the small pale-blue room.

There was a whole compartment labeled EGGS.

There were no eggs in it.

He poked his hand inside, squinting. "Sure, this damn thing's got a false bottom."

Scrib whipped out one of the two borrowed screwdrivers he'd also brought along.

In under five minutes he got the false floor of the egg compartment off.

"Hot damn!" There was a business-sized manila envelope on top of stacked packets of cash. The top bills were all hundreds. Judging by the thickness of the packets, there was at least $250,000 here.

"Half of that to Hoogly leaves us $125,000 to split."

But hold on a minute. Hoogly didn't have to know. Scrib could get the dough out of here, hide it, and claim they'd never found it at all.

In fact, even Salty didn't have to know.

With a quarter million of his own, hell, he could start up his own agency just about. At least he could clear out of Amthrax & Associates.

64   Adam and Eve on a Raft: Mystery Stories

Letting the money lie, he picked up the envelope. There might be more cash in it, or negotiable bonds.

He tucked his flashlight under his arm, let the refrigerator door swing shut, and leaned against it to examine the contents of the envelope.

Scribbled across the front of it was: *Some interesting facts about my wife's past life.*

So it wasn't money then. Scrib started to open the envelope.

"Don't bother," suggested a feminine voice.

He looked up to see a handsome red-haired woman in the galley doorway. She had a new-looking .32 revolver in her hand and pointed at him.

"Mrs. Hoogly, isn't it? Allow me to express my deepest sympathies to you in this moment of grief and then explain that this isn't what—"

"The envelope, schlepp," she requested, "hand it over."

"This? Sure. But I think you—"

"Beauford's so bloody obvious, isn't he? Hiring a private dick to hunt this down and trying to pretend you're just a lover of that scrawny Salty Warbeck."

"She's slender, but not exactly—"

"The envelope, jerko."

He held it out to her. "Sure, here."

Sabrina Hoogly snatched it. "I do wish I could allow you to live," she said, sounding not at all sad, "but you know about this damn thing and you probably suspect what's inside it."

"I never even peeked inside," he assured her. "And your secret, whatever it is, is perfectly safe with—"

"No, you'll simply have to have an accident. Just like poor Munson."

"You pushed him?"

"He fell, but you're going to expire in the boat explosion," she told him. "I'm very good at arranging accidents, as this damned dossier Munson compiled makes very clear."

"Don't blow up this yawl, because there's—"

"Please don't plead and grovel, Mr. Merlin. Die like a man."

"That's not what I'm groveling about, Mrs. Hoogly. I'm trying to tell you that there's—"

"Relax," she advised. Stepping forward, she slammed the pistol butt hard against his temple.

It took six, maybe seven smacks to make him fall down and pass out.

✗

Scrib awakened to find himself bound and gagged. He could see the refrigerator from his position on the galley floor.

He also smelled smoke.

Indicating the *S.S. Tutti-Frutti* was on fire.

He'd had some bad luck on his previous investigations, but nothing like this.

Biting at the gag, he struggled from side to side in an effort to loosen the ropes.

"Aren't you ashamed of yourself for sneaking out on me to go treasure-hunting?" Salty came hurrying into the galley. "I saw you go pussyfooting off from your room. At first I couldn't believe you were doing this, but I decided to get dressed and follow you and a darn good thing I did, considering all the mess you've gone and gotten—"

"Mum, mum," Scrib said anxiously, striving to nod at the refrigerator.

"Well, plenty of time to apologize, Scrib, after I get you clear of here. This whole dippy boat is ablaze and it's likely to blow up any minute. Not that—"

"Get this gag off me, you dimwit!" he tried to tell her.

"Yes, yes. Don't moan and groan. I'm going to save you." She took a deep breath, bent down, and picked him clean up off the floor. "I've been, did I get around to mentioning, practicing weight-lifting for quite some time now. I expected it to build up my bosom, which it hasn't, but I'm one heck of a lot stronger than I look."

"Take the damn gag off! Quit babbling!" All that came out was a muffled gargle.

Grunting once, Salty carried him free of the galley and then along the rainwashed deck. She carried him down the gangway and deposited him on the dock a safe distance from the brightly burning yawl.

Flames were crackling high up into the darkness, along with black billows of thick smoke.

"If we'd gone in there together, you wouldn't be in such sorry shape now, Scrib. Imagine Mrs. Hoogly, who I imagined was flat on her back in her room from grief and gin, bopping you on the coco and trussing you up like a—"

"The money! The money! It's on the boat!"

"Don't make so much noise, I'm going to untie you!"

"The gag first, dimbulb!"

"Boy, I wonder if she was a Sea Scout or what. Can you be a girl and join that? Or maybe, being on the social level she is, you learn to tie knots because you know you're eventually going to own a yacht or a yawl or something impressive." She was kneeling next to him on the wet planking of the dock. Her lean fingers struggled with the knots in the ropes.

"The gag!"

Salty frowned at him. "Is that gag bothering you? Yes, maybe I better get that off you first." She eased his head up and began working on the knots in the toweling gag. "This knot's quite a puzzler, too. I think it's maybe a granny or possibly a half hitch if that's a knot at all and not something you serve in the Navy. As I said, I'm not much on sea lore or— Ah, there we go. You can speak now."

"Salty, get back on the boat! To the galley!" Scrib shouted. "The money's in the refrigerator there and Mrs. Hoogly didn't take it!"

"The money?" She started to get up, staring across at the burning yawl. "That's terrible, because I don't think I can get—"

There was a great whomping explosion that knocked her flat down across Scrib.

Several more came booming across the rainy night.

A jagged hunk of railing came smashing down onto the dock near them, followed by a half dozen brass bolts.

"Damn," said Scrib, "there went $250,000."

"It was that much, huh?" She rose carefully up off him. "Well, let's look on the bright side. You're still alive."

"If you'd taken the gag off while I was still aboard, then we'd—"

"I was more interested in getting you out of there."

"That's the trouble with you," he said, angry.

"Yes, I guess it is," she admitted, and went back to untying him.

IT'S SO COLD IN CHINA

At first Scrib Merlin didn't recognize the dying man.

He was much better dressed than he used to be, looking almost dapper as he lay there writhing on the grass behind the big green-and-white-striped tent.

Scrib had been out at the edge of town, supervising the taping of a television commercial that was using a picturesque covered bridge as a setting. Deciding to walk back to the picturesque inn where he was staying, Scrib was halfway across the late-afternoon lawn of the library when he noticed the sprawled man. He was on his back, thrashing around next to a sign announcing that this was *Meet the Local Authors Day* at the Brimstone, Connecticut public library.

"Professor Champion!" realized Scrib and went running down the slanting library lawn to him.

Roger Champion was a tall rough-hewn man of sixty, white-haired and bearded. He was wearing a very expensive suit and expensive Italian shoes and his craggy face was a strange greenish color.

Up in front of the tent a Dixieland band was in the midst of playing "When the Saints Go Marching In."

Dropping to his knees beside the stricken professor, Scrib asked, "What's wrong, sir?"

Champion's glazed eyes looked up at him. "Merlin, isn't it?" he gasped. "Gad, it's been ten years since you were in my dramatics classes at Brimstone and we used to—"

"Fifteen years. Are you having some kind of attack? Is there some medication you—"

"Been poisoned," explained Scrib's old dramatics teacher, gesturing feebly at the paper cup tumbled over on the grass beside him. "Something slipped into my punch. Didn't think it'd be tried out in the open like—"

"Who? Who did—"

"Imagine running into you, Merlin. You were always one of my

68

favorite students. Shame you never got anywhere."

Scrib had slipped his arm around the dying man's broad shoulders. "Hey, in the tent!" he shouted at the blank wall of striped canvas. "Hey, help!"

"I was thinking about you only the other day, Merlin. Odd—"

"Listen, Professor, tell me who did this so—"

"You think of me as a man of honor—but salary's not that princely. My latest book—plugging it here today—is a flop—"

"I'm not doing all that well as an advertising copywriter in Manhattan," Scrib said. "Right now, though, do you have any idea who put the poison in—"

"Been doing things I shouldn't have— Caught up with me—"

"Oh, my God!" A plump blonde woman had stepped out through a flap in the tent. "Oh, dear Lord!"

"Quick, get a doctor!" urged Scrib.

Instead, the woman screamed, dropped the fat hardcover novel entitled *Kiss Me, Love Me, and More!* she'd been clutching to her bosom, and fainted. She landed, bouncing slightly once, a few feet from the stricken Professor Champion.

Now others were out into the late afternoon from within the green-and-white tent.

"Don't need a damn audience now," muttered the professor.

"Go get a doctor," Scrib told the half-dozen bystanders.

"What's wrong?" inquired a hefty moustached man.

"Poison," answered Scrib. "Hurry up, huh?"

Nodding, the dark-haired man went running off up across the wide green lawn.

"Merlin, please—" said the professor in a fading voice.

"What?" Scrib leaned nearer the froth-smeared lips.

"Maybe you can do better—make the right decision—" gasped Champion, his voice fluttering. "Here's how to find—what you need. It's so cold in China, the birds can't hardly sing."

"What?"

"It's so cold in China, the birds can't hardly sing," Champion repeated, sighing out the words. "You remember—" His body jerked, arched. Then he went slack and was dead.

A plump man with thinning blond hair came over. "I'm Dr. Denis Gilford — "

"Too late, Doctor." Scrib stood up.

"I'm a Ph.D. sort of doctor," explained Gilford. "The president of Brimstone College. Roger is—was on our staff."

Nodding absently, Scrib said, "I graduated from B.C. fifteen years ago."

"Before my time. I've only been here three years, coming from a similar position in the Midwest." Gilford was looking down forlornly at the body. "I suppose we'd best notify the police."

"Yes," said Scrib. "That's the standard procedure with a murder."

✗

Scrib's room at the Benedict Arnold Inn was small and looked out on a duck pond. He got back there as dusk was giving way to night, after having hung around at the *Meet the Authors* tent until Detective Ferro of the local police had gotten around to talking to him. There had been five local writers, three Friends of the Library volunteers, and four civilians in the tent when the fatal dose of poison had been slipped into Professor Champion's punch. As of nightfall, none of them had admitted doing the deed or even seeing it done.

While Scrib'd been out, the maid had tidied up his room, making up the four-poster bed and stacking his loaves of Chemical Farms Old-Fashion-Style White Bread in neat rows atop the antique-looking desk. Scrib had come out from New York this morning to spend two days in his old college town taping three one-minute commercials for Chemical Farms.

"A mistake," he murmured, seated on the edge of the bed and gazing absently out at the darkening pond. "A dire mistake."

Standing up, he paced the small beam-ceilinged room. He walked back to the windows, paced again, then picked up the phone off his bedside table and dialed a New York City number. Another dire mistake, no doubt.

The phone wasn't answered until the ninth ring. "Hold on a minute, whoever you are. I don't mean to be rude but I'm in the midst of a crisis." The receiver was dropped on a hard surface. Next Scrib heard lusty Beethoven music booming out, plus an ominous hollow thumping and an exuberant metallic whanging. Abruptly, the music faded, the thumping and then the banging ceased.

"I had to turn down the hi-fi and then that idiot sculptor downstairs was banging on the ceiling with a barge pole because of the *Eroica Symphony* and I also had to go hit the toilet with a roller skate, although actually a wrench or a hammer would be better except I loaned mine to— Who is this, anyway?"

"Salty, don't hang up. It's—"

"Oh, ugh!" remarked Salty Warbeck. "It's you, the unspeakable Scrib Merlin."

"I know you don't much like me, Salty, but—"

"Don't *like* you? I loathe you," she explained. "I'd rather talk to all Four Horsemen of the Apocalypse than—"

"Okay, the last encounter we had I annoyed you."

"You didn't annoy me, Scrib. Rather you filled my very being with chagrin and clammy revulsion. I mean, I ask you to do me a simple favor—"

"That business out on Long Island a few months ago wasn't exactly a small favor," he cut in. "I solved a murder, located a stash of money. Just because the dough got burned to a —"

"Oh, it isn't the money," said Salty. "Well, it is, yes, in a way, but not the losing of it just. What stings me to my innermost core, and I may be slim but I'm just as deep as some of those hefty bimbos you—"

"You're skinny, actually, is what you are, Salty. But the point of this long-distance call is—"

"Where are you?"

"In Brimstone, Connecticut. That's only about an hour's drive out of—"

"That's where you went to college, isn't it? Even though I've tried, because of your dreadful, mercenary approach to life, to sponge every solitary fact about you from my mind, I do seem to recall you attended Brimstone College. Are you back for an alumni gathering, a fun-filled reunion?"

"No. My ad agency, Amthrax & Associates, sent me out here to oversee some Chemical Farms Old-Fashion—"

"That stuff. I had a loaf of that once and it killed every darn cockroach in my pantry. I found the little things belly up with Chemical Farms crumbs on—"

"Listen, Salty, one of my old professors is dead. He was murdered."

She was silent for a few seconds. "Don't tell me you found him while he was expiring," she said. "Don't tell me he gave you a cryptic dying message."

"I did, though," answered Scrib. "And he did."

"Honestly, Scrib, don't you think there's something awfully wrong and strange with a life in which you are continually and forever stumbling over murder victims who can think of nothing better to do with their last minutes on earth than to impart some dippy phrase to you with their last gasps?"

"Matter of fact, I do," he admitted. "I went into analysis right after that business on Long Island. So far, though, Dr. Gernsback and I—"

"What's your psychiatrist's name?"

"Dr. Egon Gernsback. He—"

"I've never heard of him. Egon Gernsback?"

"No reason you should've. He—"

"Hasn't he written a book, a paperback even? Doesn't he have some revolutionary theory that—"

"No, he's just a psychiatrist," Scrib replied, staring out at the pond. "The thing is, Salty, I want to solve Professor Champion's murder because—"

"Course you do. You probably figure there's a fortune involved somewhere or some shady way you can solve the crime and then blackmail the killer into—"

"Nope, no, really. I'm changing," Scrib assured her. "But since I have this ability, this talent almost, for unraveling mysteries like this one, there's no reason I shouldn't use it. So I intend to solve the murder of my old prof simply because I liked the guy. He was my drama teacher and back when I wanted to be a comedian he—"

"You sound, over the phone anyway and I can't see your dippy face, almost sincere."

"I am. And I need your help."

"My help? Where did you say you were calling from?"

"My room at the Benedict Arn—"

"This is not, you swear, a sneaky plot to lure me back into your clutches?"

"Look, years ago—fifteen and more—I used to drop over to Champion's place after class quite a lot. Several of us would. We'd drink wine and he'd play us records from his unlimited collection. What Professor Champion collected and loved to play for us and discourse upon endlessly was blues records, on 78 and LP. I don't mean rock and roll or rock stuff, but, you know, ancient black music played and sung by guys with off-key guitars and names like Memphis Fred and Sonny Boy Marschall and Nearsighted Slim."

"There were never any blues singers with those dippy names."

"See? You know this field and I don't. I remembered that when you and I were dating you used to inflict—used to play some of that stuff from your own vast collection, Salty. I consider you an expert on that sort of—"

"Ah, I see it now. The dying message this time involved some old blues singer or a line from a blues song, right?"

"I think so. Champion probably figured I'd paid a lot more attention that I did at those sessions we used to have. There were people around while he was dying and he had to pass on this information in such a way—"

"You don't have to explain the ground rules for dying messages to me, Scrib. I've been through enough of these things with you and, on top of that, I encountered that one myself out there on Long Island."

"Okay, and that time you called on me for help. I dropped everything to rush to your side. Now I need somebody who—"

"I have a full-page spread of cartoons due for the *National Buffoon* in just three scant days."

"This'll only take a few hours."

After a short silence, Salty inquired, "What was the message?"

"I'd rather not blab it out over the phone. Could you maybe come out here tonight?"

"Tonight? Now? All the way to Connecticut?"

"It's an hour's drive on the parkways. Even in that clunky VW of yours."

"And you solemnly swear you've reformed? You want to do this simply to avenge the death of an old friend and mentor?"

"So help me."

"Well, I don't quite believe you, Scrib, but I'm going to call your bluff," Salty said. "Give me the directions on how to find my way to that tacky motel you're holed up in."

✗

"Who are the suspects again?" she asked as she guided her venerable Volkswagen through the misty night lanes of Brimstone. She was a slender blonde young woman, clad in jeans and a candystripe shirt.

They were en route to the home of the late Professor Champion.

"All of them can't be suspects." He reached, as best he could in the bouncing, shivering passenger seat, into his coat pocket for the wad of yellow copy paper he'd made notes on. "These are just the people who were in and around the tent at the time. The poison was a relatively fast-acting one, probably started working within a few minutes." He fished out a pen flashlight and clicked it on. "There was the Organic Red Hot Peppers Dixieland Jazz Band, consisting of six—"

"Cute," she commented.

"What's cute?"

"Their name. It's a play on Jelly Roll Morton's band's name."

"I didn't know that. Anyway, they were apparently finishing up a half-hour set when Champion died, indicating none of the band members could've— Left at this next corner."

"Whippoorwill Lane. Everything's got a sylvan name out here."

"It's the suburbs."

"C'mon, c'mon," she urged the car, "you can do it. Sometimes it stalls on curves. Read the list."

"Suppose you just concentrate on the dying message. Don't you have any idea where it's from?"

"A vague notion is percolating in the back of my head," she assured him.

"But you're supposed to be a blues maven."

"I am, but there are thousands of lyrics."

"You do think that's where it's from, though? My feeling is that the professor thought I was attentive to all that stuff back then."

"Yes, it is from a blues lyric. I'm certain, but I just can't put my finger on it. Go on with the suspect list."

"In the tent were Sally Ann Jitney, a rather full-figured blonde lady and author of the bestseller, *Kiss Me, Love Me, and More!* She fainted when—"

"Full-figured? I've seen pictures of her. She's a blimp. No wonder you're always accusing me of being skinny and not having a chance of being a girlie-magazine model, the career I really crave. I mean, if she's your idea of just full-figured, then—"

"The other authors present were Alfonso DiRoma, whose new cookbook is *Eat Lotsa Pasta*," Scrib went on. "Virgil Whorf, author and illustrator of a new kid book called *The Pussycat Princess Joins the Navy*. Roger Jericho, a writer I know nothing about, and a local romance novelist whose real name is actually Rosemarie Firebaugh. There were three library helpers, two men and a woman, and four visitors, who were all standing in line to have Whorf autograph copies of—"

"Didn't you say the president of your alma mater was on hand, too?"

"That's right, I forgot him. Dr. Denis Gilford. He— Professor Champion's place is at the end of this road. Drive on by, slowly."

"I don't have much choice on these dippy roads, I have to go slow."

A widower, Champion had lived alone in a modest stone cottage that was nearly hidden by a half acre of brush and maple trees.

Squinting as they rattled by, Scrib said, "No sign of lights or of the police."

"Good. I'll park under those droopy trees up ahead," she said, "and then we can sneak over and break into the place."

✗

"Someone was certainly looking for something." Scrib took another slow turn around Professor Champion's living room.

It was hexagonal in shape, with leaded windows and shelving taking up all the wall space. Nearly all the books had been pulled off their perches and they lay sprawled across the threadbare rug, some open and on their backs and others steepled. Champion's desk, the same heavy dark wood one Scrib remembered from his visits years ago, had been ransacked. Every drawer had been yanked out and upended, leaving a thick scatter of papers, letters, pencils, pens, and paper clips on the floor.

The professor's record collection, however, hadn't been disturbed. Hundreds of albums stood side by side on shelves along the front wall.

By the light of the single floor lamp Scrib had risked turning on, Salty sat scanning the titles. "What do you think they were looking for?"

"Something too big to hide in a record album but small enough to slip into a desk drawer or a hollowed-out book."

"That could be almost anything."

"True." Scrib settled into a fat armchair, the same one he used to slouch in on those long-ago afternoons. " 'It's so cold in China, the birds can't hardly sing.' What the hell was he trying to tell me?"

"Did you notice his car in the garage when we were sneaking in? A Mercedes, fairly new."

"Yep, and he was wearing a high-price suit, too. That doesn't go with this modest house, these rundown furnishings."

"Meaning the professor discovered an extracurricular source of income recently."

Scrib stood. "He was probably blackmailing somebody," he said. "The victim decided, since Champion had no immediate kin, to knock him off and hope the blackmail would die with him."

"I wonder who inherits his records. He's got a terrific collection. All these Label X ten inches, just about the entire Prestige Bluesville series." She rose to her knees to start scanning another shelf.

" 'It's so cold in China, the birds can't hardly sing,' " Scrib repeated. "Doesn't make a hell of a lot of sense as lines go."

"Lots of blues lyrics are like that. Most of that old stuff was passed around orally for years before anything got recorded. Garbling happened."

"Finding anything?"

Frowning, Salty selected an LP, then two more. "Okay, these maybe," she said. "And this one."

Crossing the room, Scrib put his hand on her slim shoulder.

Salty shrugged free of his touch. "Don't use this crisis as an excuse to get intimate," she warned.

"What have you got?" He squatted, glancing over the blues albums she'd pulled. "Blind Boy Fuller, Blind Willie McTell, Blind Lemon Jefferson, Blind Willie Johnson. How come they're all blind?"

Salty was rubbing a thumb knuckle over her chin. "I've heard that line before and I think, the best I can recall, that it's from either a Blind Willie McTell blues or from one by Blind Lemon Jefferson. I picked the others in case my memory's even fuzzier than I believe it to be. I'm darn sure it's a singer with Blind in his name."

"These guys could've used an ad agency, naming themselves like that. Blind is a negative word to—"

"Let's try Willie McTell." Sliding the record from its sleeve, Salty tapped at the grooves while studying the titles on the label. "Turn on the turntable, will you?"

"Sure." After a few false flips, Scrib got the hi-fi system ready to play.

"Fourth track, 'Three Women Blues.' "

He obliged and started listening.

"Not Top Ten material," he observed after two verses.

"Hush." When the track ended, Salty shook her head. "Nope, that isn't it. Here, try the first track on this one."

" 'Got the Blues,' " he said, placing the Blind Lemon Jefferson on the turntable.

The song came out dim and scratchy, sounding like it was coming to them across a wide gulf of time. The singer-guitarist had a strong, keening voice and he slurred and swallowed some of his words.

When the third verse began, Salty clapped her hands. "Bingo!" she exclaimed.

"So cold in China, the birds can't hardly sing," Jefferson sang. He repeated the lines and ended the verse with, "You done made me mad and broke my diamond ring." Or at least that's what Salty told him the words were. All Scrib caught on the first hearing was the "So cold in China" phrase.

He played it twice more, then turned off the machine. "Okay, we've identified the line."

"Does it mean anything to you?"

"I guess I recall his playing this for us a few times." Scrib was holding up the LP. "He told me the line to make me come and find the record."

"That seems logical."

"Nothing extra written on the label, no code scratched on the disc."

"The name itself, Blind Lemon Jefferson? Does that trigger something?"

"Nope." Sitting next to her on the cluttered floor, Scrib picked up the album sleeve and examined it. "No papers inside, no pictures or anything extra hidden in it or slipped between the layers of paper and cardboard. No special words singled out on the liner copy." He got up, letting the empty album drop to the rug. "Damn. What was he trying to tell me?"

"The quote from the lyric was his way of leading you to Blind Lemon Jefferson."

Scrib wandered to the window. "Why didn't I pay more attention back then?"

"Fifteen years is a long time."

"Yeah, but Professor Champion had faith in me. He thought I'd understand what he was talking about, though nobody else in that tent would."

"Well, you did understand. In a way. Not that it's gotten us any forwarder, as they're always saying in old British thrillers."

"Scoot over, unobtrusively, and turn off the light."

"Hum?"

"Kill the light."

Casually, Salty walked to the lamp and turned it off. "What's wrong?"

After a moment he answered, "Nothing, I guess. I thought I saw someone out there in the bushes. I guess not, though."

"Shall we depart?"

"Might as well. We'll take the album."

"Since it's so late, I won't drive back to Manhattan tonight. I'll bunk at that quaint inn."

"Good idea."

"But," she added, "in a room of my own."

✗

Scrib, absolutely alone, sat up in bed at a few minutes after 3:00 a.m. "Of course, of course," he said aloud. "That's it. It's got to be."

Leaping from his antique bed, he dressed quickly. Then he eased out of his room and walked rapidly into the night.

The campus of Brimstone College was less than a mile from the inn. Scrib walked the distance in under fifteen minutes, puffing some by the time he arrived at the woodlands surrounding the four acres. He slipped silently into the woods, thankful it was an overcast, moonless night. The night patrolman wouldn't spot him if he was careful.

Scrib hadn't bothered to visit the campus this trip. Walking the old pathways would've only tended to remind him how he'd fouled up his life thus far, how he hadn't done what he'd promised himself he was going to do. *Tune in tomorrow for another installment of "Scrib Merlin, Pitiful Wretch,"* he said to himself as he walked along a shadowy pathway to the building he was aiming for.

There it was, brownstone and ivy, looking exactly as it had fifteen years ago. Jefferson Hall.

He dashed from the path to the doorway. He stood still, glancing around. No sign of anyone.

The door's lock was a simple one and he got it picked without any trouble, using his pocket knife and a couple less orthodox gadgets he carried.

Once inside, he pushed the door almost but not completely shut. Ready for a quick exit if need be.

Then he flicked on his penlight. The corridors smelled the same, a mixture of floor wax and college-kid musk.

The art gallery was on the second floor. The door wasn't locked.

The painting, since this was a permanent collection, was still hanging where he'd remembered it. *Three Lemons on a Plate* by an obscure nineteenth-century American still-life painter.

Holding the light between his teeth, Scrib lifted the framed canvas carefully off the gallery wall.

Turning the backside of the canvas to him, he said, "Yep, I was right." Taped there, with strips of black electrical tape, was a large fat 9 x 12 inch manila envelope.

Crouching, Scrib worked the envelope free. After leaning the painting against the wall, he started to open the envelope Professor Champion had kept hidden there.

"No need to do that."

He glanced up, the flash dropping from his mouth.

The Jefferson Gallery's overhead lights blossomed on.

Dr. Denis Gilford, president of Brimstone College, stood on the threshold. His .32-caliber revolver was pointing straight at Scrib.

"This envelope," Scrib inquired, "is chock full of stuff about you, huh?"

"Unfortunately, yes."

"Serious enough to kill about?"

"Yes, and serious enough for me to pay Champion $43,000 about over the past year and a half," Gilford answered. "Champion somehow got the notion I was a fraud. Which I am. He very cautiously gathered material proving all my credentials are false."

"Why didn't you just take off?"

"I could've moved on, I suppose—assumed yet another identity. Fooling people has been my life's work and I'm quite good at it," said the college president. "However, I'm getting along in years and had decided to end my days here. There's a very liberal retirement and pension setup."

"That's not likely to happen, now, though. I'd say your academic career has gone flooey."

"Not at all, young man. Once I have all the documents poor Champion so patiently gathered, I'll be safe. For a while, if not forever."

"You can't—"

"Bribe you? Certainly not. I put you down as an honest fellow the moment I saw you," said Gilford, smiling. "And from what I heard at the professor's house tonight, after you interrupted my search and caused me to lurk in the shrubbery, I am certain." He gestured with his gun. "No, you I'll have to shoot."

"Is that one of your perks here? You get to shoot somebody now and then?"

"I can certainly shoot a vandal who broke into the Jefferson Gallery and attempted to steal a valuable though ugly painting," he replied. "No doubt, in desperate need of money for something or other, you hatched this scheme to—"

"I'm not the only one who knows about this."

"You're alluding to the skinny Miss Warbeck? She doesn't know much," the grinning Gilford told him. "I've been trailing you since you left Champion's digs. You didn't even tell her you were coming here."

"She knows enough to—"

"No, that won't wash, Merlin." Gilford stepped into the big white room. "Two quick shots ought to—"

"Let's not do that, Dr. Gilford, sir."

Sighing, Scrib got to his feet. "Evening, Detective Ferro."

The policeman was a small curly-haired man of forty-one. His gun was a .38. "I didn't quite believe the lady at first, Merlin," he said, coming into the room. "But she's very persistent and she convinced me you'd solved the murder and had gone off to do something about it on your own. I thought I'd best drop over here."

"She followed me here, too, huh?"

"Right, then called me on the phone."

"Yeah, I think I know why." Scrib handed him the envelope as he moved to the doorway.

"To save your bacon obviously," said Ferro.

Shrugging, Scrib left the gallery and stepped into the hallway. He nearly bumped into Salty. "Thanks," he said.

"I heard most of the end of it from out here," she told him.

He started down the stairs. "I guess I should've confided in you."

Catching up with him as he descended, she asked, "How do you feel?"

"Alive."

"No, I mean, didn't you really sneak over here to find that black-mail stuff and then use it yourself? Then you'd have enough money to drive your own Mercedes, wear Italian shoes, dress—"

"If I had money I'd start my own agency, you know that," he said from the bottom of the stairs. "But in this case I wasn't after any money. I just wanted to see justice done. I liked Professor Champion. Back when I knew him, he wouldn't have blackmailed anyone."

"You know, I didn't know the president was trailing you. I mean, I did notice him walking across the campus in the same direction as you, but I assumed college presidents did things like that, even at three in the morning. I suppose if I'd had a college of my own," she said as they left the building, "I'd take walks through it at all hours. I really phoned Detective Ferro to make sure you turned over anything you found."

"Yeah, I deduced that." The cold of the morning hit him and he shivered.

"Then you really are satisfied with the way things worked out?"

"Yep."

"How come you're not smiling?"

"I am."

"Not much of a smile."

"I'm doing the best I can," he said.

She hesitated for a moment, then took his hand.

ADMAN

ORCZY MUST GO!

As to why they found him floating off Malibu, dead, wearing those odd shoes, it was, basically, because of the rubber stamp. Rowland Pinemount showed me the rubber stamp the same day he got it from the shop on Western Boulevard. We were having coffee at a drive-in delicatessen down at the ocean end of Santa Monica, in my car. Rowland's girlfriend, Kinny, had lost his car again.

"Where'd she lose it?" I asked him.

This was in June or July, smoggy and up in the high eighties, and Rowland had his dark glasses perched on top of his crew-cut head and was rubbing his eyes. "Don't you want to know how?" He was a large, loose-fleshed man, thirty-four, with a small fuzzy beard.

"I know Kinny, so I can imagine how. But I wonder where."

"Portland, Oregon." Rowland finished his smoked salmon sandwich, wiped his mouth and then jabbed a plump hand into his pants pocket. "She says she loaned it to a fireman."

"To go to a fire?"

"Yes, she says."

"Doesn't he have a fire truck?"

"He's a volunteer fireman, she says." Rowland pulled a paper bag bound with a rubber band out of his pocket. "I don't think she's really in Portland. I think she's shacked up with Alden Orczy."

I didn't reply. I chewed on some ice from my paper teacup.

Alden Orczy was one of Rowland's obsessions. Rowland was, at that point in June or July of 1970, a pretty good script writer for television, and successful. He had a knack for dialogue and a tremendous gift for verbally setting an idea. Myself, I was in the advertising business, which doesn't involve talking to many people directly. Alden Orczy was a television writer, too, about our age. Orczy was more flamboyant than Rowland, a lot thinner. Ever since Orczy had butted Rowland in the stomach with his head one night a block from The Daisy, Rowland had been obsessed. He didn't like

Orczy: He didn't like his pranks. He didn't like his work. Rowland would watch every show Orczy wrote and copy down the dialogue. He claimed Orczy wrote the worst dialogue in Hollywood and he kept a cardboard box full of steno notebooks of Orczy's terrible dialogue. He loved to quote his favorite awful patches. Rowland usually described Orczy as a combination of Sammy Glick and Woody Woodpecker. Besides his dialogue, there was the fact that Orczy was apparently dating Rowland's girl on the sly.

"Look at this," Rowland said.

I'd been leaning back watching the giant plastic bagel rotate over the place, swirling in the brown air. "What?"

He shook a rubber stamp and an ink pad out of the bag, thwacked the brand-new pink stamp into the fresh ink, grabbed up the check and stamped it. "I ordered it last week and it was ready today."

On the back of the check it now said: *Orczy must go!* I read it aloud, grinned, "You starting an advertising campaign against him?"

Rowland said, "I'm going to use it on all my letters and envelopes and checks." He laughed and stamped *Orczy must go!* on my palm, then on the windshield and on his own pants' knee. "Nobody who writes such awful dialogue deserves to live."

At times Rowland's sense of humor was quite a bit like Orczy's. When he had finished trying out the stamp, I asked him, "Have you heard about the new series yet?"

"*Slum Doctor?*"

"I thought it was *Ghetto Medic?*"

"Changed the title again," said Rowland. "Yes, it looks like I'll get to do at least six segments for next season. I have to check back next week."

The waitress came over to collect and Rowland re-inked his stamp and put *Orczy must go!* on the plump part of her arm just above the elbow. We laughed for a while. Then we left and I dropped Rowland off on Wilshire near his agent's and went back to my ad agency.

I saw the billboard before I saw Rowland again. I'd been back in Connecticut and Massachusetts looking for a covered bridge which we needed for an instant-mush commercial, but we couldn't find one they'd let us paint blue to match the box and so I came back. The billboard was up over Sunset Boulevard, near where that giant girl spins around. It was a big one-color run, black on white. In large black sans-serif letters it said: *Orczy must go!*

A couple of days later I had lunch with Rowland at the Afromat, a soul-food cafeteria off Wilshire. "You've gone beyond the rubber-stamp stage," I said when we'd seated ourselves at an outdoor table in the patio behind the Afromat.

"That pipsqueak," said Rowland. Then, "Would you like to buy an electric typewriter?"

"No," I said. "Yours?"

"One of mine." Rowland liked to have at least two electric typewriters in his house out in the Valley in case one went on the fritz. "I used most of my savings-account balance to buy the billboards."

"Plural? You bought space on more than one?"

"You get a better rate if you take six," explained Rowland, wiping a dab of grits off his beard.

"I only saw the one on Sunset."

"They didn't give me the best locations."

"Aren't you going to get some money from *Slum Doctor*?"

"*Black Intern* is the name of the show now," he said. "And, no. That pipsqueak Orczy went in to Neff and got the assignment away from me."

"How'd he do that?"

"Orczy stole all my diseases."

"Diseases?"

"You know how I pitch ideas for scripts. I go in and hit them with one-liners. 'Crippled baby stuck in elevator,' and so on," said the still-plump Rowland. "So I was all set to hit Neff with six terrific diseases for this intern to treat in six successive episodes. Neff tells me he just signed Orczy to do the same six diseases."

"A coincidence?"

Rowland snorted, setting his Powerburger down with an angry slam. "Kinny must have told him in a rash moment."

"You're really sure your girlfriend is seeing Orczy?"

"She admitted it. Orczy's house out in the Palisades is one of the places she goes when she borrows my car."

I drummed my fingers on the tabletop for a minute. "Look Rowland," I said finally, "why don't you forget about both of them, Kinny and Orczy?"

"Not a chance," he replied. "I love her and I hate him. Don't worry. I'm going to keep up my campaign and drive that pipsqueak into the ground."

"I notice a couple of the trade papers have mentioned the billboard. So far your campaign is giving Orczy publicity and you nothing."

"Don't start talking like a professional ad man," said Rowland. "The kind of advertising I'm doing I know more about than you. I feel this."

"So how are you going to pay for it?"

Rowland traced his moustache with a plump forefinger. "I'm about set to pitch a movie to Lenzer out at Conglom Pictures. I won't even tell you the idea, but it's a sure sell."

I wished him luck.

In the latter part of September I had to fly to Omaha and spend three weeks looking at experimental cornfields. These were growing indoors, and one of our clients was exploring the idea of introducing organic corn flakes. I missed the next phases of Rowland's advertising campaign against Alden Orczy. From what Rowland and some of my friends and a girl who used to work at the same model agency as my wife told me, I put together what must have happened next; and my wife had clipped out all the *Orczy must go!* newspaper and local magazine ads and she showed them to me when I got back from Omaha.

Apparently, in a moment of creative elation, Rowland had told his girl Kinny the basic premise for his movie. Pacing excitedly around his big house in the Valley, Rowland had bellowed, "The first drug peddler in the Old West. Isn't that beautiful? It'll be bigger than *Easy Rider*."

Kinny really was dating Orczy on the side and she must have mentioned the idea to him. At any rate, when Rowland walked into Conglom to sell them verbally *Marijuana Cowboy*, he discovered they'd signed with Orczy the day before to do *High in the Saddle*. They were going to give Orczy $100,000 for his drugs in the Old West script, plus five percent of the gross.

Rowland didn't attempt to prove his idea had been swiped by Orczy. He didn't bother the Guild with any charges against him either. Instead, he decided to step up his campaign against the prankish writer. He took out a loan and bought space in newspapers and magazines. A few of Rowland's closer friends and associates suggested, as I had, that he drop the campaign and let Orczy have Kinny. Rowland told everybody that this wasn't an obsession but simply a quite rational campaign to purge the Los Angeles area of

Alden Orczy.

Mostly, though, the *Orczy must go!* ads added to Orczy's stature. He began appearing even more frequently on the local talk shows. Orczy had adopted a youthful style of dress, favoring bell-bottom pants, leather vests and polka-dot shirts. Seeing Orczy on television, in full color on both of his two TV sets, antagonized Rowland further. Nevertheless, he patiently wrote down all the inane things he felt Orczy was saying and filled several more notebooks. Many of the people Rowland knew had shared his initial dislike for Orczy, but now they weren't prepared to spend as much time loathing him as Rowland was. Rowland was more often at home as a result. He bought mailing lists from some mail-order advertising firms and sent out *Orczy must go!* broadsides to selected groups of people in the Los Angeles area.

Kinny was a tall, slender, blonde girl, an actress who once in a while did small parts; very pretty in a frail and vaguely nasty sort of way. Sometime around the middle of October she stopped seeing Rowland at all and moved in with Orczy. She then took all Rowland's furniture and appliances and had them moved out to Orczy's place on the cliffs above the Pacific. During one of his divorces, Rowland had had Kinny buy all his furniture in her name, so that his wife or some creditor couldn't attach it. Only one typewriter, a rug and a desk chair were left to Rowland, and possibly one small black and white TV set. He blamed Orczy for what Kinny did. Orczy's home was already completely furnished and the frail blonde didn't need any more furniture there. Rowland mortgaged his house and went into television commercials in his campaign against Orczy. At first he used only ten-second spots, showing him sitting in his empty house and saying once, somewhat plaintively, "Orczy must go!"

This didn't satisfy Rowland for long and he began producing minute commercials. This gave Rowland a chance to advertise against Orczy and an opportunity to try out some of his own ideas about cinematography. His sixty-second commercials were quite beautiful, in brilliant color, and reminding you of both Fellini and the young Orson Welles. In fact, only last month one of his commercials won a certificate in a Los Angeles advertising-art director's show, but too late to help Rowland.

The last time I saw Rowland was early in December of 1970 at a hotdog bistro on La Cienega. Rowland was thinner, his beard quite shaggy. He was living in a character actors hotel off Sunset and trying to get some fiction assignments from a girlie-magazine chain in Hollywood. He'd spent over $100,000 on his *Orczy must go!* campaign. I was getting ready to leave for New York to supervise a cigar commercial that required a snowstorm and was thinking as much about that as I was about Rowland, so I suppose that's why I didn't think he was serious about his plan for raising quick money.

"Mary Maclin's golden slippers," he said, finishing a Pizzafurter.

"Who? The old 1930s musical actress?"

Rowland nodded. "You remember the famous golden slippers she wore in *Sleeping Beauty* in 1939. People still talk about her sleep-walking tap dance up the palace steps."

"So?"

"A lot of movie buffs put a tremendous value on stuff like that, memorabilia," said Rowland. "Look at what some of that stuff at the MGM auction brought in. Anyhow, I ran into some collector at a cocktail party out in Brentwood who said he'd pay ten thousand dollars for those slippers."

"Why doesn't he buy them from Mary Macklin? She's still got them, I heard."

"The old broad won't sell."

"That ends that."

"I've been thinking," said Rowland after ordering another hot dog. "You know Mary Macklin has that big mansion out in Pacific Palisades. She has a personal museum in back of the place. There's a life-size dummy of herself, wearing those famous golden slippers. The thing is, she's going to be in Europe all this month and she's only got one seventy-six-year-old caretaker looking after the whole setup."

"How come you know all this?"

"Well," Rowland replied, "Kinny told me."

"You're really seeing her again?"

"Oh, once in a while. She comes over to the hotel to see me sometimes. I don't know if she's contrite or slumming. I still love her. With ten thousand dollars I can get out of the hole and back on my feet."

I asked, "Are you talking about stealing those shoes?"

Rowland shrugged his thinner shoulders. "Maybe."

"Come on, Rowland," I told him. "Campaigning against Alden Orczy is one thing. Even there, he could have sued you if he hadn't enjoyed the whole thing so much. Burglary is something else again.

Now, forget it."

Rowland shrugged once more. "Will you see me to a third hot dog?"

I did.

He went ahead with the idea, however. The rest of this happened while I was back in New York. I've been able, from various sources, to put together an account of what happened. Around midnight of the 20th of December, Rowland drove out to Pacific Palisades in a rented car. He was dressed in a black pullover, black jeans and dark sneakers. He'd rubbed soot on his face and was wearing gloves. Somewhere he'd got hold of a .38 revolver and had that tucked in his waistband. Kinny, whom he'd seen that afternoon, told him the old caretaker at Mary Macklin's estate always bought a bottle of discount scotch on Friday afternoons and by midnight he'd be safely asleep.

Rowland parked a block from the mansion and went skulking silently through the night, keeping in shadows. He had cased the area a few days before and knew where he wanted to go over the wall. Rowland climbed up into a gnarled cypress at the edge of the grounds and swung to the top of the stone wall circling the estate. He was much lighter now, which increased his agility. He got over the wall with no trouble and went along it toward the house.

Mary Macklin's mansion was all spires and turrets, ivied stone walls, stained-glass windows and wrought iron. Her private museum was located in a converted greenhouse at the back of the main house.

Rowland approached the glass museum so quietly the gravel surrounding it did not even crunch. Mary Macklin had considerable faith in the old caretaker and had never bothered to install burglar alarms. Rowland was able to get one of the doors unbolted.

The big room smelled of dusty cloth and its jumble of nostalgia all glowed pale blue in the night. Rowland stalked by steamer trunks and clothes racks, parasols, hoopskirts, Oriental gongs, pith helmets, fat scrapbooks, a suit of chain mail, three saddles. Then, on a low wooden pedestal, he saw the golden slippers on the feet of a figure in a yellowing white ball gown.

"Ah, the sleeping beauty," murmured Rowland as he reached out for the shoes.

"Guess again, you stupid idiot." The shoes danced away from him, off the pedestal. Alden Orczy tossed aside the ball gown and laughed. "I've got you this time, Rowland, you poor simp. Burglary, breaking and entering, grand theft, carrying a concealed weapon. You're all washed up, simpo." Orczy gave a little leap and kicked his gold-slippered heels together. "I've had all the laughs out of you I can stand, Rowland. Now I'm tired of you and your advertising campaign."

Rowland nodded. "Yes, there's only so much you can do with advertising," he said, and he shot Orczy dead.

PLEASE DON'T HELP THE BEAR

They couldn't imagine why he died with that particular look on his face.

Not that they wasted much time on the case—it was so open-and-shut. There was the victim with three slugs in him, and there was the murderer still wandering around and waving the gun when the police his wife had called arrived. And they figured they knew what the motive was.

The fact he'd been killed in that room and not one of the others didn't mean anything to them.

Leah Wentz knew what it meant, but she claimed to be in shock and never did get around to telling anybody about it.

I'm probably the only other person who knows exactly what happened that night at the Wentz Dynavision Cartoon Studios. Even Wentz didn't know.

I met Chuck Dancer about a year and a half ago in the big sunny offices of Dr. Warloff over in Santa Monica. Warloff is the best allergy man in Southern California and I'd developed a very embarrassing allergy. I was the senior account man on the Snarl Dog Food account. Every time lately I opened a can of the stuff my hands got all tingly and I started breaking out in red blotches.

Since I was trying to convince the client that our "so meaty it bounces" campaign was the one to go with, I had to open a lot of cans of Snarl. Open them and bounce the stuff on the conference table for the junior account men and on the drawing boards of the Food Art Department. So I was tingling and splotching all the time and the client, or at least old Henshew, was eyeing me in that odd way which means your loyalty is in doubt.

There I was then on that bright August afternoon, sitting in Warloff's waiting room with a copy of *Doctor Vacation News* open to an article on Swiss spas. Actually I was watching the long stripe of blue Pacific out the windows.

Chuck came in, sat down next to me, and started sneezing. "Excuse me," he said, sniffling. "Did I sneeze on your mag?"

"No, that's okay." I closed the magazine.

Chuck sneezed three more times, loud body-shaking sneezes. "You don't have a dog, do you?" he asked.

"Yes, I do. I have to."

He was a long lean man, about 30, and casually dressed. He sniffed, his Adam's apple bobbing, and said, "I've heard of people being told they *couldn't* keep dogs, but never that they *had* to have one."

"I'm in the ad game," I explained. "I handle the Snarl Dog Food account and they expect me to have a dog of my own. Actually I don't care much for dogs, especially this one. He's always attacking squirrels and burying my shoes and—"

"I love animals," Chuck told me. "I love to draw them. But when I get within ten feet of one—whammo!"

"You an artist?"

"Animator. I was with Wentz Dynavision when I first got out here, now I'm with Sensational-McClosky. Hey, you ought to take a look at our sample reel. I do great dogs."

I'd been hearing good things about Sensational-McClosky. And they were supposed to be a lot cheaper than the big studios like Wentz. I think they'd recently won the Calcutta Art Directors Award for a 20-second toilet-bowl cleaner spot—you've probably seen it, the commercial where the toilet seat dances. So I invited Chuck to bring their reel in and screen it for me and our Food Art people.

✗

I had lunch with Chuck about four weeks after that. He'd showed the S-M stuff to our agency and we'd hired his outfit to do three 30-second Fake Milk spots—the ones with the dancing cows, if you remember.

The first thing he did after sitting down opposite me in the booth at the Mexican Quickie Restaurant was to sneeze—six times, shaking the formica table and rattling the napkin holder. "Remember Elsie St. Clair?"

I've lived over twenty years in Southern California, but I'm not much on movie nostalgia. "The nineteen-thirties' movie star?"

"That Elsie St. Clair, yeah. Just saw her out in the parking lot and she's a very stunning woman." He sneezed loudly twice more.

"You allergic to old actresses?"

"No, to her leopard. She goes around with one on a leash. Animal hair, any kind of animal hair." He grabbed a fistful of paper napkins and wiped his nose. "Hey, listen. Good and bad things are happening to me."

"You haven't checked your allergies?"

"No, Dr. Warloff says I'm severely allergic to all types of animal hair. I can't even go near a fur coat without sneezing. It's going to be a long slow process to desensitize me." He wiped his nose again. "While sitting around there a week or so back I met the most incredible girl, another patient of his. She's a redhead, a real authentic redhead. Freckles, the coppery hair, the beautiful skin that some redhaired women have, and fantastic green eyes. She's not exactly zaftig, but I prefer the willowy type. I'd love to get her coloring into a cartoon. The exact shade of red contrasted with the green of—"

"What's the bad part?"

"Wouldn't be necessarily bad, these days," said Chuck, swallowing. "You know, new morality, open marriage."

"She's married?"

"Yeah, and it's incredible who she's married to. She's Wentz's new wife. Married him last year. Her name used to be Leah Taplin. Did you ever see her in the movies?"

"No. Was she in the movies?"

"Well, she made two films. *Cry of the Blood Bathers* and *Diary of a Loathsome Fiend*. You didn't see either one, huh?"

I shook my head. "You're in love with her?"

"Oh, sure, there's no doubt about that."

"How's she feel, how does Leah Wentz feel?"

"Wentz has got to be fifty, and she's only twenty-four. Boy, the things people get themselves into." He crumpled, one by one, the napkins into tight balls. "Yeah, she likes me. We've had dinner twice and—yeah, she likes me. Trouble is, Wentz is one of these wildly jealous types. Wants to know where everybody is every minute, practically asks her to phone in every hour when she's not with him."

"Where's she tell him she is when she's with you?"

"If it's Tuesday she says she's at Willie Nolan's acting lab. Remember him in the movies back in the Forties?"

"No. And if it's not Tuesday?"

"Thursdays she's supposed to go to a lecture on Existential Meditation at that temple out by Malibu." He crumpled a few more napkins. "Mostly so far I've been seeing her on Tuesdays and Thursdays." He put his sharp elbows on the table and leaned toward me. "You ever commit adultery?"

I looked away from him. "Well, in the advertising business—"

"No, I mean love, not business."

"Oh, in that case, no."

"It's pretty terrible," Chuck said. Then he laughed. "But it's great too."

✗

I was in the East for the rest of September and almost half of October. Dr. Warloff's treatments had eliminated the splotches, but now every time I opened a can of Snarl I coughed. The agency decided I'd better switch to another account for a while.

I spent a few weeks touring the Schweitzer Brothers brewery in the Bronx and meeting the three brothers and their assorted sons and nephews. Back in 1949 they'd paid out $10,000 to have six man-size beer bottles made—the kind girls put on and danced in. It took me a week of long heated meetings to convince them the only way to show dancing beer bottles nowadays was with animation.

I came back home with the idea of calling Chuck and giving Sensational-McClosky a chance to work on some beer storyboards for us. My wife told me Chuck had been calling our house three or four times a day for the past week, anxious to know when I was going to return.

On the phone he wouldn't tell me why he was so agitated. When I got to the Scow bar out in Malibu he was already in a booth with a bottle of beer in front of him. I noticed it wasn't Schweitzer's. "What's wrong? If it's Leah maybe you ought to—"

"You know what Wentz is going to do?" Chuck asked.

"You mean he's found out?"

"No, no, he's so busy moving into his big new studio in the valley and getting his new series ready for TV he's got no time to be insanely jealous." Chuck, his Adam's apple fluttering, turned suddenly to stare across the smoky room. "That guy looks damn familiar. I've seen him someplace lately."

The man was squat, balding, and sitting at the bar alone and apparently staring up at the starfish and seashells tangled in the netting over the liquor shelves. "An old actor?"

"Don't think so. Well, that's not what I want to talk about." He moved his bottle an inch forward. "Did I ever tell you about Bubber Bruin?"

I said he hadn't and Chuck went on to tell me. When he'd worked for Wentz some four years ago, he'd invented a character named Bubber Bruin. The animated bear was supposed to be a sort of underground, anti-establishment type, real shaggy. He was continually plaguing a more conventional suburban raccoon. The theme song of the show was an old folk tune called "The Preacher and the Bear."

The preacher gets treed by a wild bear while in the woods and he climbs up a tree and asks the Lord for help. He concludes the prayer with a line something like, "And, Lord, if you can't help me, please don't help the bear." In Chuck's show the raccoon was continually quoting that last line.

Wentz had liked Chuck's idea well enough to let him do several storyboards for a half-hour show and he'd finally allowed him to do a five-minute animated segment. Then Wentz had decided Bubber Bruin was too controversial for the Saturday-morning kid slots.

"Now, four years later, he's sold the damn thing to TV," Chuck concluded. "Leah told me all about it—it hasn't been in the trades yet. She didn't even know I had anything to do with Bubber. Hell, my own character?"

"If you did it while you were working for Wentz, it's his," I told Chuck. "Legally, no matter how much you feel you've been bilked, it's Wentz's character now."

"I'm not talking legal, I'm talking moral," he said. "Wentz promised me a piece of the show. If it got going I was to get ten percent of the take. Ten percent."

"Did Wentz put that in writing?"

"No, of course he didn't."

"Only other thing you can do is talk to him."

"I've been trying to phone him for a week. He's never in, they tell me. He never returns my calls."

"Maybe you need an attorney. A friend of mine—"

"I don't need a lawyer," Chuck said. "You forget, I've got Leah on my side."

✗

I had to fly back to New York again a few days after that. One of the younger Schweitzers insisted we take a look at a piece of film he'd made with his girl friend as a dancing beer bottle. I don't know what the girl looked like out of the bottle, but her legs didn't match. One was fatter than the other. I had to have five separate meetings with all the Schweitzers before any of them would admit that, yes, the left leg was a little chunkier.

While I was still in New York I noticed an item in *Variety* about Wentz opening his new studio out in the San Fernando Valley. Three separate buildings covering ten acres. The main building had 65 rooms, including a fully equipped movie theater, a museum housing a thousand of the best animated cartoons of all time, and even a room to keep Wentz's collection of stuffed animals. Wentz, or one of his PR people, claimed he actually got cartoon ideas by sketching from his many examples of the taxidermist's art. The story concluded with the news that Wentz had signed his biggest contract yet with TV for a new show entitled *Bubber Bruin and Company*.

Back in L.A. I couldn't get hold of Chuck for almost a week. He wasn't at the Sensational-McClosky studio, he wasn't at his cottage up on Scenario Lane, and his answering service implied that he'd vanished from the face of the earth without a word to them.

Two more days passed before, at just about midnight, Chuck called me. "I wanted to say goodbye," he said.

"You going somewhere?" I was hunched on my side of the bed, trying not to wake my wife.

"I'm phoning from a booth out in the valley, so I guess it's safe to talk."

"Talk about what? You in some kind of trouble?"

"No, I'm fine. Leah and I are going to Mexico in about three hours. As soon as we pay a visit to the studio."

"You're going to Wentz's studio?"

"Leah has keys, and she knows the combination of the safe in Wentz's private office."

"The safe? Chuck, what the hell are you—"

"Tell them to call you in the morning," murmured my wife.

"It's not the agency."

Chuck said, "Huh?"

In a lower, but more intense, voice, I told him, "You can't take anything from Wentz's safe, Chuck."

"Going to take what Wentz owes me. Leah thinks there's about $100,000 in there," he explained. "That's maybe not—"

"Time. Signal when you're finished," cut in the operator.

"Yeah, sure. $100,000 isn't enough really, but we know a place in Mexico where—"

"The last time I talked to you you were going to get a lawyer and talk this over with Wentz."

"Nope, that was your idea. As far as talking to him goes—well, he knows about me and Leah. He's had detectives on her trail for weeks. Remember the guy at the Scow bar I thought looked so familiar? One of Wentz's boys."

"You can't rob the man of $100,000!"

"See *Daily Variety* yesterday? See what the network is paying him for twenty-six Bubber shows? Anyway, Leah's his wife, so—"

"That doesn't mean you can—"

"I'll drop you a letter when we get settled. Won't use my real name, but I trust you not to tell Wentz where we are."

"Obviously I'm not going to do that, Chuck. But you can't—"

" 'Bye." And he hung up.

✗

What happened next I'm guessing about, at least part of it. I've talked to one of the cops involved and I'm quite certain things went about as I've imagined.

Chuck, at exactly the agreed-on time of 12:30, climbed over the back wall of the studio grounds. Wentz didn't have a watchman. Hurrying, panting from the exertion, Chuck made his way to a side door of the main building. He tapped three times and Leah opened the door.

She looked incredibly pretty standing there in the corridor, her long auburn hair tied back with an emerald-green ribbon, her green eyes bright with excitement. She kissed him once, her lips warm, and led him down the grey-carpeted hall. "His office is right along here," she said, her hand tightening on Chuck's.

The office was enormous, even for a Hollywood studio, and it seemed to take them a long time to get across it. The safe was behind an oil painting—an oil painting of Bubber Bruin.

"Oh, that's perfect," remarked Chuck. "Just perfect."

Leah reached up and swung the painting away. The sound of brakes squealing came from outside.

A few seconds later they heard a voice bellowing in the night. "You cheap bimbo! I'm going to kill him right in front of your two-timing eyes!"

Leah pushed the painting back in place. "He won't do anything if he can't find you."

"He sounds mad enough to keep looking."

"No, he'll get over it in a while. I know him. I can persuade him to calm down, but you've got to keep out of his sight."

He touched her cheek, spun, and ran out a door of the office.

He could hear Wentz stomping into the other end of the building. "One bullet in the knee! One in the stomach! One through the heart! Nobody swipes a wife from Wentz!"

Obviously the private detectives, despite all of Chuck's lying low, were still up on what he and Leah were doing.

Chuck, his throat dry, went two-stepping up a pipe and plastic stairway to the second floor of the studio building. All was dark up there, so he had to go more slowly.

He felt his way to the end of the dark corridor, found a door, and tried it. The door opened and he stepped into the black room beyond. Chuck sensed several large shapes in the darkness. He ducked behind one, crouched, and listened.

It was a big studio. Sixty-five rooms, wasn't that what the stories said? Yeah, sixty-five, and Wentz would probably never have the patience to search them all. If Chuck kept silent and stayed hunched down behind this big black object his chances weren't bad. Better than breaking from the building and maybe running into one of Wentz's private detectives. Leah probably would be able to calm Wentz down and get him headed for home.

Chuck listened hard. Was that Wentz coming up the stairs?

His eyes were getting used to the darkness. He was able to see things in the faint moonlight coming in through the tightly blinded windows. It was then Chuck realized where he was.

Rising all around him, in life-like poses, was the famous Wentz collection of stuffed animals. Raccoons, pumas, cats, dogs, a leopard, a lion, and, the big object he was trying to hide behind, a grizzly bear. Stuffed animals, every one rich with animal hair.

Chuck clenched his fists, gritted his teeth, fought against the impulse which was tearing at him and growing stronger.

The impulse to sneeze. And sneeze. And sneeze ...

NOW HE THINKS HE'S DEAD

There was really very little left of him.

They finally figured out who he was. Then they began to wonder why his remains ended up where they did.

I could have told them, but I didn't. It's always been my policy, as you probably know, not to fool around with anything like this.

Beau Willet brought it on himself, more or less. His killer is still running around free, true enough, but the police have written Beau's death off as nothing more than a bizarre accident. It's best to leave the whole thing like that.

It was about a year ago that I first met Beau. We became friends, which is somewhat odd since I'd got in touch with him initially to offer him a bribe. Well, not a bribe exactly. Simply some money to stop writing about the actress we'd hired to do all our SoyHammy commercials. Less than a week after we'd signed the contract with Panky Zeffer, Beau had an item about her in his *Hollywood Daily* column. She'd been thrown out of a Beverly Hills boutique, Beau reported, for punching a salesgirl in the snoot, tossing an overpriced suitcase smack through a plate-glass window, and kneeing the store manager in the groin.

When old Mazden—he hadn't had his stroke then and was still running the whole SoyHammy operation—read that item he got on the phone from Chicago and howled. I, being the Account Supervisor on SoyHammy, had to listen to the howling, then go over and talk to our actress. That took awhile because her maid couldn't find her right off.

I located the girl finally in the bathtub, fully clothed, and passed out, smelling strongly of Manhattans. I revived her, at least partially, and she admitted Beau had printed the truth. Having little hope of reforming Panky in the four days we had before we began shooting the commercials, I decided to approach Beau.

He was a middle-size man, slightly plumper than he appeared in the photo accompanying his column every day. About 34, he'd come down to Los Angeles from Portland, Oregon, eleven years before.. Besides his column in the *Daily*, he did pieces for *TV Look* and *Newsmag*. The possibility of our SoyHammy girl's adventures also appearing in magazines with such large circulations unsettled me.

Beau, very politely for him, turned down my veiled offer to provide him some money if he didn't write about Panky Zeffer any more. "You know what your trouble is?" he asked at that first lunch, which took place at the Microwave Tamale on La Cienega.

"Beg pardon?"

"You hate your work."

"No, I don't. I love it," I insisted. "My work in the advertising profession has brought me numerous satisfactions—a spacious home, an enchanting wife, who by the way used to be a fashion—"

"I know that. I know everything about everybody," Beau cut in. "You won't get anywhere denying my insights into how your head works. Besides knowing lots about psychology on my own, I'm Lisa Rubinchek's Number One Lover."

"Lisa Rubinchek? Oh, you mean Dr. Lisa Rubinchek."

"That Lisa Rubinchek, yeah. Don't you watch her show every night on KMA-TV? She's got the highest rating of any local show in the slot. Beats out *Bowling for Big Dough,* the *Chicano Hour*, and even the reruns of *Olaf's Pig.*"

"Very impressive," I said. "By being around her some of her psychiatric experience rubs off?"

"If you ever catch my lady on *You Think You Got a Problem*, you know Lisa. Besides being one of the most stunning and willowy blondes in this goofy town she's a damn good shrink. With one exception."

"I bet," I guessed, "that exception is you."

"You got it. Lisa's fantastically off base when it comes to figuring me out." He settled back against the serape-striped leatherette of the booth. "Immature, impulsive, lacking in judgment. Ha! Does that sum up Beau Willet? Well, you can't put too much faith in psychiatrists. Like that joke about the guy's wife who takes him to a shrink—you know the one?"

"I've heard most of—"

"She drags hubby in, informs the headdoctor that the guy is all the time sick, but regular medicos can't find a blessed thing wrong. So the psychiatrist gives the guy a forty-five-minute show-and-tell session.

Then he has the wife in and explains there's nothing physically wrong with her husband, it's all in his mind. With a few more headshrinking sessions he'll be tip-top. 'He only thinks he's sick,' he says. 'Remember, he only *thinks* he's sick.' So a couple weeks pass and the patient doesn't come back. One day the shrink runs into the wife on the street and he asks her how her husband is. And she replies, 'Now he thinks he's dead.' " Beau chuckled, rubbing his hands together. "Very profound, right?"

"Well, to me—"

"Tell you something else. I'm pulling down $100,000 a year and I'm only thirty-two. More than you make, and you're pushing fifty."

"Actually I'm forty-four," I told him.

"Too much boozing in the bistros then, plus maybe some grabby time in the wee small hours. Gives your chin that sag it's got and makes those spooky hollows under your eyes," he explained, scrutinizing my face. "Speaking of that, do you know who I saw punch out the doorman at Karlo's Nudibar last midnight? None other than kindly old Mercer Fracklen, who plays Father Finnigan on ABC's top-rated *Saints Preserve Us*. Drunk out of his coco and swearing like a crazed sailor."

I was rubbing my chin. "I drink very moderately."

"Sure, sure, everybody claims that. Right before they fall off their stools." He grabbed up his serape-striped napkin. "Hey, you know what the next big fad is going to be in this wacky burg?"

"Probably something like—"

"Peewee golf. You heard me right. Miniature golf, the craze for it is going to be as big and lucrative as it was way back when in the dim dark days of the Depression. Lisa says I'm goofy, but my gut-feeling for business trends never fails me. I'm putting a wad into buying up six courses out in the Valley. It's the wave of the future."

✗

Talc Henkel's name started showing up in Beau's *Now What?* column a couple of months later. By that time, as far as I've been able to find out, Henkel was already Beau's chief rival for Lisa. He was a—well, you know what he looks like if you saw him starring in *Rotten Cop*, *A Bloody Mess*, and *Kill 'Em All*. Before getting into pictures in the late Sixties, Henkel had been a mercenary soldier, fighting in Africa and Latin America.

Beau didn't accept much of Henkel's bio. He ran at least two items a week about him, the "so-called soldier boy." One would pick Henkel's alleged military record apart, the other would imply Henkel used a double for all the hazardous stunts in his films. Now it's the usual thing for a stuntman to do the dangerous stuff. Talc Henkel's publicity, however, made a point of stressing that he performed absolutely all the stunt work himself.

About this time I had to fly back to Chicago. Old Mazden had decided he wanted a soypig in our SoyHammy commercials. It was a very stressful trip, since I was originally scheduled to take Panky Zeffer back with me. But she'd punched the bartender at the airport cocktail lounge minutes before we were due to board our plane. I had to abandon her in Burbank, flying alone to Chicago several hours late.

Old Mazden began howling immediately upon my arrival. He'd hired an actor to dress up in a pig suit and meet me at the airport in Chicago. The guy broke out in a prickly rash from hanging around so long inside the suit. Once we ironed out that problem, two full weeks were taken up in persuading Mazden the soypig idea was no good. Even after the actor brought a note from his allergist saying he couldn't wear the pig suit ever again, Mazden kept insisting the concept was basically sound.

I had just about convinced the old man that Panky was reforming when one of his minions brought in a copy of the *Hollywood Daily*. An item in Beau's column was circled with a thick, angry-looking red line. It dealt with our actress falling off a merry-go-round during a charity fundraiser at an Anaheim amusement park. Anybody can fall off a merry-go-round, but Panky managed thereafter to sock a fairly prominent bishop in the face.

I can still see myself sitting there in Mazden's immense office, which always smells strongly of real bacon, and feeling very chilled. Despite that I was able to notice the gossip item underneath the fatal one. Beau had written, " . . . Soldier boy Henkel's double ought to get extra dough. He not only did all the stunts in the just-lensed *Dum Dum Bullets*, he picked booze-buff Henkel out of three different gutters about town . . ."

✗

When I returned home to Los Angeles I had to devote nearly all my time to auditioning new actresses to do the SoyHammy spots. This made Panky angry and she stormed up to the ad agency and conked me over the head with a wine bottle. In fairness to her I have to say it wasn't her wine bottle. It was one of the Busino Brothers' new ones she snatched from a passing Account Supervisor who was carrying it to the Art Department.

For nearly a week I was in the hospital, with actresses and their agents popping in and out of my room. I shared the room with a mortician from Glendale, who came to fancy himself a casting expert after the second day. He became quite upset when I turned down the redhaired girl you've probably seen doing the Featherweight Toilet Tissue commercials and he tossed a couple of potted plants at me. Plants, I'd like to mention, given to me by the agents and actresses. All in all I didn't think about Beau Willet for quite a spell.

Then he phoned me after I'd been out three days and suggested we meet for lunch at the Salty Dog down near the beach in Santa Monica.

"You look awful," he said by way of greeting when I came strolling into the hot dog bistro. "Been in another slug match with your lady?"

"A mortician did most of this."

"You're not a bad guy," observed Beau, his eyes on the foot-long menu. "You've sold your soul to the forces of mammon, but you're still one of the few people in this crazy metropolis I can talk to honestly."

"I wasn't aware—"

"Trust me, I sense things about you. From being so much around Lisa."

"Talc Henkel must be about ready to practice therapy, too," I couldn't refrain from saying. "I hear he and Dr. Rubinchek are seeing a good—"

"That pseudo-soldier? He's nothing more than a barnacle on Beau Willet's love boat." He paused to frown over the menu. "I'm torn between Doggie Number 16 and Doggie Number 27."

"How's the miniature golf business?"

"Oh, I'm out of that. Didn't lose too much," said Beau. "Of course Lisa has it all figured out. Why I bought in, how come I lost my shirt, and so on and so forth. All off base. What do you think?"

"About what?"

"Doggie Number 16 as opposed to Doggie Number 27."

"Compromise and get one of each."

"Naw, then I'd end up with a doubledecker chin like yours. Do I want sauerkraut or sour cream on my dog? Oh, it's good Lisa isn't here to see me so undecided."

Eventually he settled on Number 22.

Halfway through it he pushed his plate aside. "Ever been in love?"

"Obviously. Since I'm married."

"There's one of the things I like about you, that unsinkable naiveté," said Beau, cackling. "Love makes you do strange things."

"So I hear."

He poked at his hot dog with his plastic fork. "Love has made me do something I never thought I'd do," Beau continued. "Incredible."

I ate my Number 6 in silence.

"Yeah, something I never thought I'd do. I faked an item."

"Everybody does that."

"Beau Willet doesn't do that. Until now. Until that lowlife Talc Henkel came along." A very sad expression visited Beau's face. "Lots of the guff I've been writing about him isn't true. Oh, he was never a mercenary soldier, as far as I know. But that smug jerk really does do his own stunting. What a sorry situation for someone like me to fall into."

"What does Lisa say?"

"The usual claptrap. It's astounding how somebody so usually astute can be so far off on me. I feel terrible about compromising my ideals—besides which that bum can sue me."

"Is he going to?"

"He's never going to have Lisa as long as I'm around. Getting me tossed in the slammer might assure him an inside track."

"Here's a positive solution," I offered. "Why don't you marry her? Then—"

"Didn't I explain that to you? She won't marry me until—"

After a few seconds I asked, "Until what?"

"Some guff about my need to mature. How can you be immature and pull down a hundred thou a year? Sometimes she's—"

"Here's another solution. Forget about her, get a new girl."

"Are you nutsy? I *love* Dr. Lisa Rubinchek."

"We were very fond of the girl we had set to do the SoyHammy spots, too. When the time came, though, I was able to fire Panky without—"

"Boy, listen to yourself. The show-biz morality is taking you over. I'm talking about love, not salami."

"Ham," I corrected. "Although we'll probably be introducing a soysalami by next—"

"The answer," said Beau, "is to make Henkel look less attractive to Lisa."

"I saw him in *Rotten Cop* on TV the other night. He's a very striking man, tall and—"

"Tall isn't everything." Beau's head began to nod up and down. "I see it now, the column propaganda by itself isn't enough. I'm going to have to attack Talc Henkel from a new angle."

"What you really ought to do is—"

"Yeah, a different angle." He chuckled, clapped his hands. Elated now, he finished his hot dog and ordered a Number 15 malted to follow it.

They removed me from the SoyHammy account around this time, mostly because Mazden reverted to believing the soypig was the best solution to his sales problem. When one of our vice-presidents called on the old man and found him wearing the pig suit himself, he realized I'd be better off handling a brand-new account.

I took over a new product called FazBalm, a bar of soap containing 40 percent anti-chapping lotion. The idea was you washed with it right before heading out into the wind and snow. The client, who was based in Colorado, demanded we produce a series of commercials with sled dogs pulling a giant bar of FazBalm across a bleak stretch of Alaska. I tried to persuade him that lacked glamour.

While I was attempting this, in Colorado and Los Angeles, Beau commenced his campaign to ruin Talc Henkel in the eyes of his love. I saw Beau only once during this period, so some of the details of what he did I'm guessing at. He did admit he was responsible for the business with the cars and also to doping the horse. I'm certain, however, he was also responsible for all the accidents which befell the actor.

Despite my policy of staying out of things like this, I did make an attempt to talk to Dr. Lisa Rubinchek. I was anxious for more information about Beau's attitudes, and I suppose I had some notion of warning her. The closest I came was her private secretary who told me Dr. Rubinchek would be happy to give me 45 minutes of her time at the usual fee. I don't know, $150 for a single session seemed excessive and I let the matter drop. I decided if she was as perceptive as Beau claimed, she'd no doubt see all this for herself eventually.

Beau had decided to sabotage his rival. I don't know if initially he was considering murdering or even seriously injuring Henkel. Beau insisted to me he only wanted to make the actor appear inept and inefficient. With all Beau's studio connections and contacts it was simple enough for him to look at the shooting scripts of both *Dum Dum Bullets* and, later, *Right Between the Eyes*. He also had no trouble slipping into the Wheelan Studios after hours and tampering with the auto Henkel was scheduled to use the next day. I pointed out to him, when he confided in me about his activities after the fact, that Talc Henkel could have been badly hurt in the car stunt.

Ignoring me, Beau laughed his chuckly laugh. "It must have looked absolutely marvelous. The cars coming down the road, Talc Henkel in hot pursuit, and then the steering wheel comes off in his hand. Straight out of Abbott and Costello." Beau bounced on his chair, one of those canvas ones they have in the outdoors section of the Gourmet Seafood Shack in Malibu.

"You're lucky Talc was able to jump clear when—"

"*He's* lucky you mean."

"What about the horse in his new Western?"

"It fell asleep," said Beau with another chuckle.

"In the middle of a jump over a chasm?"

"Yeah, that really must have made him look lovely. Oh, the expression on that phony soldier boy's puss must have been a delight to behold. Going to have to catch a look at the footage for that day."

"The horse broke its neck."

"So? They got a lot of horses in Hollywood."

"You better knock this off, Beau, before—"

"Can't yet. Not having its full effect."

"Meaning Lisa isn't impressed?"

"She's still dating that turkey," he acknowledged. "Why can't she see him for the fake he is, that imitation warrior? Sometimes Lisa is absolutely dense. I mean, if you've read her book, *You're Okey Dokey*, you know this is one very bright broad."

"What about Henkel? The way you keep heckling him in your column about his accidents, he's sure to tumble you're behind them."

"Not that nitwit. A pretty face he's got, and he's tall, but there's nothing in the old cabeza. Talc Henkel's never going to get wise to the source of his troubles. Sooner or later, Lisa's going to see him for the fake clown he is. And she'll see me for—"

"For what?"

"For what I really am."

"Be careful," I cautioned.

✗

We couldn't come up with an Alaska satisfactory to the client. The one we built at the ComFactors Studios didn't please him. I then made a deal to use the set left over from Val Klint's $12,000,000 remake of *Nanook of the North*. To me when those huskies came barking across that realistic snow, bravely pulling an enormous bar of soap, it made a heck of a convincing shot. The client wouldn't buy it. So I had to fly up to Alaska and use the real Alaska for our Alaska. Not half as good as what we had in Hollywood, as you'll probably agree if the commercial ever airs.

The whole experience consumed a month. When I returned home I found Beau Willet's obituary in with the other items my wife had clipped from the *L.A. Times* for me not to miss. She always does that when I'm away—sort of a family tradition. So there was the final notice about Beau in with an account of a show of billboard art at a Westwood gallery and a piece about sludge delaying the shooting of the pilot for the *Beachcomber* show my agency was thinking of sponsoring.

I sat in the sunlit breakfast room with the obit dangling in my hand for a long while. The morning was warm and there were flowers all around outside. I felt very cold.

Not that I really could have done anything to prevent what happened. Even if I hadn't been up in Alaska with those dogs. No, because Beau must have been planning what he was planning from the start of his personal campaign against Talc Henkel. He was going to kill his rival and make it look like an accident.

To do a perfect job he began, after the first few accidents didn't succeed in doing away with Henkel, to study. I learned this from a bookstore clerk in Beverly Hills. Beau bought all sorts of books on bombs, guerilla warfare, and weaponry. His final try, which he was certain would succeed, was inspired by Henkel himself.

Beau had escorted Lisa to the opening of *Nanook of the North*. At the cocktail party afterward up in Val Klint's Bel Air mansion they encountered Talc Henkel. Beau was, I'm fairly certain, hoping the lanky actor would get mad, lose his temper, and take a swing at him—behave the way most of the other people Beau wrote about did.

Not Talc. He came over, gave them both his familiar bony grin. "Been meaning to thank you for all the terrific publicity you been handing me, Beau. Keep it up. You're looking splendid this evening, Lisa."

"Thank you, Talc. Would you like to join us for a nightcap after this shindig?"

"Like to, Lisa, but can't. We're shooting the big mine cave-in scenes for *Right Between the Eyes* bright and early tomorrow morn. Since, despite what you read in the papers, I do my own stunts I'm going to have to get a good night's rest so I can go into that shaft bright-eyed and bushy-tailed."

Beau blinked. "Tomorrow?"

"Tomorrow, very early. Well, keep up the good work, Beau. Raincheck on that nightcap, Lisa love."

They weren't supposed to begin the cave-in sequence until next week. Beau had acquired all the extra explosives he'd need, but he wasn't figuring on setting up the mine accident for Henkel until Sunday night at the earliest.

"Lisa, hon, I have to rush back to the office. Just remembered a—"

"Beau, why mask your true feelings so? What do I always tell you? Isn't it the same message I've given the millions of readers of *You're Okey Dokey*? Yes, you mustn't let your feelings suffocate inside," said blonde willowy Lisa. "You're annoyed by Talc, by his obvious deep affection for me, and by my quite innocent invitation to him. Therefore you're burning to retaliate with a nasty dig at him in your column."

Sometimes it was almost more than Beau could take to hear all that guff coming out of that lovely mouth. He came near at such moments to understanding why the people he wrote about were always socking each other.

He didn't go to his Hollywood office when he dashed out of the Nanook party early. Instead he rushed, driving at the very edge of the speed limit, to his place in one of the canyons. There he gathered up the explosives that he'd purchased on the sly as soon as he read through the final script for *Right Between the Eyes*. No one, so far as I can determine, saw any of what happened next.

Beau drove out to the San Fernando Valley location they were using on the film. There was only an old watchman in a wooden shack to worry about, and he'd fallen asleep long before Beau arrived. He'd checked that out a few days earlier, the fact the old guy wasn't one to stay awake.

Leaving his car at a safe distance, Beau stole silently to the area being used as the old mine. There was a real shaft opening dug there, its mouth looking very dark in the cloudy midnight.

He approached the entrance to the shaft. A weathered sign had been hung over the entrance, reading *Lucky Susan Mine*. Picks and shovels, a dented canteen, and other tools were scattered over the gritty ground.

Carrying his explosives and equipment very carefully, Beau entered the dark shaft.

Three steps in he tripped the wire which had been strung across the opening. The explosives already there went off and that was the last of Beau Willet.

Talc Henkel wasn't as dense as Beau had imagined. He had fairly soon realized who was rigging his accidents. Motivated by a desire for revenge and, I imagine, wanting to get rid of his only serious rival for Lisa, Henkel set about arranging an accident of his own. This one to eliminate Beau.

Beau was wrong about Talc Henkel. All of the actor's biography was true. He had been a mercenary and had fought in several wars. One of his specialties was demolition.

AND THE WINNER IS—

He shouldn't have confessed in front of all those people. But when he saw the man he'd murdered starting to come up on the stage to share the award, it unsettled him.

Everybody, since the awards banquet was televised live from Hollywood, knows what Oscar Kornfield did next. Some are even aware of what Joe Tackery was up to and what exactly his last words meant. Hardly anyone, though, knows about the trunkful of money.

I'm probably the only living person, besides perhaps Jana, who has the knowledge that there was $400,000 in cash involved in this business. As to where the trunk is now, I have no idea. Jana doesn't either, so far as I can determine without openly discussing it with her. Which I never will, since I don't want to get entangled any further. Let the money stay lost; there's very likely a curse on it anyway, a jinx.

Joe Tackery and I had lunch the day Kornfield fired him. We met at the Vegetarian Dragon, the health-food Chinese place in Westwood. A few of the tan and healthy-looking patrons gasped, a couple shrieked, even one of the usually unmovable waiters let out a frightened sigh when Joe came strolling in out of the smoggy yellow midday toward my booth.

"See, and he claims I'm unbelievable," Tackery said as he dropped down opposite me.

Lowering the dragon-shaped menu, I told him, "Coming to lunch in your makeup is—"

"Gauche, yeah, I know. Thing is, I didn't have time to remove it and still get over here on time. Because of the fist fight."

"You were in a fight? A real fight?"

"With Kornfield, after he fired me. Ha." When he laughed some of the scar tissue on his face cracked. Tackery poked at it, then toyed with his dangling left eyeball. "Should have seen what I did to him." He inspected his fingertip. "Huh, there's some *real* blood. I didn't think that turkey hit me hard enough to—"

"Why were you trading punches with the head of Magnum-Opus Productions? No, thanks."

Our waiter had brought a hot towel and a finger bowl for Tackery to use on his seemingly ruined face.

Tackery grinned up at him, flashing blackened fangs. "All make-believe. Illusion," he said, and the waiter went away, leaving the scented towel behind. "You saw me in *Dr. Dementia*. Now, forgetting the story line, you have to admit I was convincing in that film."

"Best bloodbeast I've ever seen."

"Hell, even John Simon on *New York* called me completely disgusting and nauseating, and you know how few things he praises." He hit the table angrily with a bloody fist, causing the hand towel to give out a slippery, squishing sound. "I was even better in *Love Finds Dr. Dementia*. Right? I've been in *movies*. Ever since I had the title role in *Horrifying Slime* I've been considered one of the best horror men in this half-witted town. Sure, doing my own makeup annoys certain people, but the hell with them. Didn't I almost get an Oscar for *Marylou's Demented Offspring*?"

"What's bothering Kornfield then?"

"He claims I'm no good, that my characterizations aren't believable. 'Wouldn't fool a cockeyed six-year-old,' is how he deftly phrased it. That, however, is not the real reason. The real reason is, that toad is consumed by jealousy," explained Tackery. "See, I was supposed to, even though my half-wit agent didn't get it on paper yet, play a running character in this new *Ghost Doctor* TV series Kornfield's producing. Hell, I was doing them a favor to play television at all. By agreeing to be the accident-victim zombie I—"

"Sounds like a difficult character to keep working into stories. Maybe that's why—"

"Naw, Kornfield gave me the ax because of Jana."

"Jana? I thought you were embroiled with a girl named Pam."

"Kim was her name and that's been over since she didn't come right back from the location shooting on *Rapist of the Range*." Absently he started removing the warts and moles from his face. "Don't you know who Jana Dayside is?"

"Sure, my oldest boy has that poster of her hidden under his bed. We used her in a toothpaste commercial couple of years back. Before she hit with *Robots Three* on TV."

"She is, without doubt, the hottest property in Hollywood at the moment."

"You dating her?"

"I am, a real love match," he said, lowering his voice. "Trouble is, I strongly suspect Kornfield is, too."

"Kornfield just married the redhaired girl who used to be part of that rock group called Advanced Stages. Item was in the *National Intruder* only—"

"You've lived in this goofy town all your life and you never heard of a producer cheating on his wife?"

"Not so soon after the wedding. According to the *Intruder* he just gifted this redhead with a diamond-studded—"

"Oy, for a man who's slaved ten years in the advertising game, you have a very feeble idea of how the world works."

"Fifteen years actually," I corrected. "Be sixteen next—"

"It's me Jana *loves*, but I think Kornfield forces her to see him. After all, Magnum-Opus is producing *Robots Three.*"

"She ought to have enough clout now to be able to say no to Kornfield. The show's been Number One in the ratings for the last month." The waiter was hovering and I picked up my menu again. "We better order. The sweet-sour parsnips are—"

"See, I'm not absolutely certain she is going out with that lecherous grunion, but I *suspect* she is."

"Ask her."

"You don't simply *ask* the hottest property in town if she's two-timing you."

"Two-timing? There's a quaint old phrase—"

"My father used to say that, and when I get angry—"

"We have very nice kelp chow mein," offered our waiter cautiously, while trying not to look at Tackery.

"Come back in a few minutes," he said.

"If you're sure Kornfield fired you for personal reasons you ought to have the Guild look—"

"Ha," laughed Tackery, causing one of his horrible eyebrows to fall off. "I don't need the guild to fix Kornfield's wagon. Once I determine what's what, I'll settle the whole thing myself."

✗

The day after our lunch I had to fly to Florida unexpectedly to untangle some problems they were having with one of our shark-repellent commercials. While the repellent was repelling sharks, it attracted hordes of ugly little blue and orange fish who kept spoiling most of our expensive underwater footage. Since I was head account man, the client expected me to come up with some way of shooing all the ugly little fish away. The first thing I worked out, with the help of a very high-priced marine biologist, got rid of the ugly fish but dyed our actor a pale lavender. What with one thing and another, including a mild case of sunstroke, I was three weeks in Florida.

By the time I returned to Los Angeles, Joe Tackery was already at work on his plan to undermine Kornfield while finding out what the producer and Jana Dayside were up to. He took to hanging around the Magnum-Opus studios out in Burbank and around Kornfield's Beverly Hills home wearing various disguises. Once he got himself up as the mutilated vampire he'd played in *Stultified*. Excessive in my opinion, but it seemed to fool Kornfield. Tackery was able to trail him all across Southern California without the producer's being aware of it.

The third day of his vigil Tackery followed Kornfield directly to Jana Dayside's new peach-colored mansion in Bel Air, thus confirming his worst fears. After that he determined to get something on his rival, something damaging enough to put him out of competition.

When he outlined all this to me over lunch at the Frozen Goatherd, that yogurt-on-a-stick place in Santa Monica, I told him it would be much simpler to abandon Jana than to trail Kornfield hither and yon.

"You forget," Tackery said, himself this particular afternoon except for a false moustache, "that Kornfield fired me off the *Ghost Doctor* show. He says I'm not good at makeup and disguise, but what I'm doing proves otherwise. You also forget he's been squiring my lady around town in a most sneaky way."

"With her compliance."

"Who would willingly date a toad like him? She's obviously being coerced. She's a very sensitive, introspective girl and a heavy like—"

"On *Robots Three* I saw her lift up a full garbage truck and heave it through—"

"Trick stuff, as you well know," he said, scowling. "I'm most certainly going to revenge myself on Kornfield. I'm pretty sure, by the way, he's trying to get me blacklisted with some of the other producers in town. He won't get away with that either."

✗

Right at this point in time I left for the Nyanya Film Festival, where one of our dandruff-fighter commercials was up for a Special Award.

Unfortunately the Nyanya rebels picked the week of the festival to stage a terror raid on the capital. Along with nearly 200 other invited guests, I was held hostage in the Royal Palace of Cinema for four and a half days. We had to get along on what food there was in the lobby, mostly popcorn and chocolate-covered raisins.

The diet and the constant threats of violence from our surly captors made my stay in Nyanya less than pleasant. Possibly you didn't see anything about the incident in the papers or on the news—Nyanya doesn't seem able to get much publicity in the outside world. Which is one of the things the rebels were grousing about.

Recuperating from the trip consumed another two weeks, so I wasn't back in the agency until the tail end of summer. My lovely secretary informed me that several strange people had been dropping in asking after me—a one-legged sailor, a very ill-looking Balkan count, a man who appeared to have suffered a severe accident, and a shaggy fellow in a bloodstained overcoat.

"Joe Tackery," I decided.

My secretary screamed just then, gesturing at the opening elevator.

A sinister-looking Oriental was shuffling into the reception area on my floor. "Do you have a moment, most celestial sir?"

"Come on into my office, Joe."

"Shall I alert the authorities?" whispered my secretary.

"Only an actor," I assured her.

"I'm still not used to this town, it's not at all like East Moline."

"Ha, ha!" remarked Tackery when we were closed in my large sunbright office.

"Is that a cackle of triumph?"

"First, how are you feeling?"

"Not bad, I seem to have—"

"Good, good." He hunkered down in the chair most of the clients prefer. "Let me fill you in on what I've unearthed."

"Don't get yellow all over the chair."

"This is smear-proof Oriental makeup," Tackery said. "I have them now, have them by the proverbial short hairs."

"Who?"

"Kornfield and that little twit of a business partner of his, Tuck Bensen."

"Bensen's about your size. He's not exactly little or—"

"Spiritually he's a shrimp, morally he's a midget. That offensive little—"

"How'd Bensen get into this? Is he going around with Jana too?"

"No, she isn't *that* goofy." He hunched lower in the chair, rubbing his gnarled taloned hands together. "I've got them on Murder One."

I blinked, dropping the soy margarine carton I'd been toying with. "Murder?"

He nodded. "Ever hear of a guy know as Mojave McWilliams?"

"Old coot who lives out in the desert, old-time prospector? Struck it rich years ago and built himself some kind of castle out there. Rumored to be fantastically wealthy."

"The rumors are true," he said. "Old Mojave had a steamer trunk chockful of cash money. $400,000 worth to be exact." From out of his robe sleeve he produced a fat wad of bills. "Money like this."

"You mean you stole the old man's life savings?"

"Life savings? Mojave was much more than a prospector—he made his dough in sundry shady enterprises. Besides which, I didn't swipe the loot. Kornfield and Bensen did."

"Then how come you—"

"They don't as yet know I have the trunk or where I hid it." He leaned back and laughed, first as himself and then as the sinister Oriental. "There's an old folksong that advises you to put your money down in your shoe before coming into a town like this, otherwise they're going to take it away from you. Mojave thought he had his cash safely stashed, but he was wrong."

"I don't quite under—"

"Let me explain."

What had been happening was this. After Tackery, in his varied disguises, had been trailing Kornfield for a few weeks he discovered the producer was making several trips out to the desert. Accompanied usually by his partner, Tuck Bensen, he visited the mammoth adobe fortress Mojave McWilliams had erected for himself when he retired from his sundry shady enterprises. McWilliams, who shunned people, had one weakness. Well, more than one actually, but one which Kornfield and Bensen could exploit. He was vain. When they approached him with the notion of Magnum-Opus doing an hour television documentary on his colorful life, the old desert rat admitted them into his fortress and invited them to return whenever they wished.

What Kornfield and his partner were really after was the trunkful of money the old man was rumored to have hidden on the premises.

Despite their apparent success and frequent mentions in such publications as the *National Intruder*, both Oscar Kornfield and Tuck Bensen were on the edge of bankruptcy. Kornfield's cash had flowed out to his earlier wives—there'd been six prior to the redhaired girl from Advanced Stages. Bensen's money had been lost at two places, Las Vegas and the track. $400,000 would be a big help.

So they went after Mojave. One night, long after he'd come to trust them completely, Bensen suddenly jabbed him in the arm with a hypodermic. This knocked the old prospector out, and a different shot caused him to speak the absolute truth. Unfortunately, right after McWilliams told them where the trunk was hidden, he died. Giving unexpected injections to old men sometimes has that effect.

Tackery witnessed all this from a ledge outside the castle living room. Besides being expert at makeup, he was a pretty fair stuntman. He managed to watch as Kornfield and Bensen hid Mojave's body in the cellar room where the trunk had been hidden. Since Mojave was a recluse they didn't expect anyone to find him for a long while. He had no servants, and kept a year's supply of simple foods on hand.

The producer and his partner, with Tackery discreetly following, next drove to a piece of land that Kornfield still owned in one of the undeveloped stretches of canyon beyond Los Angeles. Working all night the two men buried the trunkful of money, intending to let it sit a week or two before making use of it. By that time they'd know if they'd got away clear.

Tackery waited until they drove off, then dug up the loot. After helping himself to enough cash to finance his campaign for a month or more, he took the trunk and hid it at a new and different location.

"Doesn't that make you an accessory to the murder?" I asked when he'd finished the account.

"No, it makes me a light-hearted Robin Hood."

"You witnessed a murder. It's your duty to—"

"Yeah, eventually I'll blow the whistle on the two of them," Tackery promised, grinning inscrutably. "Right now, however, I am going to have some fun."

"Fun?"

"Did you know Kornfield has taken to carrying a gun?"

"No, it wasn't in the *Intruder*."

"While little Bensen is consulting Madame Olga down in Manhattan Beach to get some tips on life on the other side of the veil."

Tackery was bouncing in the chair, hugging himself, trying to control his amusement and elation.

"You've been making up like Mojave McWilliams," I accused. "Yes, that must be it. You've been getting yourself up like that old prospector and haunting Kornfield and Bensen."

"Merely giving them little flashes," he said. "You know, at a premiere I'll be at the edge of the crowd where they can only catch a glimpse. Or I might stroll across one of their lawns during a cocktail party. A cinchy impersonation—all you need is lots of whiskers."

"Listen, you're going to—"

"Wait now. I couldn't possibly fool them. Right? Because Kornfield is on record as saying how bad I am at makeup and character work. I'm no good, so I couldn't make anyone believe I was Mojave."

I wasn't happy about all he'd told me. I felt, somehow, as though I were also an accomplice. "How does what you're doing help you with Jana Dayside?"

"Once I've toppled Kornfield, turned him into a quivering wreck, he'll leave her alone. Since I started this game I haven't had much time for her, but that'll soon change."

"If he and Bensen go under, that could ruin Magnum-Opus and probably spell the end of *Robots Three*."

"Naw, they can be replaced. Anyway, M-O is secretly owned by a syndicate of Arabs. They aren't about to let a hot show like Jana's fold."

"Seems to me there are moral issues involved—"

"Come on, don't start laying that kind of talk on me. I confide in you because I know you're above morality."

"Even so—"

"Even so, you get ready to see that toad Kornfield go right down the chute."

✗

Maybe, since I'd made the mistake of mentioning moral issues, Tackery began to feel differently about confiding in me. I know I saw him much less from then on, though it may only be because I got heavily involved in refilming six of our dog-food commercials. The client didn't feel the original canines were lively enough. While attempting to reshoot with livelier dogs I was attacked by one of the German shepherds, and a St. Bernard tried to eat part of one of the cameras. It was a hectic period, causing me to forget about Joe Tackery and his situation.

As it turned out, that meeting in my office, when he was in his Oriental getup, was to be my last encounter with him. I saw him once more, as millions of others all across America did, on the Lulu Awards Show. Except, I guess, most of those who saw him didn't realize it was Joe Tackery. They thought they were seeing Tuck Bensen.

None of what follows I am absolutely certain of. Some of it I didn't even find out about until weeks after the telecast. This is, however, what I believe must have happened. Tackery continued to follow Kornfield, now and then giving him a glimpse of himself as Mojave McWilliams. Kornfield grew increasingly nervous and finally drove out to the desert. A hot wind was roaring on the night he let himself into the fortress. He ventured into the cellar and found the body of the dead prospector exactly where they'd left it. Tackery couldn't quite see the producer's expression from his vantage point, flat out on the stones of the courtyard, yet he sensed it must be an exquisite one. Here was Mojave dead, so who had he been seeing? Was it a ghost? Or was he crazy?

The next thing the worried producer did was hurry to the spot where he and Bensen had buried the loot. This time, hidden behind scruffy brush and thin trees, Tackery did see Kornfield's face. It was indeed an exquisite expression which touched the producer's features when he discovered the trunkful of money was gone.

Kornfield went to the home of his partner. Tuck Bensen denied moving the money, which was perfectly true. Kornfield didn't believe him. They quarreled and Kornfield strangled the smaller man to death. He was unhappy on realizing what he'd done. Now, so far as he knew, he'd never find the $400,000. His only piece of good luck was that, since Bensen was in such terrible financial shape, there were no servants in his big Moorish home. Kornfield searched it thoroughly, twice, and found not a trace of the missing money.

Lugging the body of his defunct partner to his car, Kornfield returned to his empty lot and deposited him in the hole where the trunk once had been. He covered him with earth and announced, on returning to Magnum-Opus the next morning, that his partner was off on a well-deserved vacation in South America. This way he'd have a few days to figure out his next move.

Kornfield still hadn't worked out much in the way of a plan by the night of the Lulu Awards banquet for the best television shows of the year. He and Bensen were up for a golden statuette as co-producers in the Best Detective Series category. Accompanied by his newest wife and attired in a sky-blue dinner jacket which concealed the revolver he always carried now, Kornfield attended. If you noticed him at his table you wouldn't have realized he was nervous or distraught. He was smiling, gracious, attentive to his guests.

The award ceremonies ran smoothly, except when they were giving out the Best Animal Actor award. During that, the German shepherd candidate chased the presenter, that platinum-blond guy who's in *City Morgue*, around the dais while nipping at his tux. It was the same nasty dog who'd tried to destroy me when we refilmed our dog-food spots. I was pleased to see, watching at home over TV, that the dog could be mean with other people. The client had hinted there was something about me which had agitated a usually amiable animal.

Jana Dayside was the one who was to present the Lulu for Best Detective Series and she looked completely stunning.

"Stunning," I said.

"Obvious," said my wife.

Jana read the nominees in that husky voice of hers, tossed her abundant blonde hair and very sensually opened the envelope. "And the winner is—*City Morgue*, Magnum-Opus Productions," she read. "Mr. Oscar Kornfield will accept."

In a very stately, for him, manner Kornfield made his way up to the dais. Jana gave him a quick hug before handing over the Lulu.

Kornfield leaned into the arc of microphones. "I'm very pleased, as well as honored, to accept this award," he began. "Obviously this honor wouldn't have been possible without the help and support of a great many people. Chief among them is my devoted partner, Tuck Bensen, who unfortunately can't be here since he's enjoying a much-deserved vacati—"

"But I'm not on vacation, Oscar."

What Kornfield saw was his dead partner, miraculously alive again, moving toward him into the limelight. "You can't be here!" Kornfield shouted. "I killed and buried you." With any angry grunt he yanked out the pistol from his shoulder holster. "And I'll do it again!"

He fired four shots into Joe Tackery's chest.

Before Tackery died he managed to say something. It was picked up by the microphones. "I told you I was good," he said.

HOW COME MY DOG DON'T BARK?

They couldn't use those final pictures of him. The photos were too much even for *Worldwide Intruder*, which is why the last picture of Kerry Dent to run in that particular tabloid showed him looking tan, fit, and relatively unwrinkled.

It was the other photos in the *Intruder* which caused Dent to do what he did. If it hadn't been for those earlier pictures, and the unflattering little stories and captions accompanying them, he wouldn't have ended up out in San Fernando Valley in such terrible shape.

Well, his wife had something to do with it, of course. And that impossible dog, too.

Dent told me his suspicions concerning his wife when I visited him on the set of his television show late in the spring of last year. I'm sure you know he was married to Sue Bee Brannigan who does all the commercials for Galz Beer. A striking girl, if not overly supportive. He was a shade over 29 years older than Sue Bee.

His suspicions and complaints about the dog I was already pretty familiar with. His feelings concerning Demon were why I was on the Wheelan Studios lot that bright, relatively clear morning. My advertising agency had bought his new show, *Demon & Co.*, for our client, the Barx Smoke Alarm. That's the one that barks and howls like a dog to warn you that your house is on fire. Dent's show seemed perfect for Barx and within three weeks of its first airing, *Demon & Co.* had shot up to the number three spot in the ratings. Not bad for a television show staring a German shepherd and a 59-year-old daredevil actor.

The trouble was, Dent had developed the notion the dog was jealous of him. He took to calling me at the ad agency, and eventually at my home in the best part of Santa Monica, to tell me how insanely jealous Demon was of him. Dent was convinced Demon was deliberately flubbing scenes, wasn't growling on cue, was mugging and letting his purplish tongue loll out during Dent's best dramatic moments and, on three occasions at least, nudging him off high places where only the actor's agility and long experience in action films saved him from serious injury. I'm not overly fond of animals, but still I found it difficult to accept most of what Dent told me.

As I approached the indoor set where Dent was supposed to be rescuing, aided by Demon, a country-and-western singer who was marooned in a flood I heard a great deal of snarling, barking, and shouting.

"Out, I want that gink out of here! Let me go, let me smack him in the beezer!"

That was Dent. You couldn't mistake his voice, which had never quite shaken his Bronx childhood.

"Easy, Kerry. Your pudgy face is getting all flushed. It's going to be coronary time if you don't watch it."

I reached the set in time to see Dent break free of the assistant director and key grip who'd been restraining him from charging at Ben Walden.

Walden was a tall, lean, and moderately handsome young man in his late twenties. He set his camera safely on a vacant canvas chair, pivoted, and stepped out of Dent's way.

"Gigolo!" accused Dent, spinning around. "I told you what I'd do with your camera if I ever caught you around me again!"

"Relax, Kerry," suggested Walden. "Your flabby body can't stand such stress."

"Flabby! I'll shove that—"

Dent, his narrowed eyes on the reporter, didn't notice the approach of Demon. He tripped over the dog and landed with a smack on the sound-stage floor.

Walden, snatching up his camera, clicked off six shots of the actor. "Beautiful, beautiful. All your chins are showing nicely." Then, cradling the camera in his arms like a football, Walden jogged away.

He was out of the place by the time they got Dent on his feet again. "Didn't I give strict orders that nobody from the *Intruder* ever be allowed near me?"

The director patted Dent on the shoulder. "The guy slips in, Kerry, he's elusive."

"And you!" Dent kicked out at the dog, missed, and nearly lost his balance.

"Why don't we take five," the director urged. "Pull Dolly out of the tank, Skipper. We'll try the scene again in a few minutes."

"I can do it now," said Dent.

"Few minutes. Go sit down and have a drink."

"I don't drink. I haven't had a drink in three years, no matter what you read in the damn *Intruder*. 'Aging Has-Been, Looking the Worse for Booze, Totters out of Gollywood Bistro on Arm of Long-Suffering Wife.' You better keep Walden off my set, off the lot. Otherwise there's going to be real trouble." He noticed me then and came hurrying over.

"You're looking well, Kerry," I made the mistake of saying.

"Why shouldn't I look well? I'm in damn fine shape. I do all my own stunts in this halfwit show," he told me, face still flushed. "Which is more than I can say for Demon, my illustrious co-star. He needs a double for all the difficult stuff. Come into my dressing room so we can talk."

I followed him through a doorway and down a corridor. "The client is a little worried about—"

"Did you see what he did just now? Tripped me so I couldn't wind Walden's clock for him."

"An accident, dogs aren't as bright as—"

"And look at this dressing room." He jerked the door open.

"Cozy."

"Cozy my fanny! It's tiny. You know who had this dressing room before me? That clunk who starred in *Cybernetic Midget*. Yeah, this is a dwarf's old dressing room." He stalked to a small refrigerator, took out a bottle of Perrier water. "Demon has a kennel the size of Pickfair, while I—"

"The client was worried by the last story in the *Int*—"

"Listen, I'm a part of your life, right?" He gestured at one wall with his glass of sparkling water.

There were framed stills from some of his old movies mounted on the wall. A shot from *The Dancing Pirate*, two from *Captain Juggernaut*, one from *Fort Gordo*, and a whole series from *The Avenging Cavalier*, which was Dent's most popular movie.

"I saw most of your pictures," I admitted, "when I was a kid."

"Ha, ha. Very funny. You're as old as I am."

"I'm forty-four, you're fifty-nine."

"Forty-four isn't that far from fifty-nine. However, I don't have the problems you civilians do." He sipped at the water. "I take care of myself, good care." He patted his chin. "That's *one* chin you see, no matter what snide lies Walden writes in the *Intruder*."

"It's not so much the lies as the photographs. The client feels—"

"That bum hounds me! He sneaks around and snaps pictures of me when I'm at my worst. He waits for some unfortunate pose, then snaps and runs."

"The picture in this week's tab is particularly unfortunate. Where you're hitting that blind beggar woman over the head with her own accordion."

"It only *looks* that way. Because of that wily jerk Walden," explained the actor. "I was helping the old bat adjust the damn thing and *snap* there's Walden and his camera."

"You were caught standing in front of the Naked Nickelodeon," I reminded. "With that poster behind you promising explicit romantic action inside."

"You don't understand what it is to be a celebrity," Dent said. "I can't take a walk or meet a friend without some nitwit reporter or photographer popping up and trying to make me look bad. The worst offender is that—"

"Maybe you should quit strolling in places like the Los Angeles tenderloin."

Finishing his Perrier, Dent turned to face me. "You recall the picture of me three weeks ago in the *Intruder*?"

"The one where you're doing a bellyflop in your pool. *Flabby Kerry Does Flop*. The client thought—"

"He climbed over the wall of my estate to snap that." The actor turned his back on me. "At least, I thought that was his only reason for being there. Now I—well, it's one of those little everyday troubles you have to live with."

I said, "I don't think the Barx Brothers can live with many more of your little everyday troubles, Kerry. What is it?"

He gestured at another wall of photos. "I've had four wives, everybody knows that. I swear the only one I ever cared for is Sue Bee."

"She's a striking woman."

"Of course she is. I only marry striking women. Sue Bee is also intelligent. How many people do you know who've read all the way through Proust's *Remembrance of Things Past*?"

"I read it in college, and my wife read it while she was in the hospital with—"

"Never mind," he cut in. "The trouble is, despite her intelligence —well, Sue Bee is being unfaithful."

I nodded. "These days, Kerry, with society in a state of—"

"Unfaithful to *me*! And do you know who the guy is?"

"No, who?"

"Him! The jerk with the camera!"

"Ben Walden?"

"That bum with the camera, yes. Walden is cuckolding me."

"You're absolutely sure?"

"Figures, doesn't it? Explains why he's trying to destroy me in the pages of that filthy rag. *Over-the-hill Swashbuckler Makes Feeble Attempt at Comeback.* Feeble? He knows we knocked off the two top shows. The network ought to have a few more feeble swashbucklers like me."

"Wait now," I said. "Do you know for certain your wife's having an affair with Walden, or do you just suppose she is?"

"I know *here*!" He thumped his handsome chest. "Look, if you're an artist you *sense* these things. I know. *Old Man Dent Takes Snooze After Too Much Booze.* He's trying to make me look ridiculous in the eyes of Sue Bee."

"But a woman of her intelligence wouldn't—"

"Just because she's read Proust doesn't mean she wouldn't have an affair with Walden."

I was silent for several seconds. "Going to be tough using any of this with the Barx Brothers," I finally told him. "If true, this is a logical explanation for why the *Intruder* seems to be picking on you. But the idea of your wife fooling around will upset them even more than—"

"You can tell the Barx boys to stick some of their smoke alarms—"

"Kerry, let me think about this. I'll see if I can—"

"Always the ad man. You can't react to anything with your *guts*. You have to write memos, take a couple dips in the think tank."

I cleared my throat. "This probably isn't the best time to ask you about the publicity stills."

"What stills?"

"Ones of you and Demon standing under a Barx alarm."

"Tell you what." Dent put a hand on my back. "We can use Demon's stand-in. That dog is an angel, a gem of a hound. Sweet, considerate, the absolute antithesis of Demon. I keep telling them to take Demon out and retire him or something and use the damn stand-in. They won't hear of it, especially Tessica Janes, the bimbo who claims to be Demon's trainer. She's got them all hoodwinked into thinking Demon is unique. He's unique all right, but—"

"Ready to shoot again, Mr. Dent," someone called outside the door.

Dent straightened, smiling. "Don't brood too much about anything that's happened today," he said to me. "I have an uncanny ability for bouncing back. And you're going to see one hell of a bounce any day now."

✗

The agency sent me to Mentor, Ohio, a few days after that encounter with Kerry Dent and I didn't see him again for nearly a month. We'd been test-marketing a new bread in Mentor, a loaf which was 20 percent sawdust and called Lumberjack Bread, and some problems had arisen. Nearly everyone who ate so much as a slice of the experimental bread had come down with a disease closely resembling the flu. There was a definite danger of the media getting hold of the story. We couldn't afford to have the whole country hearing about a new blight know as the Lumberjack Bread Disease.

I was able, with a mixture of diplomacy and bribery, to keep the whole mess hushed up. Working very covertly we got all the test loaves out of the supermarkets and dumped into a handy river. That dumping gave us another problem, since it turned out that Lumberjack Bread was capable of killing fish even with its wrapper on.

As I say, I didn't get back to Los Angeles until a month or more after my meeting with Kerry Dent on the *Demon & Co.* set. Not that I hadn't been in communication with him, or rather he with me. Dent, possibly because he knew I'd been a fan of his swashbucklers in my youth, decided I was the one person he could confide in.

The phone in my slightly mildewed Mentor motel room rang at all hours. Dent's complaints were all variations on ones I'd heard before. Sue Bee continued to be unfaithful with Ben Walden of *Worldwide Intruder*, Demon loathed him and was making enormous efforts to sabotage his comeback, Walden was so audacious that when he sneaked into Dent's mansion to woo his wife he managed to snap unflattering photos of the dozing actor. Despite his claims of renewed vigor, Dent seemed to nap a good deal, as the frequent pictures showing up in the *Intruder* attested.

One particularly bleak morning in Ohio, just after my lovely secretary had rushed in to tell me 5000 dead fish had been sighted floating down the river with several loaves of Lumberjack Bread leading the pack, Dent phoned me collect. He claimed he had absolute proof that Demon not only hated him but was actually trying to kill him. In a scene for the eleventh episode of their show the dog was supposed to remove a smoking stick of dynamite from the vicinity of the bound-and-gagged Dent. He swore, and claimed to have witnesses, that Demon switched a real stick of dynamite for the prop one. If Dent hadn't sensed something was wrong and gone rolling over a low precipice he would have been blown up.

I pointed out that real dynamite could just as likely have blown up the dog when he snatched it up in his powerful jaws. Dent told me the dog had deliberately dawdled instead of rushing in to pick up the dynamite stick. Pacifying him as best I could, I went out to do something about all those dead fish.

✗

My last, although I didn't know it at the time, encounter with Kerry Dent took place by accident. I was out in San Fernando Valley to call on a well-known sci-fi writer in Woodland Hills to see if we could persuade him to endorse a new pizza line the agency was involved with. The author, an extremely surly man, was not at all impressed by the Unidentified Flying Pizza and came close to punching me. Feeling very much like someone in an *Intruder* gossip item, I slunk away from his home and dropped into a valley restaurant for a cup of coffee to calm my nerves.

It was a noisy place, because of the prerecorded whip cracking and pistol shooting, and at first I wasn't aware of the hissing.

"Hsst, over here."

It was Dent, wearing a nylon jumpsuit and dark glasses and without his hairpiece. "Are you incognito?" I inquired, joining him in his booth.

"Used to know Whip in his heyday and I stop by here now and then."

Whip Wigransky's Burger Rancho was one of six such spots in the valley. It didn't seem to me that a nostalgia for the old B-Western actor was what had brought Dent here. "You have," I mentioned, "paw prints all over your front."

He glanced down, frowning, and brushed off some of the muddy spots. "Ho, ho," he said.

"You sound happy. I take it those prints aren't the leftovers from another attack by your co-star."

"That dumbunny isn't a co-star. I'm a star and he's only a bit player." Dent appeared considerably more relaxed than he'd been lately.

"I'm glad you're in a jovial mood. I thought maybe the picture in this week's *Intruder* would have—"

"Ho, ho, ho. That sort of guff rolls off my back. *Fat Old Actor, Looking Terrible, Escorts Stunning Much Younger Wife to Premiere.* Walden'll have to do a lot better than that to dampen Kerry Dent's spirits."

"I'll pass that news on to the Barx Brothers."

"Give them my love."

I watched his partially masked face. "What are you up to?"

"Having a Bar-B-Q Burger, Owlhoot Style," he said, smiling. "That's all."

"You're out here, disguised, looking smug. It's not like you."

"You didn't know me in my heyday," he replied. "I often went around looking smug. Recently I've found a way to return to the happier moods of yesteryear."

"Are you drinking again?"

"You can't drink and do your own stunts and keep a crazed hell-hound from destroying you." He chuckled, relaxing even more. "I was stupid for a spell, now I'm getting all my old smarts back. There was a rock-and-roll tune I used to be fond of years ago. About a guy who suspected his wife was two-timing him. He asks the suspected lover, 'How come my dog don't bark when you come round my door? Maybe it's because you been here before.' I was like that, stupid. Now I see things as they really are. I've devised a plan to bring me complete and total happiness."

"You haven't gone and joined some lunatic cult?"

"Cults join me." He locked his hands behind his head. "You and the Barx brood need have no fears. In a short time I shall have everything worked out to the satisfaction of one and all."

"Tessica Janes lives out here in the valley somewhere," I said, recalling the fact all at once. "You haven't been visiting her and making threats?"

"That bimbo and I have little to do with each other," Dent assured me. "She trains Demon, I am forced to act with him. That's our only link."

"She's a pretty large young woman. Doesn't look as though she could be intimidated."

"I don't blame Tess for what Demon does. He hates me and plots against me entirely on his own," he said. "Say, look who's coming in. It's old Whip Wigransky himself. Excuse me while I go wrestle with him. It's a long-standing custom."

"Sure, certainly." I sat there, not even turning to watch the good-natured horseplay which was amusing all the other customers. Deep inside I felt very uneasy. I had a premonition something was going to happen, something which would affect the show and annoy the Barx Brothers.

✗

Immediately after this I had to leave town again. There'd been a disastrous fire in the Barx Brothers' main factory in Trenton, New Jersey. The place had burned to the ground and not one of the 10,000 smoke alarms sitting in there had so much as yelped. The wire services had picked up the story and both *Newsmag* and *Tide* were sending people in. The Barx Brothers, with the exception of Carlos who refused to come back from Bermuda, met with me for two days while we worked out a rush campaign to counteract the effects of what had happened.

By the time I came up with a copy approach which satisfied us all, except for Jocko who went off to join Carlos in Bermuda, and wrote some commercials three weeks had passed. I was on the plane back to L.A. when the news came through. I learned about it because my stewardess was sobbing and I asked why.

"The poor darling old man," she managed to say between sobs. "He's been a part of my life since earliest girlhood. I simply adored his swashbuckling films and his TV shows and—"

"Wait a minute. You can't be talking about—"

"Yes, isn't it awful? Kerry Dent is dead."

"Kerry Dent is dead?"

"I heard it on the news just before takeoff."

"How did it happen?"

"Oh, it's too terrible."

She was referring of course only to the official version of Dent's passing. Nobody ever released the true story, which was fortunate I suppose. It's possible that Ben Walden knows most of the truth, but he won't be writing it up in the *Intruder*. Not unless he can figure a way to make his own part in the events seem admirable. Which isn't likely.

As you probably know, I don't like to get too involved in affairs of this sort. Since I was curious, though, and since I felt I owed it to the agency to find out why the star of our top-rated show had been torn to pieces, I did some digging.

What follows is, I believe, a relatively accurate account of how Dent met his end. Some of it I've had to guess.

Dent had come up with a plan to remove the two prime sources of grief in his life—Ben Walden and Demon. He was certain Sue Bee would return to him completely when there was no more Ben Walden around. He also believed Demon could be very easily replaced on the show by the stand-in, a much more admirable dog. He figured it would be to the benefit of all concerned not even to let on there'd been a switch. One German shepherd looked pretty much like another.

He arranged things so he could put his plan into action the night Tessica Janes, Demon's trainer, was not at home. The girl was scheduled to attend a screening of the punk rock remake of *Boys Town* on the night in question. Dent, with the help of Whip Wigransky, had already planted in Ben Walden's mind the idea that Dent was having an affair with Tessica. That fateful night Whip phoned Walden with a tip that the girl was going to skip the screening and spend the night with the aging actor. Dent assumed Walden wouldn't pass up a chance to get pictures of him in such a compromising situation.

Dent had been, very secretly, working out in San Fernando Valley at a seedy dog-training school. That was where he'd been the day I ran into him. The paw prints I'd noticed had come from the vicious German shepherd that Dent was training. This dog was designed to be a watchdog, eager to kill anyone his master ordered him to kill. Dent was his master.

Actually it wasn't a bad plan. Lure Walden to Tessica's place and set this killer dog on him. The police would find the body of a snooping reporter who'd obviously been torn to pieces by a mad German shepherd. There would be Demon in his cage looking sheepish.

Even if Tessica claimed the dog had been locked up all night, the evidence of a dead *Intruder* reporter would contradict her.

Dent arrived a half hour before the ten-o'clock assignation time that he'd had Whip pass on to Walden. It was an exceptionally clear night with more stars out than you usually see in Southern California.

Parking his rented van in a wooded area behind Tessica's spread, Dent led his killer dog out of the vehicle and down to the ranch. By diligent spying earlier he knew there was only one old servant to worry about. The man was in his late sixties and slept in a cottage near the main entrance of the ranch. There was a cyclone fence around the three acres, but it wasn't electrified. Dent had no trouble clipping a section out of it.

The police would naturally assume that Walden, hot after a hot story, had done the snipping.

Up to here Dent's plan went well. He crossed onto the ranch grounds with his dog.

There was an arbor to the left of the ranchhouse. He took the German shepherd there and crouched in the shadows to await Walden.

He debated whether or not he ought to let Demon loose after the killing. He decided it would be safer not to. As he'd already figured out, no matter what Tessica and the old servant might claim, they'd never convince the police that it wasn't Demon who'd done the killing. There were only two collies and a Spaniel in the kennels here. None of them could be blamed. The frame would fit only Demon.

Unfortunately there were three things Dent couldn't have anticipated. For one thing, he couldn't have known that Walden, who was spending some time with Sue Bee, would be late by about 20 minutes. Nor did Dent know that on the evenings when Tessica was away the old servant let Demon loose for a romp around the ranch.

The third thing he couldn't have expected was that his killer dog, while aggressive with people, was fearful of other German shepherds.

So when the roaming Demon, sensing the presence of Dent and the dog in the arbor, came galloping in there, the killer dog yelped and ran away through the hole in the fence.

Demon then leaped straight at Dent.

I'd always thought Dent was exaggerating about the animosity Demon felt toward him. It turned out, though, Dent was absolutely right.

That dog really hated him.

THE DECLINE AND FALL OF NORBERT TUFFY

Twenty-six million people saw them die, and that's not counting reruns.

Real murder is rare on television, particularly on a talk show. If you weren't one of those who caught the actual broadcast, you probably saw the pertinent footage on one of the evening network newscasts. The killer, who also appeared briefly on the talk show, eventually did a lot of explaining and so most everybody, including the police, thinks they know just about the entire story. Actually, the murderer himself barely knew half of what was going on.

I knew the victims and the killer, although I didn't realize until too late that they were going to be the victims and the killer. Since the authorities have the killer in custody, and since I hate to get myself tangled in public messes, there's no reason for me to volunteer the information I have as to the true causes of the effect all those millions of viewers witnessed. Sometimes when we're filming a commercial with Glorious MacKenzie and I notice her between takes, staring forlornly into her cup of Wake Up! coffee, I'm tempted to tell her all I know. But I resist the temptation.

It was because of the lovely Glorious, one of America's top five models, that Norbert Tuffy concocted his whole caper. We'd been using the stunning redhaired Glorious in our Wake Up! coffee television spots for nearly a year, ever since the Wake Up! lab back in Battle Creek had made their scientific breakthrough and we'd been able to use the very effective slogan, "Wake Up! The only coffee that's 100% coffee free!"

Norbert and Glorious were living together in his mansion out on the Pacific Palisades when I first met him at a cocktail party that my advertising agency gave for all our commercial talent. Norbert, who was very good in a scrap despite his size, helped me out when the actor who'd just been fired from our Grrrowl Dog Grub account tried to bite my ankle. I'd been expecting trouble from the moment I noticed the actor had crashed the party wearing his Grrrowl police dog costume. At any rate, the small feisty Norbert and I became friends as a result of that incident.

It was several months later, over lunch at the Quick-Frozen Mandarin in Santa Monica, that he first alluded to the Blind Butcher affair. I was already in the booth when Norbert came scurrying in out of a hazy spring afternoon.

He was clad in one of those maroon running suits he was so fond of for daytime wear. "It was an omen." He plopped down opposite me and poured himself a cup of lukewarm tea.

"What?"

"When my house fell down the hill and into the sea last month."

"I thought the house only made it as far as the middle of the Pacific Coast Highway."

"The symbolism was there to be read by one and all. The decline and fall of Norbert Tuffy."

"Still haven't picked up a new scripting assignment?"

"I haven't had a TV script credit in four months. I am definitely on the proverbial skids."

"Maybe I can get you some freelance ad copy—"

"Ha," he said scornfully. "That would really finish me. It's bad enough my house fell into the Pacific because of a mud slide, it's bad enough my favorite Siamese cat was eaten by the pet wolfhound of a noted rock millionaire, it's bad enough Glorious is now living alone in a Westwood condo, it's bad enough I haven't won an Emmy in three years, it's bad enough I am virtually blacklisted because it's rumored I am suffering from writer's block, it's bad enough I'm being robbed of potential millions by a swine calling himself Macho Sweeze—and now you suggest I top it all by working in a cesspool such as that ad agency of yours."

"We pay as much as—"

"Forget it. I'd rather play piano in a bordello."

"You'd have to join the musicians union to do that."

"Funny as a funeral is what you are," he observed as he snatched up the menu.

"Listen, you're letting a temporary setback cloud your whole—"

"Don't give me slogans. Do you realize Glorious and I may never get back together?"

"I wasn't even aware you two weren't living together. When we shot the last Wake Up! commercial with her the other day, she seemed happy."

"Sure, dumping me makes her euphoric," he said, summoning the waiter in the silk kimono. "Bring me the Number Six lunch, and pronto."

"Being on the skids sure hasn't helped your disposition, Mr. Tuffy," remarked the waiter. "And you, sir?"

I ordered a Number Five. "You and Glorious have parted before, Norbert, and always—"

"Oh, I'll get that incredibly lovely bimbo back," he assured me. "I know exactly how and when. When I collect the $54,000."

"$54,000?"

"Happens to be the exact sum I need to pay off my debts and get back on my feet again."

"Then you are going to get the assignment to do the pilot script for *My Old Man's a Garbage Man*?"

"Naw, they double-crossed me out of that gig, too, even after I laid an absolutely socko treatment on 'em," Norbert said. "I intend to acquire the $54,000 in question from Macho Sweeze. It's one half of $108,000."

"It is, but why's Macho going to give it to you?"

"You know that scum?"

"We had some commercials for 150 Percent, the Headache Pill for a Headache and a Half on a movie of the week he wrote and I met him at the—"

"Wrote? That goon couldn't scrawl an X without help."

"I sense a bitterness in your tone."

Norbert fell silent until after our freshly thawed Chinese lunches had been placed before us. "Ever hear of a series of spy novels about a guy known as the Blind Butcher?" he asked me. "Allegedly penned by one Dan X. Spear. Published by Capstone Books."

"Vaguely." I poked my eggroll with my plastic fork and caused it to make a squeaking sound. "Why?"

"I created that series and wrote all six of the paperback novels."

"So you're Dan X. Spear?"

Norbert's teeth gnashed on his stir-fried tempeh. "Macho Sweeze is Dan X. Spear," he snarled. "See, this was all four, five years in the past, before I'd reached the dizzying pinnacle of success which I am presently toppling from. Macho had this vague nitwit idea for a series and he was going around with the granddaughter of Oscar Dragomann, the publisher of Capstone Books. A spindly broad of about seventeen summers, but Macho's always gone in for ladies with underdeveloped minds and bodies."

"What did you do, Norbert, sign some kind of agreement with Macho that gave him all rights in the project?"

He snarled again. "Norbert Tuffy doesn't, not ever, do anything dumb," he told me, pointing his plastic fork. "I was, let us say, injudicious. Something I have been known to be in moments of extreme financial deprivation. Some people get woozy when you take away oxygen, I get careless when I'm suffering from lack of money."

"Where does the amount of $108,000 come from?"

"The series was less than a hit," explained Norbert. "In fact, the final book in our series, *The Spy Who Broke His Leg*, never even got out of Dragomann's central warehouse down in Whittier." He paused to gobble a few bites of food. "We now dissolve from back then to now. Macho, Lord knows how, is presently a dazzling star in the Hollywood writing firmament. Furthermore, he has become, possibly because of their mutual interest in young ladies who've only recently shed their braces, a close chum of ex-king Maktab Al-Barid."

"Him I've never heard of," I admitted.

"Another reason I wouldn't let anybody chain me to an advertising agency—turns your brains to jelly. Anyway, Maktab Al-Barid ruled the Arab country of Zayt until some fanatic holy roller led a revolt and took over that oil-rich little spot," said Norbert. "Before Maktab Al-Barid skipped the country he managed to stash away something like a couple of billion bucks in various banks around the world. At the moment he resides in ex-kingly splendor in a Bel Air mansion once owned by a silent-screen lover and more recently by those rock poets of the platinum records, Honey and Hank."

"This Arab king is financing Macho in something?"

"The peabrain is going to make movies," replied Norbert. "His first motion-picture venture, announced but a few days ago in the Hollywood trades, is to be—we'll skip the trumpet fanfare—an adaptation of *The Spy Who Went Through the Meatgrinder*."

"One of the Blind Butcher novels?"

"One of *my* Blind Butcher novels, yeah. Second one in the series." The plastic fork suddenly snapped in his clenched fist. "See, under that dumb little agreement I injudiciously signed with him back then,

Macho retains *all* subsidiary rights. All I ever saw was half of the paltry initial advances. Maktab Al-Barid has paid Macho $108,000 for the screen rights and he's going to hand over an additional $216,000 for a screenplay."

"He seems to favor multiples of 54."

"That's the kind of sympathy I need."

I shrugged. "Norbert, you made a mistake," I said. "Maybe with a good lawyer you can do something."

"Good lawyer? There's no such being," he said. "No, to get my share—and Macho can keep the screenplay money—to get my share of that $108,000 I intend to start applying pressure. I may even drop in on Maktab Al-Barid himself, although I hear he keeps himself very well bodyguarded because of a fear, perfectly legit, that terrorists from Zayt may be dropping in. Seems they'd like to have Maktab Al-Barid star in a trial for treason and sundry other misdemeanors."

"I still think an attorney could—"

"I already talked to three of them."

"What did they say?"

"I haven't got a chance to collect."

✗

As it turned out I phoned Norbert less than a week later. Locating him was a little difficult, since his answering service had just dropped him for being three months in arrears on his bill. His agent swore he'd never heard of him, then offered me five other writers who were currently hot properties. Finally I got Glorious to admit she was still in contact with him and that he, having just checked out of the Beverly Glen Hotel in another economy move, was residing in the back half of an old duplex down in Manhattan Beach.

"Hello?" he answered that afternoon, using a completely unbelievable British accent. "You are speaking to Mr. Norbert Tuffy's confidential secretary, what ho."

"Hey, Norbert, listen," I said, and identified myself.

"Old chap, you're making a bally mistake. Mr. Tuffy—"

"The agency doesn't like me to waste too much time on personal calls," I went on. "But there's something I better talk to you about."

"Not a penny less than $54,000, if you're acting as go-between for your buddy."

"Macho Sweeze? Haven't even seen him since you and I had lunch last week." From my office window I could watch a handsome highrise building being constructed, its topmost floors lost in pale smog. "This has to do with a guy named Fritz Momand."

"What a sappo name. Who is he?"

"Don't you know?"

"I have no recollection of the name."

"Fritz Momand is a freelance commercial artist who specializes in fruit. I happened to—"

"In what?"

"Fruit. He's doing a series of ads for us for FrootBoms Cereal. That's the stuff shaped like little hand grenades which explode with flavor when you pour milk over—"

"What has this Fritz guy to do with me?"

"I was at his studio over on La Cienega yesterday, to okay his painting of an orange, and he got to talking about his wife. Her name is Frilly Jonah." I paused, anticipating a response.

"Anybody who'd voluntarily call herself that must have show-business aspirations."

"She does. She's a country-and-western singer who hasn't had much success."

"Probably sings on key, which is a great handicap," said Norbert. "You're not the greatest yarn spinner on the face of Los Angeles, pal. Not that I don't enjoy chit-chat and pointless blab—"

"You don't know Frilly? You haven't been seeing her on the sly?"

"Eh? Norbert Tuffy does nothing, absolutely *nada*, on the sly," he said loudly. "Besides which, my heart is still in a sling over Glorious MacKenzie."

"This is the truth?"

"Do I ever lie? Don't try to tell me this fruit vendor claims Norbert Tuffy has been fooling around with Frilly while he's been slaving over a hot persimmon?"

I cleared my throat and turned away from the view, which was making my eyes water. "Fritz Momand is a big, violent guy who likes hunting," I began. "Very tough, extremely jealous. He's grown suspicious of late that Frilly has been seeing someone else. In the course of ransacking her room while she was off singing at the Back in the Saddle Club in Ventura, he unearthed a complete set of the Blind Butcher paperback novels. Each one was inscribed to his wife in glowing phrases. One such said: *To the apple-cheeked delight who's brought a new kind of love to me, with the passionate regards of the author*."

"You actually thought Norbert Tuffy could write gush like that?" he asked. "Using a fruit image to woo the guy's wife is a nice touch, though. How old is this Frilly?"

"Never actually met her, but she's quite a bit younger than her husband. Probably about nineteen or twenty."

"So use your coco, chum. It's obviously that scoundrel Macho Sweeze who's putting the Dan X. Spear pen name to yet another sleazy use and giving the horns to your pushcart Picasso."

"But you wrote the books."

"True, true," said Norbert, "except, as I made perfectly clear to you when last we net, Macho loves to claim the credit. I am sure it's he who's using the books to impress this honkytonk bimbo now that one book is a movie-to-be."

"You're probably right. Just wanted to warn you to watch out for Fritz Momand, since he seems the kind of guy who likes to do violence to those who fiddle with his wife," I said. "You haven't had any luck getting a settlement out of Macho, huh?"

"The amount of luck I've had in any area of late, pal, you could insert in a flea's nostril and still have room left to pack in an agent's heart," he answered. "I approached Macho and, politely for me, suggested he ought to do right by me. He was cordial, for him, and swore he'd see to it I got a little something. That is, *after* the film is released, which will be a good two years hence."

"You don't believe he'll do even that?"

"Most of Macho Sweeze's sincere promises could go on that list of the world's most famous lies, the one that commences with 'The check's in the mail.' "

"So now?"

"Since you are sincerely interested in my fate, unlike the circle of Judases I used to run with, I'll tell you what Norbert Tuffy has in mind. I have always been hailed, and justly so, as one of the most brilliant plotters in this nutty town. Even now, in my temporary exile, I have not lost the knack."

"You have a new movie idea in the works?"

"Naw, I'm working out a foolproof way to get the money Macho owes me."

✘

The very next day I was stuck back on the SoyHammy account. That's

The Decline and Fall of Norbert Tuffy **139**

about the only account in the shop, as you may recall, that I don't really enjoy. But this was a full-scale emergency and I had to fly to Chicago the same afternoon. It seems the head of SoyHammy's own advertising department had just been killed in a freak accident. He'd been having a drink at one of those revolving bars in a penthouse night club when the darn thing started to revolve three or four times faster than it was supposed to. When it suddenly stopped, he was flung clean off the terrace and fell to the street thirteen stories below.

His employers at SoyHammy had come up with the idea of giving his remains a lavish funeral, and since he had been associated with SoyHammy for many years, they figured it would be a nice touch to have all six pallbearers in pigsuits like the one the announcer wore on our SoyHammy commercials. To halt that before anybody in the media got wind of it, I was speeded eastward.

Talking all concerned out of the pigsuits and then sitting in while they interviewed candidates to fill the deceased's job consumed over two weeks. That spell in Chicago coincided exactly with Norbert's execution of his plan to get what he felt was owed to him.

Since I only spoke to Norbert once, very briefly on the phone, most of the details of his caper are what I got from the newspapers and television. Not that any of them knew who was really behind the scheme. He really was a good planner and the whole deal went smoothly.

What Norbert did was to kidnap Macho Sweeze. He then convinced Maktab Al-Barid that the snatch was the work of Zaytian terrorists from his homeland and that unless the ex-king came up with $55,000 in cash for the Zayt Liberation Fund, he'd start receiving packages containing various choice cuts of his favorite author. That extra $1000, by the way, was to cover the expenses of the snatch itself. Norbert wore built-up shoes, a padded coat, and a stocking mask when he grabbed Macho, and even his rival author didn't recognize him.

"He was a tall skinny guy, must've been an Englishman from the way he talked," Macho told the police and the FBI later.

Norbert gave Macho a shot of horse tranquilizer, something he'd swiped from the location of a Western film, and that kept him out cold for most of the twenty-seven hours that Norbert held on to him. In a way I contributed—unwittingly, to be sure—to Norbert's final plan. He took Macho out of the parking lot behind that country-and-western club in Ventura where Frilly Jonah appeared now and then.

Maktab Al-Barid was warned not to go to the law or Macho would be treated exactly as the Blind Butcher treated gangsters and subversives in the novels. To the ex-king, of course, $55,000 was nothing at all and he was even a bit puzzled as to why the fanatics asked for so little. It was a small price to pay for the safe return of one of his dear friends, and he paid it readily.

Once Macho was returned, his agent gave out the story. It was terrific publicity for the upcoming movie. There had already been a few small mentions in the trade papers about the movie, some of which had even mentioned that Macho Sweeze was Dan X. Spear. Now, however, the whole country was talking about the Blind Butcher and his brilliant creator, about how life had imitated art, and what a narrow escape he'd had. You could never really trust terrorists—they might well have taken the $55,000 and butchered Macho anyway.

The kidnaping made a celebrity of Macho. He began to show up on local talk shows, to get his picture in the magazines and the papers. The last time I ever spoke to Norbert was the afternoon the issue of *Persons* hit the area newsstands, with Macho's dark, roughly handsome face beaming from the cover.

"Did you see it?" Norbert asked.

I was fresh back from Chicago, suffering jet lag and what I suspect was a serious allergic reaction to nearly two solid weeks of SoyHammy for breakfast. My head was throbbing, my eyes were watering, and I didn't really respond very sympathetically.

"See what?"

"That smug leering face on the cover of *Persons*. Gosh, it's disgusting. When writers of real talent can't even get their pictures on a roll of—"

"Macho's had a lot of publicity lately," I reminded him, careful of what I said over the phone. Sometimes they listened at the switchboard. "Thanks, I imagine, to you—that was your touch I noted, wasn't it?"

"Who else?" I could almost hear his broad satisfied grin. "You going to inform on me?"

"None of my affair." I surveyed the pile of stuff that had gathered on my desk top in my absence; there was even a nine-pound SoyHammy. "Norbert, I have a lot of—"

"I'm back with Glorious," he told me.

"Good, I guess. Where are you living?"

"New place in Malibu. Very classy. Used to belong to Honey and Hank."

"So things are pretty much going okay for you again?"

"I have some bucks for the nonce, yeah. But I am not being bothered by the sound of eager producers pounding at my door to demand scripts. The only nibble I've had is from some guy who claims he's bought the rights to revive *Death Valley Days* on the tube," said Norbert, the momentary joy fading from his voice. "Boy, if I could've gotten all that publicity that Macho grabbed. After all, I wrote the books. Not him."

"Macho's new fame is a side effect of—well, of what happened to him" I said. "Look on the bright side. You and Glorious are back togeth—"

"That'll last about six minutes longer than my supply of loot."

"Still you ought to—"

"He's going to appear on the Mack Naydell Show tomorrow morning, live from Fish World in Laguna."

"That's one of the fastest rising talk shows in the country." I pressed my temple to try and control the throb. "But now, Norbert, I ought—"

"You bet it's a hot show. Naydell's going to knock Douglas, Carson, Donahue, Davidson, and Arends right out of the box any day now." Enthusiasm had returned to his voice. "They've been running teaser spots all day about Macho's appearance mañana."

"Don't watch, it'll only—"

"Remember that the Mack Naydell show is done absolutely *live*," he said. "Meaning they can't edit it for most of their markets. I prevailed on one of my few remaining chums in Hollywood and got a ducat for the broadcast."

"You'll only upset yourself."

"Ah, tune in and see," chuckled Norbert.

✗

Macho Sweeze appeared as scheduled the next morning. The show was broadcast live from the big outdoor amphitheater at Fish World. The day was clear, smogless, bright blue. There were some five hundred people circling the open-air stage where the prematurely grey Mark Naydell chatted with his famous guests. A very handsome setting the show had—the tree-filled hills around the outdoor theater framed it nicely.

Up in the forest, stretched out among the tall trees, was Fritz Momand. He had one of his high-powered hunting rifles with him, equipped with a telescopic sight. He also had a small battery-operated TV set, the earphone to his ear. Anything said down there on the stage he'd hear.

Frilly, early that morning, admitted she had indeed been having an affair with the man who had written the Blind Butcher novels. Fritz knocked her cold before she got to give him many more details. He left her sprawled, still in one of her fringe-trimmed cowgirl suits, on the living-room floor and took off for Laguna with his favorite rifle. He was a violent man who believed there was only one just punishment for a man who took advantage of his wife.

I watched the show from one of the screening rooms at the agency. My secretary was with me so I could dictate letters while I watched.

"Oh," she exclaimed just before a commercial break, "isn't that your friend there, in the second row of the audience?"

"Who?"

She pointed to the screen. "The belligerent little fellow who drops in for lunch sometimes."

By the time I looked up from my pile of papers they were showing a SoyHammy commercial. "You mean Norbert Tuffy?"

"I think that's his name. He won an Emmy or something years ago. What's he doing these days?"

"Sort of difficult to explain."

After the block of commercials we got a grinning close-up of Mack Naydell. "This next guest's long been one of my favorite people and a damn fine writer. I'm kicking myself it took a near-tragedy to remind me to have him drop in to visit us," he said. "Let's welcome a very talented guy, Macho Sweeze."

They cut to a medium shot to show Macho come striding out to shake hands and sit in an armchair next to the affable host.

"Happy to be here, Mack," Macho said.

"He's got a sexy voice," said my secretary.

"Before we talk about your recent experiences," said Naydell, leaning in the direction of his guest, "I'd like to talk about the Blind Butcher books."

Up in the woods above the theater Fritz Momand made the final adjustments to his rifle. He had Macho in the crosshairs now and was waiting for just the right second to fire. He figured he'd have time for two, maybe three shots. As he waited he listened to them talking.

"Up until recently," Naydell was saying, "no one knew you'd written these great suspense novels, Macho. One of which will soon be a major movie. But now you've come out from behind the Dan X. Spear pen name."

"Yeah, I got tired of hiding my light under a bushel," said Macho, grinning. "Now I am openly admitting that I am the author of the Blind Butcher series."

Fritz's finger tightened on the trigger.

Then up out of the audience leaped Norbert Tuffy. Before anyone could restrain him, he hopped right on the stage and ripped the lapel mike off Macho's checkered jacket.

"That's a lie!" Norbert shouted, and turned, arm raised high and facing the audience. "My name is Norbert Tuffy and I'm the true and only author of the Blind Butcher books!"

Fritz hesitated. He wasn't sure which one, Macho or Norbert, had written the books and had an affair with his wife.

He decided to play it safe.

He shot both of them.

WOOING CHIPS TORTUGA

They never did find all of her.

But they did find enough, along with a few fragments of a parcel of explosives, to convince them Sheena Mayday was responsible for blowing up that majestic old steamboat as well as her chief rival. Neither she nor the Sacramento police could plausibly explain why Sheena had set as many as three explosions aboard the *River Belle*, but they finally wrote that off to temporary insanity. As it was, they missed noticing a fourth explosive charge entirely.

Since I know what really took place up there on that little tributary of the Sacramento River and since Sheena was a good friend of mine, I was, for a short while anyway, tempted to speak out. Actually, she wasn't a murderess and she *didn't* cause the explosion of that authentic riverboat being used in the filming of *Plantation Fury*. But since speaking up would only antagonize quite a few people, silence seemed best. And being thought a murderess has given Sheena's popularity a tremendous, though unfortunately final, boost. Two of her earlier movies were run the other night on KWOW-TV and her poster of two seasons ago is selling impressively again.

Sheena talked about that poster the last time I saw her alive. She'd come back to L.A. from the Sacramento location to do a new Pantz commercial for my advertising agency. During a break in the shooting she and I went out for a late lunch at a favorite place of hers, a vegetarian spot on La Cienega called Eats of Eden.

"Notice that?" she asked as we walked through the near-empty restaurant.

"The one-eyed guy ogling you?"

She slid gracefully into a vine-covered booth. "Not ogling me, ogling my backside." Sheena was a very pretty woman of twenty-nine —tall, tan, and authentically redhaired.

"He probably saw one of the Pantz commercials," I suggested, settling in opposite her. "Or one of your films, or maybe the poster."

145

"That thing." Frowning, she picked up the menu, which was diecut in the shape of an enormous carrot. "What a disgusting piece of exploitation that dippy poster was. Why I ever let my agent con me into—"

"It was attractive, reminded me of the old Betty Grable pinup from—"

"Who?"

"Betty Grable, she was noted for her—"

"Legs or something, wasn't it?"

I nodded. "Your poster sold well, didn't it? So you shouldn't—"

"Am I in this only for the money?" Snorting delicately, she tossed her menu aside. "You don't understand what it's like to be famous because you have a sexy rear end. Nobody gives me credit for having any intelligence. I try to explain it's genetically possible to have a brain and a fanny, yet—here's another thing. There is no polite word in our dippy society for the human backside."

"Posterior?"

She gave one of those snorting laughs of hers. "Oh, really? Would you say that in a mixed crowd of conservative halfwits? 'My wife has a lovely posterior, don't you think?' Not that your wife *does*, but—"

"She used to be a model."

"A fashion model, They don't need buttocks."

"My wife happens to be a very—"

"For a woman of fifty, sure."

"She's barely forty-three," I said. "Listen, Sheena, you seem awfully grumpy today. Did something go wrong at our filming this morning? I noticed Sardonsky patted you on the—posterior—but he does that to everyone he directs in a commercial, male or female."

"Or anything in between." She retrieved her menu. "The sprout ragout is good here."

"What is bothering you then?"

She sighed. "*Him.*"

I tried to recall who she was living with. "You mean that actor who rides the star motorcycle on the *Goon Squad*, Tuesday nights at 8?"

"I dumped him months ago." Sheena shook her pretty head impatiently. "I mean the only man I've ever honestly loved. Are you ready to order?"

A gaunt young man in a camouflage suit was hovering beside our booth with an order pad in one lean hand.

I told him, "I'll have the Vegie Reuben."

"The usual," Sheena said.

"Beg pardon, Miss," the waiter said, "but since I've never seen you before in my life bringing you the usual will be rather—"

"See, that's Hollywood," said Sheena. "One season you have a hit TV show and a top-grossing film, the next even callow halfwits don't—"

"I'm very nearsighted," explained the waiter, "so even if you are famous I probably wouldn't recognize you. On top of which, I have absolutely no interest in motion pictures, television, or any other aspect of show business."

She asked, "Then why the heck did you come to Los Angeles?"

"I was born here."

"You aren't just working here until you get discovered?"

"No, I'm working here because I got fired from my job in a missile factory."

"I'll have the Spinach Surprise."

He wrote it down and left us. I said, "You were saying something about—"

"The only man I've ever loved. It's a pity he's such a schmuck." Sheena eyed me. "You mean you really haven't heard about me and Chips Tortuga?"

"I know he's directing *Plantation Fury*," I told her. "But since your part isn't all that large, I assumed—"

"He threw me aside. Just before casting began on the film," she said. "It's rough to have your career skidding at the same time as your love life."

"My wife is close to the wife of Risk Mundy, the star of *Plantation*—"

"That meathead.

"From what I hear, though, Chips isn't all that attractive. I know in newspaper and magazine photos he—"

"Oh, you're falling into show-business judgment patterns, which I suppose is natural after your forty-some years in advertising work—"

"Twenty-five years," I corrected. "Twenty-six next February."

"I admit Chips is short. Squat actually. And he's grossly over-weight. He dresses like a sharecropper and smells like the underside of a pier. He has ugly, unsightly blotches all over him and the hair on his misshapen skull would look better on the backside of a porcupine. He has little wartlike growths on most of his fingers and a temper like Jack the Ripper. Still, there's something about him."

"What?" I inquired.

She shrugged one lovely shoulder. "It's hard to pinpoint," she said, a sad smile touching her face. "I love the man, that's all I know. The thirteen and a half weeks we lived together were idyllic. When he wasn't throwing things." She shook her head, red hair swirling. "He's a real genius, you know, and I suppose that's part of the magic of it all."

"He's over budget on *Plantation Fury*, isn't he? And behind schedule?"

"Well, yes."

"How much over?"

"Oh, around twenty-six million."

"Twenty-six million?" I sat upright. "He's twenty-six million over?"

"You don't understand what it's like to be a genius."

"I sure understand what twenty-six million bucks is," I told her. "I thought United Media recently announced they weren't going to have any more pictures go beyond budget."

"Those goniffs have been making life very rough for poor Chips," she said. "They're always phoning him at the paddleboat to—"

"Which paddleboat?"

"The one for the film, obviously," Sheena replied. "Chips had it flown in from Mississippi somewhere. The *River Belle* is its name." Her tan hands made fists. "I absolutely hate to think of Chips living on that boat with—Yes?"

Our gaunt young waiter had returned. "Would you mind standing up and turning your back toward the kitchen door?"

"I would, yes," she answered with a faint smile.

"The chef thinks you might be Sheena somebody or other and if he could get a good look at your—"

"Posterior?"

"Right, then he'd be certain."

"I am Sheena Mayday," she said evenly. "And I want to know where in the bloody blue blazes my lunch is."

"Coming right up." He scurried off.

"Chips Tortuga is living on this boat?" I asked her.

"He loves to do things like that. When we made *Blood of a Gunfighter* we lived in a cattle car on a siding near Sweetwater, Texas. For two glorious weeks."

"Was that during part of your thirteen—"

"No, last year. Our romance, like most great ones, recurs. Three weeks last year, thirteen this—"

"I remember now," I said. "My wife told me. Right now Tortuga's romancing the girl who stars in *Plantation Fury*. I can't recall her—"

"Her dippy name is Chili Redondo," snarled Sheena. "She's twenty. Can you beat that? A mere twenty. If I were twenty again I—"

"Is she one of the reasons Tortuga's so late and over budget?"

"Chili's brain is the size of, and has the capabilities of, a jumping bean," explained Sheena. "If you stand close to that scrawny little bimbo you can hear it rattling around in her coco. When Guinness adds a rating for Dumbest Starlet in the known world, Chili Redondo will get a whole page. Comedy writers in need of routines for Vegas standup comics have but to spend fifteen or so minutes with her and they'll have enough inspiration for a ton of she's-so-dumb-that jokes."

"You don't like her."

"I loathe, detest, dislike, and can't endure her," said my redheaded lunchmate. "What's worse, she's ruining Chips' marvelous movie with her stupidities. The other day they shot one whole morning at Magnolia Hills—that's the name of the old plantation house—before they found out Chili'd parked her chewing gum behind her ear and it showed in the close-ups. She ruined seventy-six takes on the farewell to the Confederate troops scene because instead of saying, 'You all hurry back, you hear,' she insisted on saying, 'Youse all.' She's always at least two hours late, she can never find her marks, she has a tendency to burp during love scenes, she—"

"There's talk of dumping Chili and replacing her."

"Won't happen," said Sheena. "Chips is completely smitten. They're living on that steamboat like a couple of bloody lovebirds. If she goes, he goes."

"Isn't there a possibility they'll can him too?"

"No, because he's still hot. Do you know how many Oscar nominations *Blood of a Gunfighter* got?"

"Seven."

"Nine, and it's already grossed near as much as *Star Wars*," she said. "As long as Chips stays stupidly infatuated with her, she'll stay on. However, I have an idea."

I made a quick stop-right-there gesture with my hand. "I don't want to listen to any plan for violence, blackmail , or—"

"What I'm talking about is love," Sheena insisted. "I intend to win Chips back. See, where I made my mistake last time was by being too feisty and independent. This time I'm going to do the domestic bit, be all frills and hot meals. I was reading an excellent article in—"

"C'mon, Sheena, that's not you," I pointed out. "You shouldn't compromise your—"

"Who's telling me not to compromise? Aren't you the bloke who wrote the voice-over copy for this latest Pantz commercial?"

"I supervised the writing."

" 'Slip yourself into a pair of Pantz,' " she quoted in a little Shirley Temple voice. " 'They're the fashion jeans that are tight like that!' " She laughed, "Didn't you ever dream of writing a great book, or at least a great script? 'Tight like that.' Oh, golly."

"Convincing people your jeans are superior isn't the same as betraying your principles for a man who smells like a porcupine."

"He *looks* like a porcupine. He *smells* like low tide at San Pedro," she said. "At least I love Chips Tortuga. You don't love Pantz."

"I respect them. Besides, the parallel isn't—"

"Be that as it may, I'm going to edge Chili out of his life," she promised. "That's going to save the movie and our romance."

I put both hands on the table top, leaned toward her. "Listen, Sheena, I hear that a good deal of the money being poured into *Plantation Fury* may be coming from organized crime. Could be the best thing for you to do is finish up your small role and get safely away from—"

"Oh, Jiggs has told me all those rumors about—"

"Who's Jiggs?"

"He's a second unit director in charge of the stunts for the picture, Jiggs Arabee," she said. "He knows this town and he says those dippy rumors simply started because of the Five Kings."

"That 1950's singing group?"

"Fifties, Sixties, some time in the dim past. The point is they're loaded, from shrewd real-estate deals over the years, and they're the main backers of the movie."

"So? "

"Well, they used to play Reno and Las Vegas a lot and so some small-minded people think they re linked with mobsters and all, Sheena said. "It's nothing but unfounded gossip."

"If it's true, though, you—"

"My mind is made up. I'm going to keep playing this dinky and quite demeaning part. In fact, I'm flying back up to Sacro tonight after we finish up this Pantz thing. I'll oust that dumb little bimbo, get her tossed clean off the riverboat, and save Chips and his career."

"Not an easy task," I mentioned.

Sheena simply laughed.

✗

She returned to the film location near the state capital and two days later I had to go out of town unexpectedly. Another of the accounts I was responsible for was having some unforeseen problems in the Cleveland area. Glimmer Toothpaste was test-marketing a new formulation there, one containing a miracle ingredient we'd christened Smilenium, and some of the customers who'd tried the new stuff were claiming it was giving them lockjaw.

This wasn't true lockjaw, I found on arrival—their mouths were merely being glued shut because of an unexpected bonding quality Smilenium developed when mixed with certain types of saliva.

As soon as I checked into one of Cleveland's finest hotels I attempted to get more details from Glimmer's chief chemist, who'd been in town supervising the introduction of the new product. Unfortunately, he'd sampled some himself and his own teeth were cemented together.

The chemist stubbornly insisted on communicating by way of handwritten memos and, since his script was as wretched as that of most medical people, it took me quite a while to comprehend that an error had been made in mixing up several thousand tubes of New Improved Glimmer with Smilenium. What was in the tubes was a very sturdy imitation of Goofy Glue.

Seeing to it that all the flawed tubes of Glimmer were unobtrusively recalled, writing up six radio spots that subtly downplayed what had been happening, and locating our client's attorney on his yacht in the Caribbean took two and a half weeks out of my life.

During those same two and a half weeks Sheena was trying out her initial scheme to woo Chips Tortuga back by attempting to be more traditionally feminine.

The fact that Chips was under increasing pressure from United Media Studios, who were under increasing pressure from their shadowy backers, didn't help Sheena's cause. Two things were the basis of the nearly continuous arguments Tortuga was having with the various studio executives who made the pilgrimage up to the outskirts of Sacramento-Chili Redondo and the *River Belle*.

"She's inept," Shackamaxon, vice-president of United Media, told him during a nervous indoor luncheon on the upper deck of the paddleboat.

"That's her style," explained the director, biting at a hangnail.

"She's wasting us a blinking fortune," bemoaned Shackamaxon, gazing out at the river which ran unenthusiastically by the moored boat. "Somebody in accounting just figured out Chili uses up an average of thirty-seven takes per shot and each one—"

"The girl is a slow starter."

"But, Chips, you're twenty-seven million over budget and the end is nowhere in—"

"Twenty-six million," said Chips Tortuga.

"Let me be candid," said the V.P. "We have faith in you, my boy, but we don't want to take a bath on this picture."

"Fear not, meathead."

"That's what they told the passengers on *The Titanic*."

Tortuga commenced singing in an off-key whine, "Wasn't it sad when the great ship went down? Wasn't it sad when—"

"What the hell is that?"

"Famous old spiritual concerning the sinking of *The Titanic*," replied the youthful director, wiping his lunch-stained palms across the bib of his overalls. "Best known from the old 78 rpm recording by the legendary Blind Willie Johnson. Now there was a man with a fascinating life. I'd love to film something about his—"

"But not in this picture," said Shackamaxon anxiously.

"Probably not."

✗

That same afternoon one of the Five Kings, clad in an impeccable 1950's-style pinstripe suit, paid a visit to Chips Tortuga during a break in the filming. "Hi, buddy," he grinned.

Scratching his armpit enthusiastically Tortuga asked, "What do you want, fathead?"

"We decided you don't need the boat."

"You're wrong. I do."

"No, you got to concentrate on the stuff up at the old plantation and the battles," the former vocalist informed him. "You don't have any time for a riverboat."

"I need this one."

"How come?"

"For the race."

"Which race is that?"

"The riverboat race I've been thinking of for the finish of the film."

"You can't have a race with one damn boat."

"Which is why, fathead, I'm seriously thinking about ordering a second one."

The swarthy singer frowned. "We wouldn't like that," he said very quietly.

✗

When, sometime after twilight, Tortuga returned to his specially furnished suite aboard the *River Belle*, he was in an unusually foul mood. "What's that incredibly cruddy smell?" he demanded of the living room.

"Pot roast," replied Sheena, very sweetly, from the nearby galley. Scowling, the pudgy little director went storming in. "Where's Chili?"

"Detained," answered Sheena in what she felt was a demure and feminine voice.

With the help of her stuntman friend, Jiggs Arabee, she'd done a few things to the Porsche Chili had used to drive into Sacramento an hour earlier—things guaranteed to cause the car to collapse and strand the rival actress for at least several hours.

"And what's that godawful thing you're wearing?"

"An apron, dear."

"You look lousy in frills, fathead," be remarked. "Now get your keester off my boat."

"But, Chips, I've cooked you a surprise dinner. Pot roast, purple cabbage, potato pancakes, crisp—"

"Stop already, you're giving me heartburn." He turned his pudgy back on her. "Anyhow, dimbulb, you ought to know I always fast during filming."

"You sure didn't fast during *Blood of a Gunfighter*. You gained fifty-three pounds from—"

"That was a western." He faced her, his quilly hair erect. "Please do me the favor of disembarking."

"You can't have been fasting all this time. I mean, you and that bimbo have been holed up here on this dippy boat for seventeen solid weeks while—"

"Who's been talking to you?" he growled, making a threatening fist with one warty hand.

"No one, dear."

"Was it that fathead Shackamaxon? Or that hoodlum tenor? Are they trying to take this film away from me?" He grabbed her bare arm. "This is the culmination, so far, of my screen career. I've got to complete this one. Something important inside me cries out to—"

"Ho ho!"

They both looked toward the doorway.

There, car grease streaking her pretty forehead and road dust spattered across her silken jumpsuit, was Chill Redondo. "Try to sabotage me, huh? You big floozie!"

The fiery actress's charge was delayed by a loose board at the threshold. Even so, she got to Sheena very swiftly. Chili was a much better fighter than she was an actress and with five or six well planted punches she decked Sheena. She then dragged her up a stairway and over to a riverside railing. "You better stay away from my man," she warned and then booted Sheena off the deck and down into the sluggish waters of the Sacramento tributary.

✗

The rest of this isn't based on fact, only on conjecture and surmise. My wife did get a few details from Risk Mundy's wife, but I'm guessing on many of the specifies. Then, too, I wasn't in Los Angeles when the explosions occurred. Our Glimmer client had decided to introduce a new glue and I had to jet to Terre Haute, Indiana, to supervise the test-marketing of the initial batches. Although early customers liked the glue's effectiveness, some of them were complaining because it smelled strongly of toothpaste. I had to im-provise a series of radio commercials that made an asset of our new glue's near overpowering spearmint odor.

Meantime, up near Sacramento, Sheena had come to the con-clusion she could never win Tortuga back while the feisty Chili Redondo walked the earth. Love, as I long ago learned, pushes people into strange corners. Sheena, too, had been talking to the stunt director, Jiggs Arabee, and she knew the Five Kings, who were almost certainly a front for the legitimate investing of mob money, were growing increasingly unhappy with Tortuga. They didn't like his continuing to use the untalented Chili and they didn't like his insisting he was going to add a very expensive steamboat race to the already fantastically overbudget *Plantation Fury*.

One bright spring afternoon Sheena was watching Jiggs supervise a Civil War battle scene in a sprawl of woodlands that had survived between two Sacramento suburbs. As the prearranged explosions simulated cannon fire and the soldiers, each man clad in a meticulously accurate and grossly expensive uniform, ran and yelled and shot at each other, Sheena suddenly snapped her lovely fingers.

"Of course," she said to herself. "An explosion."

An explosion, cleverly done, would eliminate Chili and the *River Belle*. With those two millstones gone from around his pudgy yet gifted neck, Tortuga would be free. With deft help from Sheena, he'd come to his senses. The riverboat sequence would be dropped and he'd take Sheena back into his life.

Fate, so she thought, provided her with a perfect opportunity just two days later. Tortuga had to fly to Las Vegas for an urgent conference with some Key investors. He was leaving Chili behind, on board the steamboat.

A steamboat, even one sitting at a simulated dock, might have an accidental explosion. And so quite late that night Sheena, dressed in a black pullover and a snug pair of ebony Pantz, jobbed the lock on the film's dynamite box and took out enough to take care of Chili Redondo. She'd watched Jiggs rig explosions often enough to be confident she could blow up the *River Belle* and her tough little rival.

There were, however, a few things Sheena didn't know as she sneaked through the moonless night toward the paddlewheeler.

She didn't know about the phone call one of the Five Kings had made to Shackamaxon that afternoon.

"Buy a dog," he suggested in his baritone voice.

"Huh? What the hell—"

"Buy a dog and a white cane. Because unless that Latino broad and that boat go, you'll need 'em."

Earlier that same day, also unknown to Sheena, a call had come to Tortuga on location.

He'd answered it with, "What's the idea, meathead, of—"

"Get a wheelchair," said the Five Kings alto.

"Listen, I—"

"Or crutches maybe. Because if Chili and that damn riverboat stay on, you'll have two broken legs. At the very least."

Shackamaxon slipped up to Sacramento late that day and, once he learned that only Chili was aboard the *River Belle*, planted a fairly sophisticated plastic bomb just under the bedroom the actress was using. After setting it to go off at midnight, he then headed quietly back to Hollywood.

Tortuga, valuing his legs more than his art or his love and knowing be could never cajole the tough-minded Chili off his picture or his boat, put a complex time bomb of his own devising inside the oven of the galley stove. He set it to go off at midnight, knowing Chili never went near the stove, and arranged to be in Vegas long before his boat and his mistress went up.

The authorities found the remains of both bombs when sifting the rubble. The one they never found a single trace of was the one Jiggs Arabee, working on the orders of the people behind the Five Kings, had concealed in the riverboat's boiler. Jiggs, the only real demolition expert in the bunch, had also set his to go off at midnight.

And just one minute before midnight Sheena, little homemade bomb in her hand and a smile of anticipation on her lovely face, went sneaking up the dark gangplank.

IT WAS BAD ENOUGH

They only believed he was the Son of Satan killer for a day or so. Then the police realized they'd made a mistake and shouldn't have gunned him down in the middle of the Sunset Strip like that.

Too late to do Beans Katzman much good. He was already lying in state in a satin-lined coffin in one of the most prestigious funeral chapels in the Los Angeles area by that time, surrounded by impressive funeral wreaths. The fancy sendoff was mostly Juliet's idea. Once he was dead and gone, she seemed to feel a bit more kindly toward Beans and, quite probably, she realized a lavish funeral would get the sort of media attention that'd provide some publicity for her upcoming book and movie.

Beans was preoccupied with that book of hers, and the possible movie, when I had lunch with him on a mild hazy spring day a little over three weeks ago. The restaurant was a small, narrow vegetarian place a block or so from the forlorn peach-colored apartment building in a bleakly rundown section of Hollywood Beans was living in at the moment. It was called Disgustingly Healthy and had only recently moved into what had been a surplus store. Signs offering *Knapsacks At Low, Low Prices* and *Desert Boots ½ Price!* still decorated the pocked plaster walls.

Beans came in out of the haze and did his swish wave. "Oh, there you are, sweets. God, but I'm glad you could ditch the wife." He switched into his truck driver and walked through the tangle of shaky tables toward where I was sitting. "Where you want that truckload of avocados?" he inquired of the lean young man with the moustache who ran the restaurant.

"How are you today, Mr. Katzman?" the young man inquired, grinning.

"How vas I? How vas I?" he inquired in his Dutch accent. "Mine poy, I'm disgustingly healthy, dot's how I vas." Bouncing twice, he settled into the chair opposite me.

As a matter of fact, he did look in pretty good shape. Nowhere near as good as he had when he'd starred on *The Funny, Funny Hour* on television nearly thirty years ago, but better than he had the last time my ad agency had tried to use him for some commercials.

"Beans," I told him, "I think I'll be able to persuade them to give you a chance to audition for the part of Mr. Mildew in our Kildew Spray spots that are—"

"Sure, sure," he said, reaching into an inside pocket of his eleven-year-old sportcoat. "Did you see this? Do you know what those gumballs are planning to do to me now?"

"Which—"

"Ex-wife." He withdrew a folded-up copy of *Daily Variety* and waved it in the air. "Let me be more specific. Since my ex-wives are legion. I mean Juliet—Juliet Fairly. Gad, how could I have wed a wench with a name like that? Well, I was fifty at the time and fifty is a dangerous— Listen, sis, are you giving me the come-on?" He'd noticed a thin girl in jeans and sweatshirt at the next table.

Putting down her sprout-and-mock-meatloaf-on-pita-bread sandwich, she glanced over at him. "You were addressing me, gramps?"

"Never mind, I realize now it's only a tick." Beans dropped the trade paper on the tabletop and smoothed it out. "Waiter, cancel that magnum of carrot juice for the beauty at the next table. Where was I?"

The girl was watching him. "You look vaguely familiar. Were you somebody once?"

"Was I somebody?" His eyebrows quivered as he reached again into his coat.

I figured the wallet was coming. "Beans, listen, I have to be back at the agency fairly soon. So let's just have lunch and then discuss the possibility of your doing—"

"Take a gander at that, girlie." The fat wallet was in his hand. He flipped it open and two dozen plastic coated photos came unfolding out to dangle between the tables. "There I am as Dr. Dingle-dangle during the 1954 premiere show of *The Funny, Funny Hour*. Next you see me politely fondling Marilyn Monroe when she guested on—"

"Oh, yes. You're Beans Katzman." She returned to her sandwich.

"I can help your show-business career, my child. I know a first-rate bordello down in Tijuana that specializes in ginks with a skinny fetish. If I put in a good word, they'll hire you like—"

"Beans," I cut in, "the client is worried you may not be dependable enough for a series of TV commercials that—"

"Not dependable? Me?" He fished in the pictures of his past career triumphs and folded them up into a neat packet. "I'm completely straightened out now. The bad days done been here and gone. I am off booze, off pills, off broads. I am a prince of good fellows. Boy Scouts ask *me* to help *them* across the street." He held out his hand and made it quiver like a hummingbird's wing. "See how steady that is?"

"Seriously, Beans," I said, "when we used you on the KleanJon commercials, you fell into the bathtub in the kitchen set not once but—"

"Three damn years ago is not now. I swear to you I haven't had a drink in over a year. Truly."

"There'll have to be an audition. About two weeks from now, if you can—"

"Squint at this item, will you." He jabbed his forefinger at an inner page of *Daily Variety*. "This is going to do more harm to my career than falling into a tub."

"What?"

"Here I am, at long last, on the comeback trail." He glanced around the nearly empty room, then lowered his voice. "I am not just being considered for demeaning parts in kitchen-and bathroom-product commercials any more, my lad. Nay, I am in contention for a lead role in a new sitcom that'll—well, I'm obliged not to give out details. The thing is, I'm still only fifty-seven. My best years are—"

"You're sixty-one," I reminded.

"Not any more. For the sake of my career I've gone back to fifty-seven. I'm fifty-seven, off the sauce, and by next week I have a full head of hair." He walked his fingers through the thinning spot at the back of his head. "I have my damn feet on the ladder again and then these gumballs come along to foul me up."

Picking up the trade paper, I skimmed the item he'd been jabbing at. " 'Juliet Fairly, actress and author.' I didn't know she was an author."

"She scrawled her name and phone number on a lot of phonebooth walls in her youth— 'Call me for a hot time.' That's the extent of her literary career."

" 'Penning *I Married a Funny, Funny Man*, autobiog of her hectic life with once top comedian Beans Katzman. Publishers in Manhattan fighting over book … ' You were only married to her for about three years."

"Two and a half, but I made the fatal error of confiding all of my past sins to her. I mean, she was my fourth wife and I figured it was my last go-round."

"Fifth wife."

"No, no. I never counted Irene."

" ' … Lonnie Sheck, Junior, dynamic prez of Paragon Pictures, is near to optioning book for a major biopic to be called *Funny, Funny Man*. When last heard from, Beans Katzman was doing the dinner-theater circuit in Nebraska and—' "

"You've already reached the heart of the item." Beans snatched the paper out of my grasp. "Do you see what they're doing? First off, there'll be a book wherein I appear as a drunken, pill-popping monster who broke windows and kicked down doors in my palatial Beverly Hills mansion, carried on with dozens of showgirls, busted my wife's arm and behaved like a vile sot."

"Maybe a lawyer can—"

"How's a lawyer going to stop her from telling the truth? In those days I *was* a drunken, pill-popping monster who broke windows and kicked down doors in my palatial Beverly Hills mansion, carried on with dozens of showgirls, and busted my wife's arm—twice in fact." He stuffed *Variety* away in a coat pocket. "Then just as the last damaging afterglow of her nitwit book fades and I once again try to overcome the vissici … the vissywissy … the bum breaks of life, the damn motion picture hits the fan. There, in a twenty-million-dollar production, I'll be seen breaking arms, pinching fannies, snorting coke, rolling in the gutter all over again. It'll ruin me for good and all." He pointed a finger at the low ceiling, like a movie senator delivering an oration. "And, my fellow Americans, do you know what is even worse? I'll tell you what is even worse. They're stealing my life! My life! Juliet steals it and makes it into a book. Next Lonnie Sheck, Junior steals it and makes it into a movie!"

"Have you actually talked to an attorney?"

"Three of 'em. They say I haven't got a chance to stop it."

"Maybe it'd be best to leave the whole thing alone," I suggested.

"A book and a movie might actually help your career. Years ago *The Jolson Story* gave Al Jolson a whole new career as—"

"Juliet isn't going to show me down on one knee singing *Mammy*," Beans pointed out.

"Even so, Beans, the best thing to do is let it alone and—"

"Nix, amigo. I've already devised a surefire plan to get Juliet to cease her pranks. Yes, I intend ... What is it, lad?"

The proprietor, who also acted as waiter, was hovering beside the table. "Might I take your orders, gentlemen?"

"I'll have the overalls," said Beans, pointing at a sign on the wall. "Two pairs for the price of one. Yum yum."

"Always kidding, huh, Mr. Katzman?"

" 'Tis me life's work, laddy. Did I ever show you the pictures of me on my—?"

"Several times."

I said, "I'll have the mock chop."

Beans took up his menu, brought it close to his face, adjusted a nonexistent monocle. "Mock chop ... phony burger ... fake steak ..." he muttered. "Is this a real fake steak, old chop? I mean old chap. Wouldn't want a bloomin' fake fake steak, wot?"

"Well, it's made out of lentils, soybeans, carrots, and kelp."

"Ah, that's exactly how my dear old mammy down in Alabammy used to make it. I'll risk that and a glass of your Disgustingly Healthy Veggie Juice Cocktail #2. That's #2, mind you, not #1 or #3. And most certainly not #5."

The owner hurried off.

"As I was saying," said Beans, "I've concocted a clever scheme. Now, I admit that when we separated, Juliet was a bit nasty—"

"She had the police drag you out of the house in a straitjacket and manacles—"

"That was a bit nasty, wasn't it? Ah, but despite that, Juliet of all my many wives really was fond of me. Yes, my son, Juliet Fairly is a sucker for the ample Katzman charm. Therefore, I intend to persuade her to give up all thought of selling this tome."

"It's going to take a hell of a lot of persuasion. They're talking about offering her something like five hundred thousand for the hardcover rights, according to this story in—"

"You underestimate my charm." Beans spread his arms wide. "Look at me—feast your orbs. I'm fit and trim again as well as completely reformed. If I put my mind to it, I can woo Juliet into abandoning the whole foolhardy venture."

"Maybe," I said, far from convinced.

✗

The next day the agency sent me up to Seattle to do a little troubleshooting. One of our clients was introducing a new diet-aid pill called Fataway Plus and some unexpected problems had popped up. Nearly twenty percent of the people who tried the new pills not only cut down on their food intake, they ceased eating altogether. Nearly ten percent of these people also became very militant and declared they were on hunger strikes in support of various extremely radical causes.

The Fataway advertising manager had also flown to Seattle, which caused me an extra problem. I had to give soothing stories out to the media, come up with some quick radio commercials minimizing the dangers of the pills, supervise the quiet withdrawal of every damn bottle of the stuff from the shelves and keep anybody with a camera of any sort from getting a shot of that ad manager. Pictures of a 360-pound diet-aid executive wouldn't do us much good. All in all, I was in Seattle for ten long days. It rained a lot while I was there.

Meantime, Beans Katzman had commenced his assault on Juliet. It was, I learned from him later, a complete and absolute flop. Since throwing him out of their mansion in Beverly Hills, she'd had a high stone wall built all around the grounds. There was an electrified iron gate and, according to Beans, chunks of jagged bottle glass all along the top of the wall. When Beans, clad in his newest suit, a conservative banker's-grey model from 1971, arrived at the gates on a clear morning two days after our vegetarian lunch, he found himself being scrutinized by a video camera mounted up above the electrified gate.

"Your business, please?" inquired a metallic voice that came barking out of a speaker embedded in the stone wall.

"I've come to pay my respects to the lady of the house." Beans waved the bouquet of yellow roses he was toting at the eye of the camera.

"Name, please?"

"Don't you recognize me?" He started to reach for his wallet full of pictures. "I'm Beans Katzman."

"Ben Katzman?"

"Beans! As in 'full of!'"

A silence followed.

The camera used the time to look him up and down.

"Beans?" A new voice came out of the speaker.

"Ah, Juliet, it does this old heart good to hear your lovely dulcet—"

"Get the hell off my property or I'll call the law!"

"Juliet, my sweet, I wish merely to—"

"I'm going to count ten. Make that fifteen for old times' sake. I'm going to count to fifteen and then turn the dogs loose. One ..."

"Dogs, m'love?"

"Killer dogs," amplified Juliet. "Mean and rotten killer dogs who go for the throat."

"I doubt they can get at me through the iron bars in the gate." He jiggled the bouquet up in front of the video camera. "Take a look at these posies, Juliet. Yellow roses, your favorite most—"

"... four ... five ..."

Sensing it wasn't the proper moment to launch his romantic campaign, Beans bowed to the camera eye. "I'll withdraw until you're in a better mood," he announced. "You may keep the flowers."

He bounded up closer to the gate, tossed the dozen bright-yellow roses over the high iron gate. There was a sentimental note attached and Beans hoped that might melt Juliet's heart a bit.

"... fifteen!"

An alarm bell started ringing somewhere up near the mansion. Metal doors clanged and he heard a loud galloping noise.

Seconds later, two huge black and evil hounds came charging down the well kept lawn where once, in better days, Beans had strolled hand-in-hand with Juliet. One dog flung itself, snarling and slavering, at the gate. The other dog paused to worry the roses, ripping blossoms, wrapping paper, and tender note to shreds before joining its partner at the gate.

Shrugging philosophically, Beans sauntered down to his rented car and drove home.

✗

Beans concluded that if he couldn't launch his romantic assault on Juliet at her home, he'd have to begin his campaign elsewhere. He considered himself a master of characterization and disguise, a fact attested to by his string of photos that showed him in sundry roles. He rented, on the cuff, a chauffeur's uniform, and borrowed an impressive Mercedes sedan from his one-time agent, who still owed him a few small favors. Beans took to cruising through Juliet's posh neighborhood at various hours of the day and night. A few times he risked parking near the gates of the estate.

On his third day of this scouting, he saw the gates come rattling open and Juliet came barreling out of the drive alone in a silvery Jaguar. Discreetly, he followed her. It was midday and Beans assumed she was on her way to lunch. If he casually approached her, after doffing the disguise, in a public restaurant or cocktail bar she certainly couldn't set the cops or those dogs on him. And Beans was confident that once Juliet got an up-close look at him, her old affection would blossom once again.

It was probably while trailing his ex-wife through the narrow, winding streets that he listened to the news on the car radio and was inspired with the alternate notion that was to prove so unfortunate to him.

" ... The Son of Satan has struck again and stabbed two to death. That story after these messages," a handsome-voiced newscaster was saying as Beans followed Juliet.

"Skip the commercials, give me the gory details," whined Beans in his adenoidal teenager voice.

After spots for SweetiSink, Fat Ed's Homecooked Frozen Pizza, Nat and Phil's Tallman's Clothing Warehouse, and the very funeral parlor he'd be buried out of, the news of the world returned.

" ... Santa Monica police believe the crazed, self-styled Son of Satan killer has claimed two more unfortunate victims, this time in a quiet residential section of Santa Monica. Late this morning, the bodies of Roberta M. Weaver, thirty-seven, and her husband, Mark L. Weaver, forty-two, were found in the couple's Santa Monica home. Both had been stabbed numerous times and all the usual tokens had been left behind. The grim crimson Halloween mask representing the face of the Devil, the three black candles placed a the head of each victim in small silver holders, the brand new set of carving knives left at the feet of the final victim. The Son of Satan killer also, as has been his gruesome custom in all seven of his previous murders, left a bloody message scrawled on the Weavers' wall. In the blood of his victims he wrote, *Why don't you stop me?* Acting Police Chief Alan Alch says the police are—"

Shaking his head, Beans found a soothing music station. "All the goofy people hereabouts aren't in show business," he observed, returning his full attention to his former wife's car.

Juliet seemed to be heading for the ocean. She must be meeting someone for lunch at one of the beachfront restaurants along the Pacific.

Juliet didn't go to a restaurant, though. Instead she drove down to the beach town of San Amaro, some fifteen miles below Santa Monica. She drove up into the low hills, and swung into the driveway of a modest shingle cottage. As Beans drove by, he saw a man come out of the little house, run across the browning lawn, and put his arms around Juliet.

"I'll be damned," he remarked, recognizing the small blond man who was kissing his former wife.

✗

I'd hoped to return to Los Angeles in time to sit in on Beans' audition for our Kildew Spray commercials, but another agency field job came up and I had to fly directly from Seattle to Detroit. The new trouble involved our Mother Malley's Zippy Zoop. There was evidence that some crank was visiting supermarkets in and around Detroit and tampering with packages of the new instant-soup mix. The problem was that most of the customers who got the tampered-with packages swore the soup tasted better than it ever had before. My assignment was to get a tampered package, have it analyzed, and find out what the devil the crank had added. I was also to come up with a series of radio spots designed to persuade the crank to give himself up. Our client wanted to offer him a job in the Mother Malley test kitchens. That kept me away from home an additional two weeks and I didn't get back until after Beans was buried. I had my wife send flowers—yellow roses—but I would've liked to have attended his funeral.

The day after the auditions, I phoned Beans from Detroit to find out how he'd done.

"I didn't bother to show up," he informed me, sounding unusually chipper.

"Why? Is something wrong, or—"

"Something is right, my lad," he said. "That deal I alluded to when last we dined at that compost heap masquerading as a restaurant has come through. I'm going in to sign the contracts next week, with thirteen weeks guaranteed. The tide is turning."

"Great. What is it? A sitcom?"

"It's *Amos & Andy*—a new version with an all-white cast. I'm going to be Kingfish."

"Well ... that's terrific, Beans. And you're certain it's set?"

"Just about," he said. "The only little snag is they want a notarized letter from Juliet in which she swears she's never going to write a book about me or a movie. See, if it looks like a lot of negative stuff about me is going to come out, even though I'm completely reformed, the people behind this new show feel it'll screw up the sales potential."

"You sound pretty elated," I said. "So you must've won Juliet over. Did your campaign—?"

"It was a total flop."

"Then how are you going to get her to—?"

"Juliet is carrying on a torrid romance with someone," he said. "It turns out, believe it or else, to be that gumball who's going to make the movie."

"Lonnie Sheck, Junior? But he's married to Tuffy Kash, the girl who plays the second nymphomaniac on *Outskirts of Houston*. One of our clients co-sponsors that—"

"Since ven don't married peoples fool mit a liddle hanky-panky, mine poy?"

Beans then proceeded to explain to me, mostly in his Dr. Dingle-dangle accent, all he'd been up to since last we'd met—how he'd tailed Juliet to the hideaway she and the producer were using in San Amaro, how he'd followed her there several times and confirmed she was in the throes of a torrid affair, how she wasn't about to cease and let Beans win her over to his cause.

"I was quite taken aback when I saw who it was Juliet was fooling around with," Beans told me, back in his near approximation of his true voice. "First Lonnie Sheck, Junior stole my life. Now he steals my ex-wife and my chance to woo her out of the idea of publishing that damn book.

"Remember that old Fred Allen radio routine? Probably before your time. The judge is asking the defendant why he killed his rival. Turned out the dead man had borrowed this guy's money, his car, his clothes, and so on. He then swiped his best suit, and, sneaking into the guy's room at night, he stole his false teeth out of the glass beside his bed. The routine ends with the poor guy saying, 'It was bad enough, Judge, him using my money and my wedding suit. It was bad enough he married my girl, using the ring I'd bought for her. It was bad enough when he drove her off on their honeymoon in my car. It was bad enough when he stopped beside me on the street and rolled down the window of my car to razz me. But, Judge, when he laughed in my face with my teeth I up and lost my temper.' That's about how I feel, my boy."

"Wait now," I said, sensing a smug note in his voice. "You aren't planning something criminal, are you? Like blackmail?"

"Me? *Moi?* Do something *crooked*? Why, that'd break the little hearts of the millions of freckle-faced boys who look to me as a role model," he answered in his handsome nitwit voice. "Besides, blackmail won't work."

"How do you know?"

"Let us merely say I did some nosing around. Turns out Tuffy knows about the affair and doesn't give a hoot."

"Then what's left to—"

"Not to worry, Guv. Be assured I'm not going to miss this last chance to get back into the limelight."

"C'mon," I told him, "this isn't your last chance. If this show doesn't pan out, you'll always—"

"This one will come through," Beans assured me and hung up.

✗

Obviously Beans never confided in me what his intended solution to his problem was. I'm nearly certain, though, from what he did tell me and from what came out in the papers and on television after he was shot down in the street, that my conclusions come pretty close to the truth.

After watching Juliet for a while longer, he was able to work out a fairly accurate schedule of when she and Lonnie Sheck, Junior got together. He knew that one of the times they always got together in the cottage in San Amaro was on Thursday nights about ten. He picked Thursday night to make his move—who knows? Maybe because Thursday was the night *The Funny, Funny Hour* had been on television back in the 1950s.

What Beans would do was simple. He would kill both Juliet and Lonnie. He wouldn't be caught or even suspected, because he'd make it look like the Son of Satan killer had struck again. He bought the carving knives at a cut-rate hardware store in Los Angeles, the candles at an occult bookshop out in Glendale. The devil mask, the purchasing of which would've probably made somebody suspicious, he swiped from a costume shop he used to patronize back when he was doing his show.

Beans didn't feel he'd have much trouble bringing himself to kill either of them. After all, he'd done a lot of fairly violent things in his time, back in the days when he was on booze and pills. He had himself one hell of a motive, too. Not only were Juliet and her lover trying to steal his very past from him, they were on the verge of botching up the best chance he'd ever had for a comeback. Nope, he was dead sure he could knife them both and leave a message in blood on the wall afterwards. Nothing to it.

To make absolutely certain he was in the proper nasty mood, Beans decided to have a few drinks before driving out to San Amaro to get rid of all his problems.

That may be why things went the way they did.

✗

At any rate, at a few minutes before nine Beans dumped all his Son of Satan props into a cardboard box and hopped into the borrowed Mercedes. He set the box on the front passenger seat beside him and drove on up to Sunset.

"The decline and fall of the West is commencing right here," he murmured to himself as he turned onto the gaudy Strip. "Hookers and hustlers by the yard."

An ebony sportscar cut in front of him and came to a sudden dead stop alongside a gaggle of six or seven young women in shorts and high heels who were congregated in front of a club called Yellow Fever.

Beans hit the brakes, yelling. "Conduct your business elsewhere, gumball!"

He smashed right into the tail of the black sportscar.

The driver was a tanned man of thirty-one. He leaped free of his car and came charging back toward Beans. "You old coot, why in the bloody blue blazes don't you watch—"

"Me? Listen, you ding-a-ling gumball," boomed Beans, climbing clear of his car; "in my day, hookers and their Johns did business behind closed doors."

"How'd you like to pick your choppers up off the asphalt, Granpappy?" inquired the young man, waving a tanned fist near Beans' nose.

"A sawed-off beach bum like— Hey, sis, get the hell out of there!"

A very pretty young blonde, possibly mistaking Beans for a

potential customer, had slid into the car by way of the door closest to the sidewalk. Giggling, she was poking around in his cardboard box. Just as she held up the devil mask, two uniformed cops drove up, stopped, and eased out of their patrol car.

"What's the frumus all about, folks?" asked the younger one. He looked just exactly like a TV cop—blond, tan, handsome, and grim.

"Nothing, officer," said the sportscar driver. "This old gentleman and I are friends and we simply stopped to exchange a few pleasant words."

Beans wasn't paying attention to the conversation. He was watching the girl stumble out of the car with the crimson mask in one hand and the set of carving knives in the other.

Both policemen saw her now.

The older officer asked, "Who does that stuff belong to?"

The girl, whose face was pale now, said, "Him. The old guy."

"Mind if we ask you a few questions, sir?" asked the younger cop.

Shaking his head, Beans moved toward the Mercedes. "Let's just forget the whole thing," he suggested over his shoulder.

"Halt, sir," ordered the young cop.

"It's him!" decided his partner. "It's the Son of Satan! We got him!"

Angry, Beans spun around to face the cops. "Don't either of you gumballs know who I am?" He started to reach inside his coat for his wallet full of pictures.

"He's going for a gun!"

Both policemen fired at him. The older cop hit him once in the stomach. His handsome partner got Beans twice in the chest.

As I said, they realized their mistake after a day or so—but it was too late to do Beans much good. Juliet was already giving him his fancy sendoff.

ALAS, MY LOVE

Lee couldn't think of much to say to the police.

Because by the time they grabbed him, he was pretty certain he'd killed the wrong person. That made it difficult to claim what he'd done was justifiable homicide.

So he kept quiet and let them book him for murder. Maybe he and his attorney can work out something for him to say.

Meantime, all sorts of stories and rumors have started circulating, some of them even more interesting than the truth. Not that I'm completely certain myself what the truth is in this case. I know as much, or maybe a bit more, than poor Lee Branner did. But even if I knew everything, I'm not going to get involved in this mess. Lee really did commit a murder after all.

✗

When he first mentioned *Alas, My Love* to me, he was feeling completely positive about the book, nearly euphoric.

We were jogging side by side along an early-morning stretch of Southern California beach and I'd remarked on the new maroon running suit he was decked out in.

"What?" He was a tall, lanky man, sunbrowned and nearly thirty-six. "I didn't catch your remark over that godawful wheeze of yours."

"Warmup suit," I gasped. "Yours. New?" I'd only started daily running earlier in the month and after a half mile I did sometimes develop a mild wheeze.

"You're wondering," said Lee, grinning and breathing evenly, "how a washed-up TV hack writer like me can afford underwear, let along a three-hundred-dollar—"

"You got," I inquired, "a new writing assignment?"

"Seems incredible to you, doesn't it? Lee Branner, six-time Emmy runner-up. Head writer on such dramatic hits of past seasons as *Hula Cops*, *Wuthering Heights Revisited*, and many more. You were sure I was on the skids for good."

170

"Never thought one way or the other. Noted sweatpants no longer full of holes. Congratulations."

"Through it all," he said, never once breaking his easy sand-pounding stride, "only one person stuck by me and continued to believe in me. That was Emily, the most loyal wife a man could—"

"What's the assignment?" I rasped.

"You sound godawful, sport." He slowed, halted beside a large sprawled hunk of driftwood. "Better rest for a spell, huh?"

"Doctor says—" I shook my head "—do mile morning before work." I'd stopped next to him, panting. "Good for heart."

"But cardiac arrest won't be good for your heart at all." Lee nodded at the log. "Sit a spell and I'll fill you in on how I'm going to zoom right back up the ladder."

"Get cramps if sit down too soon after running."

"Suit yourself." He gazed out at the hazy blue Pacific, laughing. "Emily knew I'd make it back, even after seventeen long months without a writing assignment. She's been a constant source of inspiration to me, through thick and thin." He turned and gestured up at the hillside. "Even when it looked as though we might have to give up our five-hundred-thousand house up there, she— Damn, did you see that?"

I was sucking in air. "See what?"

Frowning, Lee pointed up at his impressive red-tile and Moorish stone mansion and at the thick foliage that separated it from its neighbors. "I thought I spotted a flash of something, as though someone was watching me through binoculars." He frowned and turned back toward the morning ocean again. "Might be my imagination. Might be some pinhead trying to spy on celebrities. They still remember Emily, you know, even though it's been three seasons since she quit TV's top-rated nighttime soap, *Heavy Breathing*, to devote herself full time to our marriage."

"What's the new job?"

"This isn't the first time I've thought I was being— Aw, you've got to watch out for Hollywood paranoia." He rubbed his hands together. "I'm not just making a comeback, I'm bringing off a *triumphant* comeback. I'm going to do a miniseries."

"Great. That'll pay—"

"Top dollar. Enough to pay off our debts, or most of them, anyway. It was really rough going there for a while. We came damn close to losing both the Mercedes. Emily didn't complain once, but sometimes I could see in her eyes that— Hi, Tag."

Tag Marlo, with a silky golden spaniel on a leash, was approaching from behind. "How you doing, Lee?" He grinned, waved, as the dog tugged him forward.

"Was that grin at all sheepish?" Lee asked me after the incredibly handsome young actor had passed.

"Didn't appear to be."

"He's heard. He knows I'm on the way back up," said Lee, nodding. "When he was doing Heathcliff in *Wuthering Heights Revisited*, we were great buddies. He and that dippy folk-rock singer he was living with dropped in on Emily and me all the time. The past year or so, though, it's been averted gazes and sheepish smirks. And he only lives a half mile down the damn beach from us."

"He's heard, you've heard," I said, checking my watch. "*I'd* like to hear before I hasten off to my ad agency."

"Sure, Tag Marlo'd like the lead in *Alas, My Love*," reflected Lee, watching the actor recede. "Who wouldn't? And he's aware that Bosco Cheever, hottest young producer in Hollywood, has hired me to do the damn script."

"*Alas, My Love*," I said. "That's a book, isn't it?"

"Is it a *book*!" He took a step back on the yellow sand, spreading his arms wide. "*Alas, My Love* is the blockbuster novel of the year, cuz. Been on every bestseller list from coast to coast for forty-seven weeks or more. Paperback rights sold for nine hundred thousand, which ain't bad in tight times like these. It's outselling books about cats, Jewish American Princesses, and how to reduce the size of your backside. It's a fantastic hit and I'm going to be turning it into a five-part miniseries."

"Have you read it yet?"

He shook his head. "I'm going to pick up a copy this afternoon. Two copies in fact, one to read and one to mark up. I imagine it's just one more fat romance, but I know I can turn it into a first-class miniseries. Tag might not be bad for one of the leads at that. I hear it's about a triangle situation."

My breathing was nearly normal. "Nobody seems to know much about the author."

"What a pen name he's got! Jason Renfrew, Junior." He laughed. "Probably a little-old-lady librarian living in Oxnard."

172   Adam and Eve on a Raft: Mystery Stories

"Well, I'm glad to hear you're working again," I told him. "I got to be heading for work."

"Let's have lunch later in the week," he suggested. "My treat."

"I'm free Thursday."

"Thursday it is. I'll phone you about the place," he said. "That's another great thing about being in the chips again. They won't be disconnecting my phone for a while yet. I think I'll do another couple of miles before getting to the old typewriter." He went running with ease off along the bright morning beach.

✗

Lee wasn't smiling when he came into Señor Legumbre's VegMex Restaurant that Thursday. He was wearing a new sportcoat, new slacks, and new Italian shoes, but he looked pale under his tan. His walk reminded you of a kid coming in after school to write something a hundred times on the blackboard. Tucked under his arm was a fat hardcover copy of *Alas, My Love.*

"What's that godawful smell?" he inquired as he sat opposite me on the sunlit patio section of the place.

I obligingly sniffed the air. "Chili powder?"

"No, no—something vile."

"Guacamole?"

When he set the novel down on the glass tabletop, I noticed his hands were trembling slightly. The dozens of tiny yellow paper bookmarks fluttered like leaves in the wind. "Are you wearing a new aftershave?" he said.

"Matter of fact, yes. One of our advertising clients just intro—"

"Smells like a lumberjack's armpit."

"It's supposed to. What happened to your euphoria of the other day?"

He glanced around at the scatter of other lunch customers. "How many people have to buy a damn book to put it on the bestseller list?"

I shrugged. "I don't know. A hundred thousand?"

"More than that probably." Lee sighed. "And there are hordes of others taking it out of libraries. That's dreadful to contemplate."

"Isn't the novel any good?"

"In less than three weeks the paperback edition'll hit the stands. Paperback book critics no doubt have review copies already." He took another look around. "Some of the pinheads right in this room have read *Alas, My Love.*"

"Possibly. But what does that—"

"It's about—" He leaned toward me, his voice dropping low. "You haven't read it?"

"Nope. I read mostly nonfict—"

"The godawful thing is about *me!*" he said in an anguished whisper. "About me and Emily!"

I scratched at my nose. "You mean about a couple sort of like you two. A television writer married to an actress who—"

"Don't I get paid handsome sums for expressing ideas clearly and concisely?" he asked. "*No*, I don't mean the damn thing is about a couple with a few similarities. I mean, cuz, the book is about me and Emily!"

"What they call a roman à clef?"

"What I call a knife in the back, a rug pulled out from under my life, a scaffold trap sprung beneath my hopes and—"

"That's right," I realized. "It's about adultery, isn't it?"

"*Alas, My Love*, old chum," he said, teeth on the verge of grinding, "is about how Emily has an affair behind my back. Emily, who I've always believed was one of the few supportive and trustworthy women in this entire godawful town. My other wife, you know, was a—"

"But this is fiction," I reminded him, reaching across to tap the book's bright dustjacket. "Even if you noticed a superficial resemblance to you and—"

"Superficial? Do you think I'd be on the verge of a total collapse if the halfwit resemblances were merely superficial?" Sighing again, he gazed at the high adobe wall around the restaurant patio. "Things had been going so well, too. The whole town knows Bosco Cheever gave me the nod for this miniseries. The trades are even hinting they'll get somebody like Richard Chamberlain for one of the leads. I'm hot again. MSG called me yesterday about working on a new series pilot for them. *Us*, *People*, *TV Life*, and *Mammon* have all called, begging for interviews. Even that pinhead Jess Rawlins wants to do a story for *The National Intruder*. Two years ago he was underfoot all the time, when I was writing *Passion* for CBS. Lately, though, it's sheepish grins and furtive nods from across the room." He folded his hands to keep them from quivering. "Then I had to go and read this damn book."

"You had to if you're going to adapt it."

"The horns of a dilemma," he said. "I don't have the heart to continue on this project, yet I need the damn dough and the credit."

"So do it," I advised.

"They'll all laugh at me," Lee said forlornly. " 'The poor cuckold, scripting his own humiliation.' "

"Most of the people in your circle probably don't know what cuckold means, so—"

"They sure as hell know the principle involved."

"Tell you what, I'll read the book. Maybe you're imagining these parallels between you—"

"This isn't the result of a deranged mind at the end of its tether," he assured me, his voice rising as he snatched *Alas, My Love* up off the table. "Bosco Cheever doesn't offer nearly twice scale to a scriptwriter who's on the verge of going bonkers—" He paused, grew thoughtful. "I wonder if Bosco *knows*. He did give me a rather sheepish look once when my agent and I were in negot—"

"Say, you airheads, this ain't a literary tearoom." The stocky moustached proprietor had come stalking over to our table. "You want to read books, hire a— Oops! Sorry, Mr. Branner."

"That's okay, Lyle."

"I know you're on the rise again," apologized the owner. "I just didn't recognize you from the back. It's my steadfast policy never to insult people unless they're on the way down." He glanced over at me appraisingly.

"My chum's neither on the rise nor the decline," explained Lee. "He's an advertising account exec and has remained on a successful dead level for untold eons."

"I got some great ideas for ads," confided Lyle to me.

"We'll order shortly," Lee said.

"Sure, take your time." He strode off, pausing to snarl at the patrons of another table.

"See? My status has improved," said Lee. "When I was in here last month, Lyle kicked me in the slats." He opened the novel to the place marked by the first of the dozens of slips of yellow paper.

I noticed that nearly half the left-hand page had been marked with a pale-yellow highlighting pen. "Maybe we ought to order pretty soon. I've got a client meeting at—"

"Listen to this." Lee cleared his throat. " 'She stood poised upon the precipitous diving board above the liquid turquoise of the sun-drenched opulent swimming pool. Her petite figure was exquisite, a nubile statue of frozen poetry capped by her desirable auburn hair, which was the color of burnished brass forged in the smithy of idolatry. Jacques Rambeau's manhood was aroused as he drank in the ravishing radiance of her lithe—' Well?"

"Vivid writer."

"The prose is godawful. But don't you recognize my wife when you hear her described?"

I shook my head. "Lots of women are small and have red hair."

"So thought I." He ran his finger along the underscored paragraph. " 'On the lush inner portion of her maddening left thigh was a delicate scar in the shape of a crescent moon.' See?"

"Does Emily have a scar the shape of a crescent moon on her thigh?"

"Surely you've noticed it, all the times you've been poolside at our place."

"We were only there once, Lee, four years ago. Tell you the truth, when I swim I take off my glasses and I can't see a—"

"Well, she does and this Renfrew bastard describes it exactly. Along with many other intimate details of her structure." He slammed the book shut. "He also recounts, as best he can in his halting prose, her speech patterns, attitudes, likes and dislikes. He even knows that her favorite after-sex snack is popcorn with garlic salt smeared on it."

"Emily's a well known actress. Lots of magazine articles might have—"

"No, this guy knows her, cuz." He flipped *Alas, My Love* open again. "How about this passage? 'He was tall and reed-slim, a Lincolnesque sapling of a man with a foursquare face and hands like slabs of raw lumber.' That's me—called Lance Bengal in this book."

"That could be a young Gregory Peck or dozens of other guys."

"Okay, I grant you some of this could be coincidence," Lee admitted, commencing to leaf through the pages. "But as Renfrew goes on and describes this disgusting and steamy affair between Emilia Bengal and Jacques Rambeau behind the noble and unsuspecting back of Lance Bengal, he—"

"Is Bengal a writer like you?"

"No, that's switched around. Emilia's the writer, her husband's a fading movie actor, and Rambeau is a hotshot TV director."

"Which isn't very close to your—"

"Allow me to continue," he requested while turning to another marked passage. "Every time Emily and—every time Emilia and Jacques meet to perpetuate their filthy relationship, all the dates match."

"What dates?"

"If Lance Bengal is out of town or stuck late at the studio the dates given in the damn book match exactly with the dates that I myself, in real life, was out of town or delayed at the studios over the past four, five years. Every damn one!"

"How can you be certain of that?"

"Because I keep a journal. I went back, once I realized what I was reading here, and double-checked," he said. "I'm going to leave all my notes and journals to the University of—"

"You're really convinced this novel is a fictionalized account of an affair between Renfrew and your wife?"

"Yes, there's no other answer." He closed the book once more. "It's tearing me apart."

"But if Emily'd been having an affair for years, you'd have suspected some—"

"Has your wife ever fooled around?"

"No, she doesn't go in for—"

"How can you be sure?"

"I just am."

"You go out of town on godawful assignments for your nitwit agency all the time. There's no way you can be absolutely certain she—"

"I trust her."

"Ah, I trusted Emily, too." He held up the thick novel. "And look."

I said, "What does Emily say?"

"I haven't mentioned it to her."

"Why not? If you're brooding about whether or not it's true, you—"

"I'm not brooding about that. I know this godawful book is true, a thinly veiled account of my trusted wife's infidelity."

"Maybe, though, she could suggest another explanation for how—"

"I don't intend to bring the subject up with her," he said firmly. "I have a certain pride and I'll be damned if I'll go sniveling to her over this."

After a few seconds, I suggested, "Maybe this Jason Renfrew, Junior, could offer some explan—"

"Oh, I'll find *him*," he said, turning the back of the book toward me. "He's a mystery man right now, but I'll track him to his lair."

The author's photo on the dustjacket was a shadowy thing, showing only the back of a man wearing a trenchcoat with the collar turned up and a sport-car cap. You couldn't get any real idea what he looked like.

"It might be better to forget all about it," I said. "Just do the script, collect your money, and—"

"*Forget?* Forget about the one man in the world who's made a mockery of my life. Emily has been my main source of inspiration all these happy years and— No, I'll find Renfrew, whoever he may be, and wherever he is on the face of this earth."

"If he's really writing about you and Emily, he's got to be in Greater Los Angeles somewhere."

"I'll find him and teach him a lesson."

"Hey, what do you mean? Doing any violence to him'll only cause you more—"

"Once I confront the man, I'll decide exactly how to handle him," he said. "There are certain unwritten laws that apply to situations such as this."

"My advice," I said, "is to—"

"This has gone beyond advice."

✗

Two days later, I had to fly to Iola, Wisconsin, and so I wasn't around while Lee Branner carried out most of his investigation to find out who the mysterious Jason Renfrew, Junior, really was. We did talk by phone once or twice, so I know what he was up to. One of our clients, Mother Zooker's Cookies, has its main offices back in Iola. You've no doubt seen pictures of the famous two-story-high giant cookie jar that houses the company's offices there. We've used, at the insistence of the company, the cookie-jar offices in quite a few of our print ads. Millions of people associate that quaint jug-shaped building with Mother Zooker's Cookies and the slogan "Nearly As Good As Homemade!"

The problem we had in Iola was that three members of a radical terrorist group called the Skid Row Commandos had waylaid and robbed a Kropfhauser Armored Car, stolen $420,000, and were, due to a complex and highly unlikely string of circumstances, holed up in the cookie jar. They'd been there for twenty hours when I was sent to Wisconsin, and by that time television-news viewers all across the country had seen the famous cookie-jar offices surrounded by armed police.

It was publicity certainly, yet we were afraid a certain percentage of people would start associating our cookies, all twenty-six Goodness-to-Gracious Varieties, with crime and violence. My job was to come up with a quick radio campaign that would cash in on the media attention while at the same time disassociating us from these wild-eyed, bearded terrorists.

The assignment kept me in Iola for close to two weeks. The armored-car robbers held out in there for seven and a half days and by the time they surrendered and came out, the cookie jar was riddled with bullet holes. I had to work out some print ads to minimize that, too, and also convince the client to patch the thing up as soon as possible. Certain members of the Mother Zooker board wanted to flaunt the holes and launch a campaign about their cookies being made while the bakeries were under siege and so on. I talked them out of that, pointing out that gunshots and cookies make for poor fusion. But it took a full three days of meetings and conferences.

✗

All the while, Lee was on the trail of Jason Renfrew, Junior. It is possible that originally he intended only to confront the guy. As the pursuit dragged on, however, his anger and outrage increased. Having written several police shows over the years, he knew how to go about his search in a methodical way. Even though he was dead sure Renfrew was a pen name, he patiently searched through all the local phonebooks and city directories. He even used his contacts with the motor-vehicle people and the phone company. There was no listing anywhere. Not even an unlisted phone for anyone named Jason Renfrew, Junior.

Next, feigning casualness, he called the producer of the miniseries.

Bosco Cheever had a thin nasal voice and a terse style of speech. "So?" was his greeting when Lee phoned him at his Burbank offices.

"I've been reading *Alas, My Love*," began Lee. "It's a—a great book, Bosco. I really appreciate the opportunity to turn it into television, it's going to be—"

"Okay, okay."

"The thing is, Bosco, I—what's that gurgling sound?"

"Toilet flushing."

"You're in the john? You're taking this call on that phone of yours in there?"

"Yep."

"Far be it from me to criticize—you're a man of culture and sensibility, Bosco—but flushing the toilet while talking business lacks dignity."

"I don't do it with everybody. What's up?"

"I think it'd be a good idea for Renfrew and me to talk over a few things. Minor character problems and—"

"Who's Renfrew?"

"The fellow who wrote the book."

"Oh, him. Impossible."

"Why?"

"Who can figure writers? It's in his contract. No direct contact with us."

"Wouldn't he make an exception if—"

"Nope. That all?"

"Who's his agent?"

"Ugh. That Lena Kapp bimbo."

"Thanks. I'll have the treatment in to you by no later than—"

"So long."

Lee heard water running as the phone was being hung up.

✗

He tried to charm fat Lena Kapp. "You're looking well, Lena. Trim and fit."

She sat, immense in a flowered caftan, behind her small blond desk. "Horse crap," she replied. "I look like a sack of lard. Who's your agent these days?"

"Lowell Swinefort."

"Lowell Swinefort." She chuckled. "I thought he'd died."

"He's alive and doing very—"

"Sure, like I'm trim and fit."

He looked beyond her. Out the windows of her tower office he saw a private plane go drifting by through the haze. "The reason I—"

"I'm not taking on any new clients."

"No, no. I'm happy with Lowell. The reason—"

"How can you be happy with a pinhead who's coked out of his nut ninety-nine percent of the time and hasn't gotten you work in two years?"

"I was only out of work seventeen months. And I've just signed to do the *Alas, My Love* miniseries."

"I know. That was Renfrew's idea. Sounded suicidal to me, getting a washed-out hack to take a—"

"Wait now." He stiffened in the low chair. "Renfrew suggested me for this scripting job?"

"It sure as heck wasn't my idea. Renfrew had enough clout with Cheever to convince him you were the one."

"Then Renfrew and Bosco have met?"

She shrugged, her massive body jiggling. "Who knows? Renfrew is too damned independent for me, but the book's already earned almost two million five so I don't kvetch too much."

"Lena, I'd like to meet Renfrew. Talk the book over with him, explain how I want to approach it for television."

"No." She stood and the floor shook. "Jason Renfrew, Junior, is a very private man. He grants no interviews, won't see anyone. It's fouled up the chance to get him extra publicity, but—"

"Since he knows my work, Lena, he'd make an exception in—"

"Listen, schmuck, he won't even see *Life* magazine. You think he's going to talk to you?" She rumbled toward the door. "See you around campus."

Lee stood, remaining next to his chair. "A letter? Can you forward him a letter in which I'll outline my questions and feelings and—"

"He doesn't want to hear anything from anybody." She jerked her office door open wide. "I don't send him anything but money."

"You've seen him, haven't you?"

Her tiny eyes avoided meeting his. "Haven't so far, no," she answered. "He's a recluse."

"Don't you even talk to him on the phone?"

"He doesn't have a phone."

"Renfrew is a pen name, isn't it?"

"Is it?" She nodded at the open doorway. "Scram now, Branner."

✗

Lee didn't do any writing on the television treatment of *Alas, My Love* over the next few days. He'd sit in his studio, gazing out at the calm Pacific far below, with the novel resting in his lap.

Every time he started to try to work on adapting it, he'd become distracted by one of the passages he'd marked earlier.

"You know what my mother used to fix me when I came trudging home from school?" inquired Emilia as she reposed in silken but sparsely clad luxury upon the languid bed in their Beverly Glen hideaway. *"Ketchup sandwiches. Yes, just ketchup spread on cheap white bread. We were disgustingly poor in my youth, dearest Jacques ..."*

"Ketchup sandwiches," he muttered. "That's what Emily's halfwit mother fixed her. She's always telling me that sad story. Even on our honeymoon, she— Hey!"

He leaped up, book thumping to the floor, and ran to the side window of his studio. Scowling, he scanned the distant trees and scrub on the nearest hillside. He'd sensed the brief flash of sunlight hitting the lenses of binoculars.

Even though he remained a the window for several minutes, he couldn't make out anything.

Finally, book tucked under his arm, he left. He drove his Mercedes over into the Beverly Glen canyon, searching for the lovers' hide-away cottage as described in the book. He had no luck, and one suspicious old lady who was out pruning her flowers wrote down his license number.

✗

Four more uneasy days went by. He hadn't found Renfrew and he hadn't written a word. When Bosco called, Lee lied, told him he was turning out pages of the treatment each and every day and would have it finished by the following week.

That evening, as dusk settled over the beach, he decided to talk to his wife about the whole business.

"Must you bring that thing to the dinner table?" she asked when he plumped *Alas, My Love* down next to his plate.

She was a slim auburn-haired woman, and as attractive and bright as Renfrew had described her.

"It's my work," he said.

"You know how much I dote on you and what you write, Lee," Emily said, passing him the salad bowl. "Still, you've been a real grump ever since you got this damn assignment."

"Can you," he inquired, watching her intently, "guess why?"

"I suppose it's because you haven't done a day's work in two and a half years and you feel rusty. That's understandable. But—"

182   Adam and Eve on a Raft: Mystery Stories

"Seventeen months. I was only without an assignment for seventeen months. Emily, I've read this damn book from cover to cover. Twice."

"I hear it isn't very well written."

"Oh, so? You haven't read it?"

"You know I read mostly anthropology and—"

"It's about us!" He'd lost control, was shouting. "About you and me and—this Renfrew bastard!" He slapped the cryptic photo of the author. "Its six hundred and forty-two godawful pages deal in minute detail with the affair this lout had with you over the past five years or so. And about how I, fool that I am, never suspected a blinking thing. Never even guessed I was being cuckolded."

"Being what?"

"Ah, that's perfect. I knew you'd pull that, avoid the major issue and pick at my language."

"Have you stopped taking those pills Dr. Hedley gave you?"

"What the hell has that got to do—"

"You're getting all purplish in the face and froth is forming on your pale lips," she pointed out. "I think you ought to take something to calm you down."

"You deny it?" He was on his feet now, waving the novel in the air. "That I had an affair with—Renfrew, is it?"

"Here I looked up to you as the ideal wife, a constant source of inspiration for me. Now—" His shoulders slumped, the book dropped to his side.

She rose gracefully to her feet. "Our relationship is better than this, Lee," she said quietly. "I won't have you accusing me of—"

"Did you or didn't you?"

"I'll be sleeping in the guest room tonight." She left him there at the dinner table with the cooling food.

✗

The next morning at dawn, while running along the grey beach alone, Lee suddenly halted. "Lena sends him royalty checks," he said, snapping his fingers.

That afternoon he went into the building on Wilshire where Lena Kapp had her offices. By hiding in a deserted conference room that had once been used by a now defunct cable-television service, he was able to linger in the building until it was locked up for the night. Then he went sneaking up two flights to Lena's suite and, after determining the agent and her staff were long gone, let himself in.

On the address wheel on her desk he found Jason Renfrew, Junior's address given as 232 Otramar Road, San Amaro Beach, California.

Lee slipped free of the building by way of a service door, hurried to his Mercedes, and went driving down the night coast to the nearby beach town.

✗

There was a prickly fog that night. Lee spent twenty minutes finding Otramar Road and nearly ten more spotting 232, which for some reason was situated between 242 and 248. Renfrew lived in a cottage that sat on the downside of the twisting road, its back hanging out over the dark beach and propped up on stilts.

He parked his car up the road from the place, sat in it for a few minutes. He discovered he was breathing openmouthed, nearly panting. Pressing his lips together, he opened the glove compartment and yanked out the .32 revolver he kept there.

He tucked that into the waistband of his trousers and climbed free of the car. Striding, he hurried down to the front door of the cottage.

Lights were on and he heard an electric typewriter going, along with a hi-fi playing Beethoven.

Lee didn't knock. He just turned the knob of the door, found it wasn't locked, and shoved his way into the cottage.

Seated at a woebegone old desk, facing the doorway, was a small sandy-haired man of thirty-one. He lifted his glasses up, resting them atop his head, and stared at Lee.

"You, huh?" Lee crossed the threadbare matte rug. "Jess Rawlins, a hack reporter for that godawful *National Intruder*."

"What brings you to my—"

"This is terrible. It's bad enough she makes a cuckold of me, but to do it with a schlub like—"

"Makes you a what?"

"It's disenchanting," muttered Lee, edging nearer to the staring Rawlins. "She, the woman who, up until now, inspired me to my greatest creative heights has a shabby affair with you. Then, you slime, you turn it all into a sleazy novel and to top it off tell them to hire me to do the TV adaptation."

"Lee, listen." Rawlins rose carefully out of his chair. "I admit I wrote the book."

"Of course you did." He tugged out the revolver and pointed it at him. "You defile my wife, brag about it in print, make me the butt of Lord knows how many cruel jokes. Now I'll get even with you for that!"

"Lee, you know I'm just a hack—a writer for hire."

Lee fired twice.

"Just the front." Both slugs caught Rawlins in the chest. He cried out and went stumbling back until he smacked into the window behind him. "I only ghosted the book for your wife. She wanted to make some extra money so—" He slumped, fell dead.

Lee lowered the gun. Then he realized what Rawlins had been trying to tell him.

BARBECUE BOB

Although he may end up in prison, he'll probably make at least $100,000 this year. That's not bad money, even these days. And the prison sentence may be light, only a few years. But, of course, what he originally had in mind was making at least $750,000 and never seeing the inside of a cell. What rankles, too, is that he'll be getting the money not for being clever and cunning, but simply because his plan got screwed up the way it did and made him an instant celebrity of sorts. Two of the television networks are bidding for the rights to turn his life into a movie and close to a dozen magazines and tabloids are anxious to buy his exclusive story.

He hadn't come up with his plan the hot, hazy morning I encountered him on Fifth Avenue. My advertising agency had sent me East from Los Angeles because one of our clients was having some trouble launching a new soft drink in the tri-state marketing area. The stuff was called NoKo, a revolutionary cola that contained no sugar, no caffeine, and absolutely nothing artificial. Initial consumer reaction had been less than satisfactory. People were saying NoKo tasted like tap water.

I almost stepped on Ezra Gates and passed on. He was sprawled on a lower step of St. Norbert's Cathedral, sound asleep amidst a scatter of weatherbeaten and trod-upon lithographs. Ezra was wearing tattered maroon sweatpants, very old Adidas running shoes, no socks, and a T-shirt that featured the faded slogan *Kiss Me! I'm Serbo-Croatian!* across its hole-riddled back. His sandy hair was too long, his beard at least a week old.

Actually, I didn't recognize Ezra right off, but I happened to step on one of the drawings and while I was freeing it from my shoe I spotted his style. Crouching, I studied the sleeping man's dirty, bewhiskered face.

"Ezra?" I poked his shoulder through a hole in the shirt.

"All my own work." He sat up suddenly, like a jumping jack who'd had his string yanked. "Unlike some so-called street artists who pass off cheesy Taiwan prints as their— Oh, the shame of it all!" He recognized me and brought one stained hand up to strike his breast.

"What's been happening to you, Ezra?"

"Incredible, isn't it?" He got to his feet, his joints making odd creaking noises. "When last we met, on your earlier trip to the Apple just six scant months ago, I—"

"It was only four months ago," I corrected.

"Ah," he sighed. "My fall from grace has been even more meteoric than I realized. Then I was the boy wonder of the advertising world, head art director of the vast and prestigious Madison Avenue advertising firm of Shestack & Bensink. Now I—"

"You weren't exactly a boy wonder, Ezra," I reminded him. "In fact, nobody can be a boy wonder at thirty-seven."

"Your long years as a West Coast account-exec have hardened your— " He paused, noticing that I'd been cautiously sniffing the air. "Save your snoz, you won't smell any booze on my breath. It wasn't liquor brought me to this, nor drugs either."

"What then?"

He wiped his nose on his wrist. "Love."

"Not again?"

"What does that heartless remark mean?"

"When I first met you, out in L.A. nine years ago, you'd followed a girl out there. That chubby redhead who was doing *I Married a Fat Girl* and—"

"Aw, that wasn't love." He hit his narrow chest again. "This is love."

"How long," I inquired, "have you been out of work?"

"I'm working." Ezra pointed at the sprawl of his drawings with one foot. "Freelancing. An old and noble profession."

"Look, let me buy you a cup of coffee," I offered, glancing around. "How about that Barbecue Bob Restaurant across the —"

"No—nope," he said, his teeth grinding. "Not there. I'm not especially fond of Bob." Eyes narrowed, he was staring across at the huge photo of Barbecue Bob that graced the front of this outlet of the nationwide fast-food chain. Bob, crisp chef's hat cocked over one eye, was grinning his famous plump grin, the one that appeared in all the Barbecue Bob print ads and on all the twenty-second, thirty-second, and minute television spots.

"What the hell does he have to do with—"

"He stole my true love."

"Barbecue Bob? They guy who hustles BQ Burgers on TV and touts his Orgy-Style Salad Bar with—"

"He's just an actor, you know." Ezra sank down to sit on a cathedral step. "There's not really a Barbecue Bob, only a conglomerate based in Texas someplace." He nodded toward the giant grinning face across the hazy avenue. "His real name is Barry Katchall. He's fifty-one years old and he's stolen Zinia from me."

I sat down next to him, pushing aside a drawing of the Empire State Building.

"Not another model, Ezra? You're alluding to Zinia Fless, aren't you? The top advertising model in America?"

"Don't you think I have the depth of character to lose my heart to, say, Zinia Zankowitz, the noted Talmudic scholar? Or Zinia Buckler, the long-distance runner?"

"No, you don't. You're always getting tangled up with skinny, dippy models or actresses with brains the size of gumdrops," I told him. "Each encounter is worse than the last, Ezra, and leaves you in worse shape."

"I'll bounce back, never fear."

"What makes you think that?"

"I have talent," he replied. "I'm an artist. Unlike that fat lout Barry Katchall. I'll win Zinia away from —"

"Geeze, is that perspective way off, mister." A lean high school boy had stopped to survey the drawings. He was pointing at one of the Brooklyn Bridge. "You futzed up your horizon line so the—"

"Take a hike, schmuck," suggested Ezra.

"The reason I mention it, I'm an artist myself. We're studying perspective at the New York High School of Comics and Graphic Arts this semest—"

"I studied at the School of Kicking Wise Punks in the Slats." Ezra started to rise. "In a moment I'll demonstrate my award-winning technique on —"

"Okay, okay," said the youth, moving away. "Personally, I advocate solidarity among artists, but you obviously don't share that view."

"A top art director at Shestack & Bensink," sighed Ezra, settling back down on the step. "Now schoolboys criticize me."

"How come you left the agency?"

"After Barry Katchall stole Zinia, I—well, I found it difficult to concentrate on my work. I wasn't sleeping nights, due to the heartache and the fact I was watching his posh townhouse on Riverside Drive for a glimpse of Zinia as she came and went. One fine day, Shestack, in the morn, and Bensink, in the afternoon, found me dozing across my drawing board."

"You were sound asleep just now," I mentioned. "Are you still dogging her?"

"Zinia spends a lot of time at his place and they use it as a base of operations when they depart for the lavish parties and glittering bistros they frequent. I've found a spot in a nearby alleyway where I can watch the rear entrance of Barry Katchall's townhouse. They use that entrance because he doesn't want the public to follow his comings and goings. I never approach them, but now and then I snap a few photos with special night film. Here, I think I've got a few of her wearing a terrific cocktail dress that—"

"Ezra, I'm tied up the rest of this week," I said, standing up. "But let's have lunch next Monday. I won't be going back to the Coast for another week at least."

"Where are you staying?"

I mentioned my hotel on the Park.

Ezra said, "Okay, I'll phone you there on Monday morning. Meantime, I'll think of a place we can go where you won't be embarrassed to be seen with me in my present shabby state."

"We can go an—"

"No, I see it in your eyes."

"Okay, call me Monday."

"I will," Ezra promised, crouching to rearrange his display of his work.

✗

We met, at Ezra's suggestion, at Chez Swann, a fairly expensive French restaurant on East Forty-ninth. I arrived first, and during the ten minutes I spent alone at our tiny table in a far corner I was somewhat uneasy. If Ezra came shuffling into Chez Swann looking as he had when I'd seen him sprawled on the steps of the cathedral last week, I doubted they'd seat him.

But it was a changed Ezra Gates who showed up for lunch — clean-shaven, hair trimmed, wearing a conservative business suit and a somber tie-with a briefcase and a moderately patronizing smile for the waiter who led him over to our table.

"I don't speak French," Ezra said, sitting, "but allow me to say *j'arrivée*."

"Arrived where?"

"On top of the world."

"You've come a long way since last week."

He chuckled. "You've grown increasingly cynical out there in lotusland." After glancing around at the other patrons, he placed his black briefcase on the crisp white tablecloth. Unzipping it, he slid a hand inside. "I've made a discovery which, in its way, rivals those of Thomas Alva Edison, Leonardo daVinci, and Dennis Wepman."

"Who's Wepman?"

"I think he's the guy who invented the paper clip." Ezra extracted a newspaper clipping and passed it across to me. "Or maybe it was the safety pin."

The heading on the six-inch one-column item read TRIVIA EXPERT VANISHES and the subhead added FOUL PLAY SUSPECTED IN AUTHOR'S DISAPPEARANCE.

Someone named Myron Zeppelin, age fifty-six, of Queens, hadn't been seen since late last week and a cousin of his had finally gone to the police. Zeppelin was the author of *Show Biz Triv*, *More Show Biz Triv*, and *Yet More Show Biz Triv*.

"What's Myron Zeppelin got to do with anything?" I set the clipping down next to my salad fork.

Reaching out, Ezra retrieved it and carefully returned it to the briefcase. "I know where he is."

"Somebody offering a reward?"

He laughed again. "Cousin's offering a hundred dollars for information."

"How's a hundred bucks going to put you on top of the world?"

"It won't, but seven hundred and fifty thousand will."

I asked, "Who's offering that?"

"Let me pep up my yarn with some visuals." Ezra's hand snaked back inside the briefcase. "This photo is cropped, for reasons that'll soon be obvious." He produced a nine-by-twelve glossy and passed it to me.

A grey-haired man, who looked unconscious or worse, was being carried along what was probably an alley. This was an enlargement, and grainy, and showed only the man and the hands of those who were lugging him. I noticed a large ring on the finger of one of the unseen pallbearers.

"This is Myron Zeppelin?" I asked.

"The late Myron Zeppelin, yes. Nice clear portrait of the fellow-one of several I was able to shoot a few evenings back."

Dropping the photo to the table, I said, "You saw somebody kill this guy, and instead of helping you took pictures?"

Laughing, Ezra said, "This is New York, old buddy, and there's a long and time-honored tradition of not getting mixed up in other people's troubles. But in this case, I didn't see old Myron getting snuffed out and shuffled off. I was merely on the spot when they were disposing of his earthly remains."

"This has something to do with Barbecue Bob," I said, "with this Barry Katchall who plays him."

"Ah, indeed it does." Ezra pointed a the hand with the ring. "Note the initials BB on that little dingus there. 'Tis the very same gaudy bauble Barry Katchall wears in all the commercials."

"You were a witness to this part, though? You actually saw Katchall toting the corpse out the back way of his townhouse?"

"I surely did." Ezra took back the photo.

"Then why haven't you told the cops?"

"You're not paying close enough attention. Remember my mention of seven hundred and fifty thousand?"

Frowning, I said, "Blackmail."

"I prefer to call it retribution," said Ezra. "One of the last times Zinia and I met she threw in my face that Barry Katchall had seven hundred and fifty thousand dollars in the bank, whereas I had at the time total assets in the vicinity of a thousand six hundred twenty-three."

"You ought to forget this," I advised. "Just turn your pictures over to the police."

"Nope," he said, shaking his head. "This is too good for the police. See, Shestack & Bensink are involved, too. Which cheers me up no end."

"That's right," I recalled, "your old agency handles the Barbecue Bob account."

"How do you think Zinia met Barry Katchall in the first place? While up at S & B visiting me."

"Where does the agency come into this business with the dead—"

"That other pair of hands in the picture. They belong to Shestack."

"He was in on the killing, too?"

"No, no." Ezra rested both elbows on the table. "Here's what happened. I was at my post as usual the other night, waiting for Zinia to show. The minutes, then the hours dragged by. I was about ready to pack up when I spotted Myron Zeppelin, looking highly furtive, skulking up to the back entry of Barry Katchall's townhouse. The hour was well after midnight."

"Why would he have been visiting Katchall?"

"Unlike some trivia experts, Myron Zeppelin did a good deal of first-hand research. Rumors have reached my ears before this that he was not above making a more direct profit from some of the unusual items he unearthed."

"He was a blackmailer, too?"

"He was a blackmailer, I'm an avenger," Ezra corrected. "Anyway, after Zeppelin had been inside the place for less than fifteen minutes, I heard what I thought were shots. Two of them."

"Didn't anybody in the neighborhood—"

"This, need I keep reminding you, is New York," Ezra said. "People don't pay attention to stuff like that. Anyway, minutes after that, a familiar limo comes barreling up and parks near the back door of the townhouse. Shestack himself alights. I, sensing the opportunity for some nice photos, ease ever closer. I get him going in and, much better even, I get him and a very disturbed-looking Barry Katchall carrying the body out and dumping it in the trunk of the limo."

"Why would Shestack be a party to—"

"Do you know what the Barbecue Bob account bills?"

"Must be about fifteen million anyway."

"It's twenty-two million," Ezra told me. "Shestack & Bensink get about twenty percent of that for handling the account. Now if Barry Katchall is arrested for murder, where does that leave S & B? Better yet, where does it leave the nearly five hundred restaurants? Fact is, the five hundredth is opening later this very week here in Manhattan. Where does that leave the Barbecue Bob chain of restaurants across this land of ours? Not to mention menus, billboards, television commercials, and a good many etceteras. That nitwit's face is on millions of pieces of advertising material. 'Barbecue Bob Murders Trivia Expert!' That's not the kind of publicity any of them want. It's worth millions of bucks to keep Barry Katchall free."

"But he obviously did murder Zeppelin."

"Sure, that's exactly what he did," said Ezra, head nodding. "Barry Katchall is a very high-strung, nervous, and emotional man, given to outbursts of temper. I learned that about him when I was still with S & B and sat in on some tapings of the Barbecue Bob commercials."

"The police," I repeated. "You have to take this to them, Ezra."

"Nope, I take it to Barry Katchall." He grinned. "Fact is, I've already started my campaign."

"Campaign?"

"I'm going to wear him down a bit," he explained. "Work a sort of teaser ad campaign on the oaf. Hints on the telephone, bits of the photos via the mails. By the time I offer to sell him the negatives for seven hundred and fifty thousand dollars, he'll rush to the payoff spot."

"That'll make you a —"

"Happy and contented man," Ezra said. "Once I have money, large amounts of it, and Barry Katchall has nothing much, then I'll be able to get Zinia back again. Although she's lovely and bright, she is, I admit, mercenary."

"She earns quite a bit on her own."

"Okay, let's say I don't win her, which strikes me as highly unlikely," he said. "Even so, I'll get even with Barry Katchall for stealing her away. And that seven hundred fifty thousand won't be bad, either."

"Listen, Ezra. I've heard a few things about this Katchall guy since I've been in Manhat—"

"Who authorized you to poke your snoot in my—"

"Scuttlebutt. Since you mentioned he'd blighted your love life, I started paying attention to what people—"

"Okay, so you had my best interests at heart."

"The point is, Barry Katchall has a reputation for being a highly vindictive man, very quick tempered," I said. "He acts on impulse and he can be violent when—"

"Don't I know that, old chum? Don't I have documentary proof of that very fact?" He patted the briefcase.

"He's the sort of guy, I hear, who'll cut off his nose to spite his face."

"Hey, there's a fresh new phrase. They pay you that outrageously high salary to come up with bright sayings like that?"

I said quietly, "He's liable to try something irrational if you goad him, Ezra. He won't care about saving his neck, only about fixing your wagon."

"Another sparkling new saying coined before my very ears." Ezra leaned back and chuckled. "Seriously, I appreciate your concern, but it ain't necessary. I can outfox that schlep with the greatest of ease."

✗

For the next few days I didn't see or talk to Ezra. I know he tried to get in touch with me, but I was tied up in endless meetings with the NoKo people. In an attempt to improve the new beverage's taste, they'd modified the basic formula. This version, when testmarketed in Yonkers, caused some unanticipated side effects. A mild euphoria was the most frequent effect, but there'd also been reports of visions, hallucinations, and, in a few instances, out-of-body experiences. While a majority of the NoKo executives wanted to downplay the incidents, a few argued that this would make a good basis for a campaign. The arguments pro and con took all of my waking hours and quite a few of those when I should've been sleeping.

Meanwhile, Ezra pressed on with his campaign. Huddled in his sparsely furnished apartment in the West Eighties, he fashioned threatening letters that blended striking typography with snippets of the incriminating photographs of Barbecue Bob and the ad executive hauling off the deceased blackmailer. He also made provocative calls to Katchall's unlisted number.

While slouched in his real leather lounging chair, a remnant of better days, he'd monitor all the shows he knew ran Barbecue Bob commercials. When Katchall was beaming plumply and inviting "C'mon to my place, folks. Gorge yourself on my Gargantua Burgers and my Bob-Chokin' Sack-o-Fries. Help yourself to free shrimp, lobster tails, and pigs' feet. Stuff crisp salad into your maw, guzzle beer and wine. All for the amazingly low low price of just—", Ezra would phone the actor.

"Yes?" Katchall sounded ever more nervous each time he answered.

"This is the voice of your conscience again, old chum. Repent!

Murder will out!"

"Listen, you. Who the hell are—"

Ezra hung up.

The mailed threats followed a similar pattern. Above and between tastefully cropped photos of Myron Zeppelin's funeral procession would be such slogans as *The Wages of Sin Is* and *Murder Will Out!*

Ezra kept this up for several days, gradually introducing hints that the pictures might be for sale into his graphics and visuals.

As I understand it, he intended to give Katchall a large shock at the gala opening of the five hundredth Barbecue Bob Restaurant on Madison in the East Fifties. Then he'd send the request for the $750,000.

After that, there'd be just one more phone call to set up a safe place for the exchange of money and negatives.

✗

It happened that I had an hour between client meetings on the evening of the opening of the restaurant. With not enough time to go out for dinner, I slipped into a deserted screening room in our Lexington Avenue offices and sent out for a sandwich. While I was eating, I turned on one of the room's television sets.

Most of the local news shows were offering live coverage of the Barbecue Bob festivities and I flipped to one of the stations just as their report came on.

"I see a lot of celebrities in this ravenous crowd," the handsome newsman was saying, "all gathered here to celebrate a fast-food triumph of— Hey, strolling in now is that jovial gentleman known as Barbecue Bob!"

Katchall's chef's hat drooped and his smile looked as though it were pinned in place as he made his way into the bright chrome-and-leatherette restaurant. Following close behind was the stunning red-haired Zinia Fless, wearing a very spare dress. She was smiling at the crowd gathered in the restaurant but seemed somewhat preoccupied.

Then I spotted Ezra. He was modestly disguised with a wispy false moustache and dark glasses. He wore an orange windbreaker over a T-shirt. The jacket was zipped up nearly to his chin. Later I learned that Ezra had silkscreened the shirt himself, using the old equipment he had in his shabby apartment. It was an excellent job.

His assumption was that neither Katchall nor Zinia would

recognize him while he made his move and then vanished into the crowd. And even if one of them did recognize him, he intended to lie low someplace until he made his request for the money. His scenario was simple. He'd catch Barbecue Bob's attention, swiftly unzip his coat, and flash him a glimpse of what was emblazoned on his chest. It was a photo of Myron Zeppelin's body being carted down the alley.

Ezra had positioned himself so that Katchall could see him clearly but not one of the news cameras could. About a minute of exposure would suffice. Then Ezra would zip up, sneak off, and slip out a side door of the brand-new restaurant. Katchall, pushed to the edge, would now be willing to pay anything to save himself.

The first part went just fine.

"Hey, Bob!" piped Ezra in a false voice. "Look at this, Bob!" He yanked the jacket open, just as he'd done when he practiced at home, and thrust out his narrow chest.

Katchall blinked, his mouth dropping open. Then a nasty scowl touched his plump face. "Okay, buddy, you think you've got me, huh?" he roared. "Well, we're going down together!"

Ezra hesitated, jacket halfway zipped up again. He hadn't been expecting this.

"I confess! I killed Myron Zeppelin!" announced Katchall. "That's right—me, Barbecue Bob! I murdered the guy!" Shaking with anger and fury, he pointed now at Ezra. "And there's the sneaking little twerp who knows all about it and has been trying to blackmail me!"

"Gee," murmured Ezra, "you're cutting off your nose to spite your face."

He tried to get out of there, but the crowd wouldn't let him.

HAVE YOU HUGGED
YOUR UNDERTAKER TODAY?

He managed to do everything he'd boasted he was going to do and more. His investigative work led to the solution of the old murder case that had baffled the Los Angeles area police for over fifteen years, he figured out the real motive for what had been thought of as a bizarre series of random slayings, and he contributed to the capture of the killer at long last. This final accomplishment Red Stebbins never knew about, though, because that unexpected razor got him just before it happened.

Although I had no way of anticipating it, I contributed to Red's death. He himself was, I'm nearly certain, planning to commit a murder of his own, and my wife says that if I wasn't so negative I'd see that what I actually did was help save a life. I'm nowhere near as easygoing and positive as she is and I seem to be having a fairly rough time handling the guilt, but even though at the time I unwittingly set him up, I believed I was doing him a good turn.

✗

When I encountered Red Stebbins two weeks ago in Westwood, I had no premonition of what lay ahead. The late-morning air was relatively clear as I went strolling back to where I'd parked my car. I'd been talking with one of our advertising-agency clients in his office in the village. What I was trying to do was convince him that calling his contemplated frozen product Italian Gangster Pizza was not anywhere near being a terrific idea. He in turn informed me that he wasn't sure he ought to remain with an agency that had no sense of humor.

As I passed the high, wide front window of Chez Télé a fist commenced tapping on the other side of the thick glass. Slowing, I glanced into the store.

The first thing I saw was Jane A. Wicker—nearly forty Jane A. Wickers, since an image of her was on every single operating television set in the store. She was smiling, running one slender hand through her long auburn hair, and looking, though a shade gaunt, quite attractive.

Then I noticed Red. He was wearing a suit the color of burnt marshmallows and making a come-on-in motion with his left hand. His thick splatter of freckles stood out on his pale puffy face, his crinkly red hair was standing up high and disordered.

After glancing at my watch, I nodded and went on into the Chez Télé.

"Good to see you after all these—"

"Listen to what this pinwheel is babbling about," he invited, pointing at Jane on several of the screens.

"Murder is, after all, the most awful act a human being can commit," she was saying to the handsome, sunbrown interviewer who shared a fat candystripe sofa with her.

"I can tell you an equally awful act," said Red. "The one you're putting on right now."

"—anxious to hear about the new bestseller you have in the works that brings you to Southern California," Prentiss C. Gunch was telling her.

"He seems more anxious to peek down her front," observed Red, starting to pace along the tiers of sets.

"The most brutal and bizarre series of killings in recent Los Angeles history will be the topic of the book I'm working on now."

"You're referring to the infamous Demon Barber of Hollywood case, aren't you, Jane? Those crazed slashings that took place fifteen years ago and—"

"I'd prefer not to apply that crude media tag to the killer." Jane's smile had tightened.

"You bet you don't," Red told the array of redheads. "Because my forthcoming book, the definitive one on the whole damn case, is going to be called *The Demon Barber of Hollywood*."

"—be calling my book *The Man with the Razor*."

Following in Red's wake, I inquired, "Are you and Jane in the midst of another feud?"

He stopped to stare up at the largest screen. "I'm enthusiastically ignoring her," he replied. "Even though she swiped my book idea and is trying to compete with—"

"You two were close a few years ago. Why don't you see if—"

"Close? I guess you could say we were close, since we were shacked up in that townhouse in Manhattan. Rented, I might add, with my royalties from *The Mind of a Serial Killer*. Eighty-six weeks on *The New York Times* list of—"

"I thought Jane wrote that one."

"Don't go turning into a goon on me," Red warned, starting to pace again while he watched Jane talking. "After cuckolding me, making off with six cardboard cartons of my latest true-crime research material, *and* failing to kick in on the Christmas presents for the doorman, the elevator man, and the super, Jane A. Wicker swiped my brilliant notion and penned a cheap quickie imitation entitled *The Mind of a Mass Murderer*. A cheesy knockoff that—whoa now."

On the sets Jane was saying, "You're confusing my earlier book with a cheesy knockoff written by a man who calls himself Red Stebbins." She laughed in a pitying way. "Can anyone who writes serious books call himself Red? I mean to say, we don't speak of Red Shakespeare, Red Hemingway, Red Ellison—"

"Listen, Princess Bimbo," Red told a row of screens, "*I'm* going to write the best book on those razor killings. And even though you managed to get a contract for your chintzy imitation of my opus, it'll be *my* book that gets all the sales. All the book clubs, all the miniseries and movie action, all the merchandising cumshaw that—"

"Um," said a sweet-faced old lady who'd eased over to us.

"Button your yap, granny. I'm drinking in every word this pinwheel is spouting, storing it up to rerun and savor whilst plotting revenge and other—"

"Be that as it may, son, you can't go monopolizing all the sets this way. I'm shopping for a small portable for my granddaughter and I want to see what my favorite game show *It's a Steal!* looks like on some of—"

"Your granddaughter must be a goon if she watches that tripe."

"Pay attention, young man. *It's a Steal!* is *my* favorite game show."

"Then it's you who's a goon, granny."

"See here, I'll call over that broad-shouldered young salesperson yonder and have him give you the heave-ho unless you—"

"Red." I clutched his arm. "Let's get going. I'll buy you a cup of coffee."

His eyes remained on the dozens of screens, on the glowing image of Jane touting herself and the upcoming book that was apparently going to be in direct competition with the one he was at work on. "If you weren't stuffed to the gills with caffeine, you wouldn't look as though you just stepped out of your coffin," he told me. "If there's anyplace in this pesthole where they serve peppermint tea, I'll tag along."

"Why, they serve a most refreshing peppermint tea right across the street at the Feast of Reason," the old woman pointed out. "Why don't you two scoot over there?"

"It'll probably be jammed to the rafters with goons and pinwheels, but okay." Red glared at several of the Janes, gave them a fingertip-kissing salute, and allowed me to drag him away.

✗

Before Red got into the fistfight with the proprietor of the Feast of Reason, which was a combination natural-foods café and bookshop, he explained more details about his latest book project.

"Now, isn't that better than coffee?" he asked, reaching across our narrow table to tap my cup.

"Nope."

"Sure, it is. Don't be a goon. And rose-hip tea is great for your—"

"How'd you and Jane come to pick the same topic?"

He took another enthusiastic bite of his soy-jelly donut. "Strange coincidence, what?" He took another chomp. "Odd how, after spending two-plus blinking years under the same roof with me, overpriced roof at that, the lovely, winsome Jane A. Wicker just happened to come up with an idea for a true-crimer that I'd been kicking around for eons. Could it be, do you suppose, that she might've seen the bulging folder packed with copious notes that I'd made on the Demon Barber of Hollywood case?"

"Did she?" I ignored my herb tea.

Red was glancing up at the bookshelves nearest our table. "That peabrain never had an original idea in her entire thirty-three years on this planet. The only smart thing she ever did was move in with me, and look how she eventually fouled that up."

"I don't recall the case that clearly. What was—"

"You should get your snoot out of *Advertising Age* more often," he advised. "Fifteen years ago, just about this same time of year, there were five bloody murders here in your own beloved, smog-ridden L.A. The crackpot killer, dubbed by the media the Demon Barber of Hollywood because he sliced up his victims with an old-fashioned straight razor, slaughtered those five over a nine-day period, then he went out of business and was never heard of from that day to this."

"Wasn't there some demonic angle?"

Nodding, Red said, "The Demon Barber was fond of scrawling little catch phrases like *I do Master Satan's work* in blood on the walls. He also—well, he did certain things to the bodies. See my forthcoming blockbuster for details."

"As I recall, the victims were from all across this area," I said. "None of them linked in any way."

"The killer apparently picked 'em at random—a foreign-car mechanic in Santa Monica, a widow in Glendale, a lady realtor in Pasadena, and so on."

I watched him for a few seconds. "You're onto something."

He strived to appear guileless. "At this point, all I have is a vague hunch. I only arrived in this posh cesspool day before yesterday. When I really start digging, interviewing the surviving kin and ferreting out facts everybody's overlooked up to now, the true story will emerge at long last."

"Jane's been out here a couple weeks, hasn't she? I know I've been seeing her on talk shows and other local—"

"Let me but allude to the old fable of the turtle and the bunny."

"You have a contract for your book, don't you?"

"Did I ever write on spec?" He'd reached the natural blueberry center of his donut. "Opportunist Press advanced me—well, a handsome six-figure advance. Okay, okay, I admit that Princess Bimbo managed to scrounge a hundred thousand more out of Peterkin & Sons. You have to remember, though, that I don't perform lewd acts with my publishers, editors, or—"

"Is there room for two books on this particular case?"

"At the top there's only room for one good one." He tapped his chest with his thumb. "That'll be mine. What's ticking me off is the possibility, remote though it may be, that Jane'll wheedle herself a movie deal on her book and beat me to all that show-biz gravy. Right now Amalgam Studios is enthusiastic about what they've seen of my book in progress, but I don't trust—"

"I know Win Ferber over at Amalgam. He's the head of—"

"Don't you think I know who runs Amalgam? I may look like a rube from beyond the Rockies, but I'm aware that Ferber owns the whole shebang." He gestured with the remains of his donut. "Now there's the kind of relationship I should've had with a woman. His wife, heiress to an automotive fortune, bought him the whole Amalgam setup some years back. Very neat."

"I'm meeting with Win Ferber and several other Amalgam people early next week," I said. "They're producing a new TV sitcom we're sponsoring part of. Show's called *Isn't It a Drag?* About three GIs in 1944 who end up having to impersonate the Andrews Sisters in Occupied Europe while—"

"Spare me the sparkling details."

"The pilot tested very high."

"Around here it would. Half the goons in L.A. are transvestites or—unk!" He'd noticed a specific book on the shelf. Rising from his chair, he grabbed it. "Do I see any of *my* books on these groaning shelves? No, nay, not at all. But here sits *The Texas Oil Millions Murder Case* by sweet little Princess Bimbo. A hamhanded steal of my *Oil and Blood*." He scowled as he scanned the jacket copy. "'Crime-of-the-Month Club selection, alternate selection of the Talk-a-Book Society, soon to be a major motion picture.' Yeah, well, that movie deal fell through but not soon enough to keep it from futzing up my chances for a miniseries on my book."

"Um, sir." The tanned, handsome, and wide proprietor had come over to our table. "The books aren't for reading at the tables. Customers often make that mistake."

"Who would *read* this compendium of pinwheel swill? Only some goon whose lips move whilst he peruses, who has to run a stubby, grease-stained finger over the—"

"Speaking of which, sir, you seem to have smeared natural blueberry jelly all over the dustjacket."

"It's an improvement."

"Usually in situations like this we ask the customer to purchase the book in question at full price," explained the muscular owner of the Feast of Reason, "but since Miss Wicker's brilliant and insightful book is over a year old, and hasn't been on the bestseller list for a few months, we'll let you have it for just $19.95 plus—"

"You can have it on the cabeza, pinwheel!" Red swung out with the fat book and bonked the bigger man on the forehead.

The fight only lasted another two minutes or so. Afterward, I picked Red up and helped him totter outside.

"That's one more bit of grief that woman's caused me." He paused to rest against the rear end of a parked Porsche.

"Maybe you ought to quit seeing everything as a contest and—"

"Ah, how apt." He was leaning down, squinting at a bumper sticker on the car. HAVE YOU HUGGED YOUR UNDERTAKER TODAY? "Yessir, very apt for dear Jane. She's going to need a friendly undertaker if she doesn't quit trying to sabotage me."

✗

The next day my agency sent me to Akron, Ohio. We'd been test-marketing a new ice-cream bar called Igloo Stix for one of our clients and the live polar bear who was taking part in promotions at malls and supermarkets had escaped. My job was to supervise the hunt for him, see that the police didn't shoot him and he didn't do anything that would jeopardize the image of the new product. I was also supposed to write some lighthearted newspaper ads about our missing bear, something that would keep local citizens from worrying about being mauled, maimed, or eaten by the Igloo Stix mascot. I wasted nearly two full days tracking what turned out to be a dancing grizzly who'd, coincidentally, run away from a traveling circus. Our bear showed up on my fifth day in Akron, sleeping peacefully in the back of a van at a used-car lot. Sales at Igloo Stix actually went up almost 20% during the week he was on the loose.

I arrived back in Los Angeles the eve of my meeting with Win Ferber and the other Amalgam Studios execs. Late that night Red phoned me.

"Wake you up?"

I was in my study pasting tearsheets of my polar-bear ads in a scrapbook. "Not at all. If you want to do that, call again in two hours."

"Sounds like you're developing a rudimentary sense of humor," he said. "Listen, I've been overcoming monumental barriers since you left for your frolic in Ohio."

"You having trouble with your Demon Barber book?"

"Dear little Janie has bribed just about every damn surviving relative of the five victims," he told me, anger strong in his voice. "Not a one of those goons'll so much as spit in my eye. Me, the dean of American true-crime writers."

"I won't mention that to Win Ferber tomorrow."

Red said, "Here's what you *can* insinuate into the chat. Despite all the nasty tricks Princess Bimbo has been playing me in her vicious attempt to sabotage my career, I'm forging ahead. I'm going to win this sweepstakes. How? I shall have not only the most detailed and spine-chilling account of the murders ever written, I'm going to have the solution to the case."

"You know who the killer is?"

"I'm close to knowing," he answered. "Because I have spotted what nobody else did—not cop, not reporter, certainly not plain Jane. I have seen what they all failed to see. And that, old buddy, is the link between the victims."

"What do you mean? Those killings were just a madman striking at random in—"

"Not at all. All the theories that've been floating about for fifteen years are completely cockeyed."

"So what's the real motive for—"

"The actual motive I haven't unearthed as yet, but I'm close," Red said. "When you're gabbing with Ferber and the other Amalgam goons, all you have to do is tell 'em that Red Stebbins will reveal the identity of the killer in his book on the Demon Barber of Hollywood case and offer absolute proof of his guilt."

"You ought not to promise more than you can deliv—"

"Quit talking like a pinwheel. Before I'm through, I'll have all that."

"But what exactly do you have now?"

He hesitated. "Don't tell anybody this part," he cautioned. "But I was going through the L.A. *Times* morgue on this case and I came across some photos of one of the victims that I'd never seen before—taken while the poor simp was alive. It took me a while, but I remembered where I'd seen him before. His name was Rollo Kneep and he worked in the mailroom at *TV Week* magazine. He was twenty-six, living in Pasadena, when he got killed. I'd met him when I was out here in the late Sixties doing a mag piece on nostalgia. There was a big old-movie fan convention in Pasadena and Kneep was one of the organizers. I even interviewed him."

"And he told you something that you now realize gives you a clue to—"

"I can't remember a flapping word the goon told me. But I had a hunch and I dug around in the newspapers for the week the killings began," continued Red, excited now. "Okay, two days before the first Demon Barber murder they held the Third Annual Greater Los

Angeles Movie Buff Convention at the Seawitch Hotel in Santa Monica. Rollo Kneep was once again an organizer and in a newspaper shot of a bunch of the fans I'm near certain I spotted none other than Carmelita Novsam."

"Another of the victims?"

"Yep. Realtor in Pasadena, age thirty-five."

"So two of them were interested in old movies."

"Yeah, but suppose they all were? Suppose those five were all at that con?"

"And?"

"All sorts of possibilities. The most obvious one is that they saw or heard something they weren't supposed to."

"The Demon Barber killed them all to keep them quiet and then made it look like the work of a madman? He'd have to have a damn strong reason to make him kill five innocent people."

"That's what crime is all about. You do it for fun and profit."

"Can you tie the other three in, or come up with a reason why—"

"Not yet, but I will," Red assured me. "If I could get those dimwitted relatives to break the code of silence Jane's imposed, I'd find out quick."

"Otherwise?"

"It'll take a bit longer," he said with confidence. "I'm a crackerjack investigative reporter and that means that if one avenue is blocked, I know how to detour to get to where I want."

"So you want me to hint to Ferber that—"

"He may not be bright enough for a hint, tell him right out. Inform him that Red Stebbins knows what the link between the victims was and that these weren't motiveless crimes—details to follow once Amalgam options *my* book and not Princess Bimbo's."

"When exactly will you have the actual—"

"Faith, old buddy, is what you got to have. Faith. Don't be a goon."

Vowing not to be a goon, I hung up.

✗

Win Ferber was impressed when I mentioned what Red was promising. So were his five associates, none of whom was taller than or as suntanned as the fifty-one-year-old head of Amalgam Studios. Ferber indicated that if Red could really deliver what he promised, the studio would be inclined to option his version of the case and not

Jane's. We didn't talk much more about the Demon Barber of Hollywood because the director and the story editor of *Isn't It a Drag?* got into an argument as to which of the Andrews Sisters was a blonde. The director swore it was Maxine and the story editor claimed it was Patty. Ferber told them that as far as the show was concerned, it was LaVerne. That caused the story editor to start shouting and then jump up on top of the conference table. What with one thing and another I didn't get home until sundown.

I was going to phone Red at his motel in Malibu, but when I played my answering-machine tapes I found a message from him.

"I'll call you mañana, old buddy," he said. "Jane thought she had me trapped, but, as I told her, it takes more than a brain the size of a watermelon-flavored jelly bean to outfox Red Stebbins. I'll be doing research all night and, comes the dawn, I ought to have most of the answers. Let's have lunch sometime."

✗

I never saw Red again or spoke to him. What follows is my account of what I'm pretty certain happened, based on newspaper stories, one brief conversation with Jane A. Wicker, and some speculation.

That afternoon while I was at Amalgam, Red had decided to talk directly to Jane. He wasn't going to give away anything about the theory he had but simply ask her to let him talk to a few of the victims' relatives she'd signed up as exclusive contributors to her book. Red figured he ought to be able to find out from them if the remaining three victims had been at that movie convention. Once he established that, he'd zero in on the events that took place at the Seawitch Hotel that weekend. With a little luck and his proven skill as a detective, he ought to be able to come up with a motive and, more than likely, the identity of the elusive killer.

"Hi, Jane, this is Red," he began.

"Oh, God." She sounded as though he'd just informed her she had a terminal illness.

"Look, it doesn't bother me that we're friendly rivals, hon," he said amiably. "After all, we're all members of the same profession."

"Bug spray."

"Is that some new teen slang you're trying out on—"

"I was wishing aloud there was a bug spray powerful enough to get rid of pests your size," she said. "Red, dear heart, don't ever call me again or come near me. It's bad enough knowing you're on the same coast." She hung up on him.

His orange hair stood up straight, crackling. "Boy, where's the Demon Barber when you need him?" He slammed down the phone. "Have I got a candidate for— Hey!"

Suppose, just suppose, Jane was found dead. Suppose her throat had been cut with a straight razor. Think of the damn publicity. The whole country would be talking about the Demon Barber again. And Red, tearful over the loss of his dear friend and colleague, would come forward and vow to track down the killer. Besides the publicity for him, there'd be only *one* book about the old murders.

The Demon Barber, fearful that such an ace investigative reporter as Jane A. Wicker would expose him at long last, would have looked her up, stalked her, and got rid of her to protect his dark secret. Terrific story it'd make. Especially with Red all over the media vowing that he wouldn't be scared off, that his book would be completed.

Okay, where would he strike? Someplace remote, quiet, out of the way.

Wait a minute. Galen Warlocksky, one of the victims, had run a garage in Santa Monica. Sure, Red had been by there just yesterday. The place was in a rundown section of town, hadn't been open for years. All he had to do was lure Jane there, use the razor, and that was it. No more competition, no more having her tell him he was an insect. And all the perks from the Demon Barber book would be nice, too.

How to get her there, though?

Ah, simple.

Red waited an hour and phoned Jane again.

"If this is you, Red, I swear I'll—"

"Miss Wicker? Miss Jane A. Wicker?" He was, he knew, great at doing fake voices and this was one of his best. He sounded deathly calm, a bit crazed, and not at all like himself.

"Yes?"

"I'm a great admirer of yours."

"Well, I suppose that's fine, but I really don't have time for every pest who—"

"But you're writing a book about me."

"What?"

That got her. You could sense it in her voice.

"Of course I can't reveal my identity, but I would like to talk to you," he continued in his convincing madman voice. "You're not like that hack Red Stebbins. You're a real artist and I trust you to present my side of the story fairly."

"Sure. Where can I—"

"Tonight. Ten o'clock. At Warlocksky's old garage. Out back and alone."

"Yes, but—"

He broke the connection. Chuckled. Waved his arms and clicked his heels.

✗

Earlier that same afternoon Red had succeeded in tracking down the group that had staged the Third Annual Greater Los Angeles Movie Buff Convention. He found out that all the records of the convention, as well as those for six others, were stored in a rundown warehouse down in Manhattan Beach.

What he'd do tonight is get the warehouse keys and drive there about seven. When he was certain it was safe, and after he'd dug around in the files for a bit, he'd sneak out and get over to the garage in Santa Monica. He'd have bought a straight razor at a pawn shop by then, disguised of course. He'd be waiting for Jane when she showed up at ten. Once rid of her, he'd hurry back to the warehouse and go on with his researches. Not a perfect alibi, but a hard one to crack.

Besides, the police were sure to think it was the Demon Barber come back to discourage Jane from pursuing the case.

Red got into the warehouse all right. It smelled as though rats and mice had been holding their conventions there. Using a flashlight, since all the power was off in the hollow old brick building, he located the cardboard cartons for the year he wanted. In less than fifteen minutes he'd found the membership roster for the convention.

"Holy moley!" Red exclaimed after scanning the rows of names. "I was absolutely right! All five of the victims were at—"

He died right then.

The Demon Barber had followed him from his motel, and after waiting around to make sure Red was alone he slipped inside the dark warehouse. He was still pretty good with a razor.

Just as Red's body hit the grey-cement floor, Jane burst into the place. She had her .32 revolver in one hand and a powerful flashlight in the other. "Freeze!" she said authoritatively.

Win Ferber turned slowly to face her. "Maybe we can make a deal, Miss Wicker. Amalgam'll buy your book and you—"

"Are you kidding?" She tossed her auburn hair and laughed. "I've just caught the Demon Barber. I don't have to deal with a dinky studio like yours now ..."

Although he never lived to get all the details, Red's basic hunches about the case were all correct. Ferber had been at the Seawitch Hotel on the first afternoon of that movie-fan convention—not as a buff, but to visit a striking young lady he was trying to end his relationship with. In a few days, his wife, a jealous woman some years his senior, was going to sign the final papers that would make him owner of Amalgam Studios. If anyone found out about his affair and told her, the deal would be spoiled for good and all.

The young lady was angry that afternoon and she chased him from her room into the hotel corridor, sparsely dressed and shouting angry remarks at him. By chance, one of the hotel elevators—it had been acting up for several days—left five movie fans off on the wrong floor. They all witnessed the scene between Ferber and his mistress.

Fortunately for him, they all wore name tags. By carefully sneaking around the convention he was able to find out who they were and where each one lived. He became the Demon Barber, took care of anyone who could foul up the studio deal, and then stopped killing.

My mention of what Red was onto unsettled Ferber. He hung around Red's motel that night and then followed him to the warehouse. And Red's call to Jane, which hadn't fooled her after the first minute or so, caused her to suspect that he was investigating something important and wanted her out of the way for a while. She drove over to his motel and followed him when he left.

She's never suspected that he was planning to do away with her. And so far she hasn't gotten around to wondering why he had an old straight razor in his coat pocket. In fact, she told me she thinks it would be a nice touch if she dedicates her book to Red's memory.

A CHECKLIST OF
THE MYSTERY WRITINGS OF RON GOULART

[Publisher's note: many of Ron Goulart's science fiction and fantasy stories skirt the edge of detection and crime. Readers are especially encouraged to check *Ghost Breaker* (1971), *The Chameleon Corps & Other Shape Changers* (1972), *Odd Job #101 and Other Future Crimes and Intrigues* (1975), and *Skyrocket Steele Captures the Universe and Other Media Tales* (1990).]

NOVELS AND SHORT-STORY COLLECTION:

If Dying Was All. Ace, 1971
Too Sweet to Die. Ace, 1972
The Same Lie Twice. Ace, 1973
One Grave Too Many. Ace, 1974
Ghosting. Raven House, 1980
A Graveyard of My Own. Walker, 1985
The Tijuana Bible. St. Martin's Press, 1989
The Wiseman Originals. Walker, 1989
Even the Butler Was Poor. Walker, 1990
Now He Thinks He's Dead. Walker, 1992
Groucho Marx, Master Detective. St. Martin's Press, 1998
Elementary, My Dear Groucho. St. Martin's Press, 1999
Groucho Marx, Private Eye. St. Martin's Press, 1999
Groucho Marx and the Broadway Murders. St. Martin's Press, 2001
Adam and Eve on a Raft: Mystery Stories. Crippen & Landru Publishers, 2001.

SHORT STORIES:

Alfred Hitchcock's Mystery Magazine

"Lost Tiger," December 1963
"The Tin Ear," September 1966
"Undertaker, Please Drive Slow," October 1967
"Granny," August 1970
"The Trouble Was," May 1971
"Orczy Must Go!," September 1971 (Adman)
"Pick Poor Robin Clean," November 1971
"News From Nowhere," January 1972
"That'll Never Happen No More," September 1973
"The Story of My Life," August 1978
"Out of the Inkwell," September 1978
"Running," November 1978
"Why the Funnies Museum Never Opened," December 1978
"Nervous Laughter," November 1979
"Big Bang," January 2, 1980
"This Race to Run," January 7, 1981
"Deathless Prose," February 4, 1981
"Suspense," July 22, 1981
"Never," September 16, 1981
"Wooing Chips Tortuga," October 14, 1981 (Adman)
"Christmas Time in Prison," November 11, 1981 (Scrib Merlin)
"Tale of the Tomb," December 9, 1981
"Private Nose," January 6, 1982
"Funny Stuff," November 1982
"Nose Job," July 1983
"How to Win at Russian Roulette," Mid-December 1994
"74 Games of Solitaire," June 1996
"A Game of Hangman," September 1997
"You May Already Be a Winner," June 1999
"The Past Almost Recaptured," September 2001

Ellery Queen's Mystery Magazine

"The Peppermint-Stripe Goodby," September 1965
"Rink," November 1967

"The Haunted Man," December 1970
"The Gold Medal Caper," March 1973
"The Laughing Chef," September 1973 (Adman)
"Please Don't Help the Bear," January 1977 (Adman)
"Now He Thinks He's Dead," November 1977 (Adman)
"And the Winner Is — ," April 1978 (Adman)
"How Come My Dog Don't Bark," September 1978 (Adman)
"Ninety-Nine Clop Clop," January 1979 (Scrib Merlin)
"The Decline and Fall of Norbert Tuffy," June 1981 (Adman)
"Six Tablespoons Molasses," July 1983 (Scrib Merlin)
"A Million Laughs," September 1983
"It Was Bad Enough," November 1983   (Adman)
"Adam and Eve on a Raft," March 1984 (Scrib Merlin)
"Alas, My Love," September 1984 (Adman)
"It's So Cold in China," February 1985 (Scrib Merlin)
"Barbecue Bob," May 1985 (Adman)
"Have You Hugged Your Undertaker Today?," April 1986 (Adman)
"Believing in Santa," Mid-December 1994

Ellery Queen's Prime Crimes

"Back on My Feet Again," Winter 1983 (Adman)
"Keep It Clean," Fall 1985
"Eavesdropping," Fall 1986

Mike Shayne Mystery Magazine

"Who Ate the Liontamer?," February 1964
"Fifty Cents to Get Out," November 1966
"She Hasn't Told You?," February 1972
"Down There," February 1973

Mystery Monthly

"You Have to Stay Dead So Long," September 1976
"They're Gonna Kill You After Awhile," January 1977

The Saint Mystery Magazine

"Where Do You Get Your Ideas?," August 1984

Separately Published

"Murder for Dummies," The Mysterious Bookshop, Christmas 1996
    (booklet)
"Murder in Studio 221B," The Mysterious Bookshop, 1999 (booklet)
"The Great Impersonation," Crippen & Landru Publishers, 2001
    (booklet to accompany the limited edition of *Adam and Eve on a
    Raft*)

Adam and Eve on a Raft

Adam and Eve on a Raft: Mystery Stories by Ron Goulart is printed on 60-pound Glatfelter Supple Opaque Natural (a recycled acid-free stock) from 11-point Century Schoolbook, a computer-generated version of a typeface designed by M.F. Benton in 1924 and based on the original design of 1896 by L.B. Benton for *The Century* magazine. The cover illustration and design are by Gail Cross. The first printing comprises approximately eight hundred copies in trade softcover, and two hundred twenty-five copies sewn in cloth, signed and numbered by the author. Each of the clothbound copies includes a separate pamphlet, *The Great Impersonation* by Ron Goulart. The book was printed and bound by Thomson-Shore, Inc., Dexter, Michigan.

Adam and Eve on a Raft: Mystery Stories was published in October 2001 by Crippen & Landru Publishers, Inc., Norfolk, Virginia.

CRIPPEN & LANDRU, PUBLISHERS

P. O. Box 9315
Norfolk, VA 23505
E-mail: CrippenL@Pilot.Infi.Net
Web: www.crippenlandru.com

Crippen & Landru publishes first edition short-story collections by important detective and mystery writers. Currently (October 2001) available are:

The McCone Files by Marcia Muller. Trade softcover, $17.00.

Diagnosis: Impossible, The Problems of Dr. Sam Hawthorne by Edward D. Hoch. Trade softcover, $15.00.

Who Killed Father Christmas? And Other Unseasonable Demises by Patricia Moyes. Signed, unnumbered overrun clothbound, $30.00. Trade softcover, $16.00.

My Mother, The Detective: The Complete "Mom" Short Stories, by James Yaffe. Trade softcover, $15.00.

In Kensington Gardens Once . . . by H.R.F. Keating. Trade softcover, $12.00.

Shoveling Smoke by Margaret Maron. Trade softcover, $16.00.

The Man Who Hated Banks by Michael Gilbert. Trade softcover, $16.00.

The Ripper of Storyville and Other Ben Snow Tales by Edward D. Hoch. Trade softcover, $16.00.

Do Not Exceed the Stated Dose by Peter Lovesey. Trade softcover, $16.00.

Renowned Be Thy Grave by P.M. Carlson. Trade softcover, $16.00.

Carpenter and Quincannon, Professional Detective Services by Bill Pronzini. Trade softcover, $16.00.

Not Safe After Dark by Peter Robinson. Trade softcover, $16.00.

All Creatures Dark and Dangerous by Doug Allyn. Trade softcover, $16.00.

Famous Blue Raincoat by Ed Gorman. Signed, unnumbered overrun clothbound, $30.00; trade softcover, $17.00.

The Tragedy of Errors and Others by Ellery Queen. Trade softcover, $16.00.

McCone and Friends by Marcia Muller. Trade softcover, $16.00.

Challenge the Widow Maker by Clark Howard. Trade softcover, $16.00.

The Velvet Touch by Edward D. Hoch. Trade softcover, $16.00.

Fortune's World by Michael Collins. Trade softcover, $16.00.

Long Live the Dead by Hugh B. Cave. Trade softcover, $16.00.

Tales Out of School by Carolyn Wheat. Trade softcover, $16.00.

Stakeout on Page Street by Joe Gores. Trade softcover, $16.00.

Strangers in Town by Ross Macdonald. Trade softcover, $15.00.

The Celestial Buffet and Other Morsels of Murder by Susan Dunlap. Signed, numbered, clothbound, $40.00; trade softcover, $16.00.

Kisses of Death by Max Allan Collins. Trade softcover, $17.00.

The Old Spies Club and Other Intrigues of Rand by Edward D. Hoch. 2001. Signed, numbered clothbound, $42.00. Trade softcover, $17.00.

The Sedgemoor Strangler by Peter Lovesey. 2001. Signed, numbered clothbound, $42.00. Trade softcover, $17.00.

Adam and Eve on a Raft: Mystery Stories by Ron Goulart. 2001. Signed, numbered clothbound, $42.00. Trade softcover, $17.00.

The Reluctant Detective and Other Stories by Michael Z. Lewin. 2001. Signed, numbered clothbound, $42.00. Trade softcover, $17.00.

The Lost Cases of Ed London by Lawrence Block. 2001. Published only in signed, numbered clothbound. $42.00.

Forthcoming Short-Story Collections

Jo Gar's Casebook by Raoul Whitfield [published with Black Mask Press].

Nine Sons and Other Mysteries by Wendy Hornsby.

The Curious Conspiracy and Other Crimes by Michael Gilbert.

The 13 Culprits by Georges Simenon, translated by Peter Schulman.

The Dark Snow and Other Stories by Brendan DuBois.

One of a Kind: Collected Mystery Stories by Eric Wright.

Problems Solved by Bill Pronzini and Barry N. Malzberg.

The Iron Angel and Other Tales of Michael Vlado by Edward D. Hoch.

Kill the Umpire: The Calls of Ed Gorgon by Jon L. Breen.

Cuddy Plus One by Jeremiah Healy.

Come Into My Parlor: Stories from Detective Fiction Weekly by Hugh B. Cave.

14 Slayers by Paul Cain [published with Black Mask Press].

The Adventure of the Murdered Moths and Other Radio Mysteries by Ellery Queen.

The Mankiller of Poojeegai and Other Mysteries by Walter Satterthwait.

The Spotted Cat and Other Mysteries from the Casebook of Inspector Cockrill by Christianna Brand.

Hoch's Ladies by Edward D. Hoch.

[Untitled collection of Slot-Machine Kelly stories] by Michael Collins.

[Untitled collection of Ambrose Ganelon stories] by James Powell.

Full descriptions of all titles and other information can be found on our website: www.crippenlandru.com

Crippen & Landru offers discounts to individuals and institutions who place Standing Order Subscriptions for all its forthcoming publications. Collectors can thereby guarantee receiving limited editions, and readers won't miss any favorite stories. Standing Order Subscribers receive a specially commissioned story in a deluxe edition as a gift at the end of the year. Please write or e-mail for more details.